First edition

Acknowledgements

Front Cover design: Paddy O'Farrell

Illustration: Justin "j-lo" Barlow

Technical back up: Antony O'Farrell

P off & F off
PUBLICATIONS

Paddy O'Farrell

He always wanted to be a writer when he grew up; one out of two ain't bad! Born in Canada in 1942 with a father born in Hong Kong and a Grandfather born in the Channel Islands, he attended 11 schools before signing up for 15 years in the RAF in Electronics.

He got demobbed and subsequently enjoyed a wide range of sales and marketing careers in finance, life assurance, pensions, electronic components, semi conductors, satellite TV, toys, reusable nappies, good food guides, gaming furniture design and internet consultancy to name but a few.

He took a degree at Coventry University at the age of fifty and added the professional qualifications: a fellow of the Institute of Business and Technical Management; a fellow of the Institute of Sales and Marketing; a qualified Sales Engineer; a member of the Society of Electronic and Radio Technicians and a Technician Engineer of the Chartered Institute of Electronic Engineers.

He has travelled in over 40 countries and in his first book, "Primrose Cottage", he draws from his experiences in life, from some of the characters he has met and from a vivid imagination.

He settled in South Leicestershire for 30 years with his Scottish wife and their two sons and has enjoyed hobbies such as Duplicate Bridge, (a two star master), making golf clubs, swimming, walking, oil painting and calligraphy. He and his wife now live in their retirement home in Spain

MCC

(Muddlecombe Cricket Club)

by

Paddy O'Farrell

This book is dedicated to my lovely wife Fay, who thinks this book is an even bigger load of shite than my last book "Primrose Cottage".

Author's note: The majorities of names used are fictitious, and bear no resemblance to anyone alive or dead unless they are called Ian Botham or are daft enough to have the same names as those used in the book then they deserve to be misrepresented.

And bearing in mind it is a fiction/fantasy there may be discrepancies in the time differences between events such as the MCC tours and the Angolan peace talks.

I apologise profusely in advance to any body that makes champagne in South Africa, a beautiful country whose wines are unrivalled, and apologies to their lovely inhabitants, the Afrikaans together with the Irish, the Indians, members of the MCC and the Knights of the Realm but, hey lighten up smart arses and enjoy.

Primrose Cottage   By Paddy O'Farrell

List of characters in chronological order

Dr Rammittin Chucknabuttee	Muddlecombe's brand new doctor all the way from India
Tendulkar Chucknabuttee	Village elder statesman from Pali, Rajasthan & Dr Rammy's Great Grand father
Krishna Chucknabuttee	Dr Rammy's uncle and Chairman of the Botswana Cricket Association
Boris Slobovitch	Chekov's old minder/assassin and W G Grace look-a-like, Chairman of "Borisky Diamonds"
Sidney Sidenose	A solicitor from Shoreditch.
Brewster Kegworth	Landlord of the "Snort & Truffle" pub
Fiona Kegworth	Brewster's Scottish wife, an accountant.
Mildred O'Riley	The doe-eyed wife of Creighky O´Riley, governess of the local school cum community college. Chekov's lover
Mrs Dimmock	A phenomenon.
Gerantinium O'Deighty III	Village elder and Chairman of the Interplanetary Standards and Ethics Committee.
Lt Col Creighky O'Riley MC OBE	Mildred's errant husband, village bore, roué & all round pain in the bottom
Chekov Yeboleksi	Head of the Russian mafia, ex KGB Interrogation expert, Mildred's lover
Dudley	Diamond cutter from the Black Country
Sharon & Tracey	CID policewomen moonlighting as "Borisky Diamonds" salesmen
Mma Xalwo	Somali beauty working for de Beers in Botswana
Sir Reginald Makepeace	British High Commissioner in Botswana
Piet & Jacobus van de Nitwit	Afrikaans brothers, very big and very stupid
Mma Kagiso	PA to Sir Reginald
Ian Botham	Sir Ian Botham

Preface

In the beginning was the word.
And the word was **BANG!**
Bloody great big bang!
And after several billions of years all the rubbish that was flung out of the explosion eventually got it's act together and sorted itself out into planets, stars, galaxies, black holes, novas and all that sort of stuff. And the Lord had a good look round and behold he looked kindly on a small innocent looking planet that was just starting to evolve.

It had everything going for it, water, hydrogen, oxygen, lots of other sorts of gasses and "oh, look, there's an amoeba! "

'That'll do nicely,' he said smugly to himself. 'I can do a lot from here.'

And so he set forth to work on this exciting new venture.

'What on earth am I going to call it? I'll think of something. There are far more important things to do right now.'

So after flogging his guts out for six days, or weeks or years, or millennia he decided to give it a rest and on the seventh whatever he rested. I'm not surprised; the poor bloke must have been knackered

'Hum, not a bad job. It looks lovely doesn't it?' he hummed to himself.

'Look at all those lovely seas and lakes and forests and flowers and volcanoes………….'
He stopped and had another thought.

1

'A tad on the hot side, perhaps I'm rushing things?' So he took the rest of the week off. After a while on one of his days off he noticed things staring to move about on planet "thingamajig" and he had a little sing song with himself

'Here we go, here we go, here we go,' and a little rhyme started up in his mind but he couldn't find anything to rhyme with "evolve".

So on his days off he watched some more. He watched things crawl out of the water; he watched things walking, running and even flying. "That's bloody clever," he thought as he watched photosynthesis and trees and plants starting to mature and things on the ground starting to eat them.

He watched Ardipithecus Ramidus starting to crawl and then walk. He watched Australapithecus then Homo Habilis and Homo Erectus and then along came Adam and Eve.

'Yes!' He gave a big punch in the air to celebrate. Of course the vines hadn't developed to such a stage yet so there wasn't a decent drop of Chardonnay to be had anywhere. 'Must remember that next time,' he thought to himself and started taking notes.

And so on this seventh day of the week he relaxed but still kept on watching.

And along came Abraham and he started begatting and then Moses and his tribe and they begat all over the place. But things were taking a turn for the worst. What with the Egyptians and the Hittites and those bloody Assyrians and then to cap it all who turned up but the Greeks and the Romans. Everything was going tit's up. Wars, pestilences, droughts, floods,,,,, 'thank God for old Noah eh?' He didn't quite understand why he was thanking himself, but hey ho.

"This is not quite what I had in mind when I started this project. I just wanted a nice quiet little place where I could rest and put my feet up on a Sunday. That Garden of Eden was just perfect but somehow it hasn't worked out quite to plan, he blamed the snake but that wasn't fair really as he didn't have a leg to stand on.

" He sighed a deep sigh and had another think about things.

"I know what I'll do. I'll send down my son. Young Jesus, he should be able to sort it all out. Now who can help me out on this one? Ah, Joseph and Mary, now they don't seem to be too busy."

Charming, just bloody charming, those bloody Romans, I ask you? I send my boy down to sort it all out, and what do they do. Crucify him! Not even Charlton Heston could help him out on this one. Jerusalem is going to end in tears; I can see it all now. And he watched the crusades and they all wanted a bit of Jerusalem, and people started chopping themselves into bits and it all got a bit messy.

Well, I'm going to build another Jerusalem where everything will be just like a piece of heaven on earth. Now where can I find this place?

And he watched and looked and quite by accident he came across and old dormant volcano and he watched as it evolved and the dark satanic hills surrounding it slowly turned

3

into woods which sheltered the valley which then became green and verdant.

"I'll start with a few butterflies, that shouldn't do much harm you'd think eh? And those flowers will need pollinating. Wasps? No, but a few bees wouldn't go amiss and some nice birdies eh?"

"Oh, this is so exciting! Now I don't won't any cock-ups here, so who's going to look after it and who's going to start begatting and breeding some nice sensible people? No, not too sensible, they'll only start asking questions. Some nice stupid simple people. I know, old uncle Gerantinium. I'll send him down and that bit of stuff he's got on the side, what's her name. Mary? Oh, Christ, not another Mary. Sorry son. So be it."

"And where is this place, my Jerusalem? England. Brilliant. They must have had enough of holy wars and they'll be pig sick of fighting the French by now and surely must have figured out which royal house is going to run the place. And they've made peace with those bloody Jocks at last and so there should be a decent drop of malt whiskey close to hand. Oh, yes!" He punched the air once more.

'Gerantinium, wake up and get your arse over here!'

Gerantinium stopped snoring abruptly and eventually made his way over to the boss.

'Gerantinium, have I got a deal for you my boy.'

Gerantinium didn't like the sound of that as the Lord stroked his nose and with a twinkle in his eye, said, 'now I've got a little job for you. Nothing too mind boggling. I just want you to set up a little colony for me. That's all I'm asking. Nothing awe inspiring. Just a nice quiet "pipe and slippers" sort of place. Have you got the picture?'

'Er, I'm not quite sure there boss. Just run it by me again can you?'

'Peace and solitude, nice gardens, lots of flowers, simple folk……..'

'Can I have a pub?' He was interrupted by Gerantinium,

'Of course you can my boy and you can have a little church as well. But for Christ's sake, don't go over the top with that religion stuff or they'll crucify you. And you can take that young Mary with you as well.'

Gerantinium had to think about this. The boss continued.

'Now look, you'll be the boss, but there's no Monarchy, there's no democracy, there's no communism, there's no Buddhism, there's no anarchy of fascism, you'll be a committee. How's that sound? Shouldn't strain the old brain cells there now should it Gerantinium?'

'A committee?' Gerantinium mused a while.

'You know, just sit there all day long drinking coffee, scratching various parts of your anatomy, making lots of notes and blethering a load of old codswallop and at the end of the day, not a decision in sight.'

Gerantinium was till in deep thought again.

'And you'd be the Chairman. How about that?'

Well, how could he refuse?

'Where exactly is it?'

'I don't know, somewhere in the middle of England.'

'Well, it's sounds ok so far. What's it going to be called?'

'Oh, I don't know, something on the lines of Shangri La, or Utopia, or, well, call it whatever you want, alright?'

Gerantinium's brain was getting into a bit of a muddle here, but an idea was slowly forming.

Chapter 1. The Chucknabuttee dynasty

In the small village of Pali, somewhere between Jodhpur and Udaipur, the inhabitants awaited the return of Tendulkar Chucknabuttee, their village headman, elder, sage and raconteur. Tendulkar had travelled far and wide and always came back from his travels with wondrous tales of far away exotic cities such as Bombay, Delhi and Calcutta. But this time he had been away for over a year and all sorts of rumours were circulating about not only his travels but also his possible health.

Committees had been formed to make decisions in his absence but couldn't come to any decisions. Premature funeral pyres had been instigated, families had gone into the pre-mourning mode of wailing without your actual weeping, a sort of practice mourn with the volume turned down.

Then one sunny afternoon (most afternoons had been sunny for the last fifteen years) a bedraggled figure was seen walking down the dusty track that constituted the main road to Pali, dressed in the traditional Khadi wraparound or "throw" as they are probably called in fashionable furnishing circles, with his sandals covered in dust as was the rest of his person.

A crowd began to assemble in anticipation and suddenly the sample mourning changed to weeping. Weeping for joy and happiness as the realisation came over everybody that their long lost leader was amongst them once more and they could relax and leave all the decision making up to him now.

The crown gathered round the tall and authoritative figure and slowly the clamour and noise subsided to await the first cherished words from their spiritual and moral leader.

'I couldn't half murder a cold beer and some decent onion bhajis!' So the scene was set for a feast to celebrate the return of the exalted one or "the father of our children" as some of the members of the female persuasion called him.

As the sun fell slowly upon the distant Hindu Kush range of mountains and the flies fell slowly off the meat, there was a great hush fall upon the assembled villagers as their leader started his tale of the mother of all journeys.

'My children,' (He probably wasn't kidding) 'I have been away from you for one whole year. I have been without your love and understanding. I have not been able to listen to all your problems. I have indulged myself in seeking more knowledge. I have been selfish in furthering my own education. I have not been able to give you governance. I have been neglecting in my duties. But fear not for I have held you in my thoughts these past hundreds of days and hundreds of nights…………´

´Get on with it you silly old sod! ´ was the cry from the more irreverent part of the crowd.

'As I was saying,' he cleared his throat and pulling himself up to the full importance of his height and continued. 'I have travelled far and wide and seen many wondrous things in our fair country but this time I have seen things that mankind cannot comprehend. I have travelled in a huge metal monster belching out fire and brimstone across the sea and oceans for many months and have been to the land of the great White Raj.'

This brought out an enormous gasp from his captive audience whose eyes and mouths were now wide open in astonishment and dribbling with exotic juices. Not a pretty sight.

'I have been to the Great British Islands. I have been to the land of plenty where the King is a Queen. Where she has more servants than a man can ever dream of. Where the servants dress in as fine a style as our own Maharajas.'

This was getting all too much for the crowd whose saliva glands were about to dry up completely.

'I have seen buildings that are more ornate and larger than anything Bombay or Delhi can dream of. But I have also seen a

9

religious ceremony that can humble even Brahma, Vishnu and Shiva.'

This was getting to the limit of the crowd's credibility. All dribbling had stopped and all eyes were now fully fixed on their great leader in an awesome silence that was heavy with respect. A respect that had never before been shown to this man who could feel it closing in on him in lumps and like the greatest of theatrical actors knew the crowd were in the palm of his hands and his to do what he wanted.

'I have been to a green oval pasture with thousands of disciples sitting around it looking towards the centre of the pasture with much awe and excitement. And then from a great white pavilion temple come the two high priests dressed in white coats who walked with great reverence to the centre of the pasture carrying holy branches or staffs of wood. And when they reached the centre of the pasture there were white markings already laid out to show the sacred ground where sacrifices must surely be made. And they took the three small trees and drove them into either end of the sacred ground and then placed upon these altars two smaller branches.'

He stopped to take a breather and survey the audience who by now were in total silence.

'And then all of a sudden my children, out of the temple came eleven of the lesser priests again dressed in white but obviously of a lower caste than the high priests. It was then that one of the high priests gathered from his sacred clothing, a small red orb made of the same finest skin from one of our Sacred Brahman Cows and dyed with the finest dyes from the side of the River Ganges dye pools in deep red. Sacred seam stitching was around this magic orb and suddenly the high priest threw it to one of the lower priests.'

The crowd were transfixed.

'The lower priests then went into a ritual of throwing the orb with much velocity to the others as if to kill or maim but they had been trained so skilfully that they moved aside and caught the orb in their hands. If they had not they would surely have gone to their deaths. And then my children, the disciples crowded around the pasture started to go into a religious frenzy as the climax of the ritual was about to take place.'

'But suddenly the crowd were hushed by the appearance of two more priests coming from the temple. It became clear they were to be sacrificed and were dressed in their full battle armour of virginal white and each carrying a great wooden sword shaped from the finest willow in order that they could die with honour. They marched bravely out to the sacrificial area between the two high priests and made much abeyance by beating the ground with their swords. '

He took another deep breath ready to deliver the climax of his story. This story would be remembered by generations, this story would go down in the annals of his village as the greatest story ever told. He looked to his audience and prepared to deliver the coup de grace. He slowly lifted his arms in the air and knew he held his audience like putty in his hands.

'And then my children, the high priest gave the sacred orb to one of the lower priests. And all the disciples around the sacred pasture were now in complete silence.'

As was his audience.

'The high priest then held up his arm, looked around the sacred pasture and shouted …………..play!'

He now filled his lungs and raised his arms up to heaven for the crashing crescendo.

'And the Gods answered their prayers,,,,,,,,,,,,,,,and it rained!'

And so it was that cricket came to the district of Rajasthan.

* * *

Four generations later the great, great, grandson of Tendulkar Chucknabuttee (one of many) was just entering the office of the Dean of the University College Hospital, Jodhpur.

Rammittin Chucknabuttee was a good looking young man, tall for his size, with the usual golden brown complexion of the Indian race. His large eyes were surrounded by long languid eyelashes. His lips were struggling to contain large pearl white teeth that flashed with a tantalising twinkle every time he smiled which was most of the time and mostly directed to the opposite sex. Rammittin had a great affection for the opposite sex as they did for him whether they liked it or not.

'Mr Rammittin Chucknabuttee, how good of you to come.'

'Er yes Dean?' came the puzzled reply.

'Please sit down. Now where was I? ´ the Dean opened a large brown folder on top of his large brown desk and started leafing through the pages. He stopped and looked up at his visitor. He slowly moved his hands forward together in a praying motion and looked up to the ceiling for inspiration. Having found the necessary inspiration he continued bringing his eyes down to look deep into Rammittin's eyes.

'I have just come from the office of the Clerk of the Courts of the Rajasthan District.' This was followed by a long silence.

'Er, have you Dean?' Came the puzzled rhetorical question which was obviously going to get a reply anyway.

'Yes.' The Dean looked up for more inspiration. 'He's a very busy man.'

'Er, is he?' A more puzzled query came from the visitor who felt he had to say something in-between the Dean's interminable search for inspiration.

'Yes.' The Dean continued now obviously full of inspiration. 'Yes, he is extremely busy, and he has a lot of paperwork on his desk which has to be dealt with efficiently and effectively. And do you know what the majority of his paperwork consists of?'

'Er, no Dean?'

'Paternity suits.'

'Er, paternity suits?'

'Yes, paternity suits. Do you know what paternity suits are Mr Chucknabuttee?'

'Er, aren't they something to do with what fathers wear when they visit their new born babies, Dean?'

'Not quite. It is to do with fathers, but not what they wear. It is a legal term for a lawsuit to determine the identity of the father of a child born outside of marriage, and to provide for the support of the child once the identity of the father has been determined.'

'Is it?' This was getting interesting to the visitor who now sat up and started to take more notice.

'It is indeed, and do you know whose name is on all these paternity suits Mr Chucknabuttee?'

'Er, no Dean?' Rammittin felt that things were starting to go a bit pear-shaped instead of getting more interesting.

'Yours. Mr Chucknabuttee. Yours!' The Dean was now fully inspired, leaning forward and looking directly at his visitor with all the total authority of his position.

Rammittin was lost for words which confirmed that things were definitely in pear-shaped mode.

The Dean leaned back into his large leather chair with a look of total satisfaction and a nasty sneery type of smile started to creep across his face.

He continued. 'In my meeting with the Clerk of Courts it became clear that a lot of taxpayer's money was at risk here in legal actions that could take some considerable time. There was also the anguish of the parents of all these young girls to be taken into consideration during these legal proceedings.'

The Dean leafed through some of the papers in the files and continued. 'You are obviously not a wealthy man. I see here you were awarded a local government grant to pay for your education. It would seem that only a prison sentence would be the outcome of any legal proceedings.'

'Er, it would?' Rammittin didn't like the sound of that.

The Dean leafed though some more papers. 'It says here your colleagues in the college campus call you "Trisexual". I have been given to understand that means you will try anything. It would appear to me that a prison sentence would only heighten your sexual deviations and that at the taxpayers' expense. And that you would be back in society well within the limit of your raging libido.'

'Er, I would?' He didn't realise he had a raging libido.

'So, after much discussions with not only the Clerk of the Court but also some of the parents of the young ladies involved, it would seem that it is in everybody's best interest that you should disappear.'

'Er, disappear Dean?' Had the medical school come up with some sort of invisibility pill?

'So we've had a sort of non governmental whip round and have found enough funds for the price of a cost effective one-way sea voyage to the great British Isles for you to stay with some of your relatives there.'

'Er, I have relatives there?'

'You do now my boy. And the voyage will give you time to reflect on your "shortcomings in life" to coin a phrase. You will be travelling "Cow Class" I believe it is called. But I understand it has nothing to do with the sort of comfort we allow our sacred cows in this country.'

Gulp, was the only thing Rammittin could say at this point of time.

The Dean closed the folder and sat back luxuriating in his chair. He put his hands together in front of him again and suddenly smiled benignly at Rammittin.

Oh shit, looks like a bit more pear-shapeness was coming his way.

'Mr Chucknabuttee,' the Dean said after careful consideration. 'I'm not an ungenerous man and your record here at the University College Hospital is academically sound. After four and a half years you have maintained a good record and it seems such a waste to throw all that professional medical training away. I notice you have shown an interest in gynaecology. Although I must say your approach to gynaecology seems to be coming from a proactive angle rather than a reactive angle. But, be that as it may, I'm sure you must be able to give society the benefit or your training here in some form or another?'

'Er, I am sure I can Dean.' It was time for a bit of sucking up now.

'I feel we may be rushing into this a little bit too fast.' The Dean said very thoughtfully.

'Er, oh, I'm sure we are Dean.' He'd got a cracking date on for tonight.

'I have been given to understand that the final of the Rajasthan district University cricket match is on this weekend.' The Dean said looking Rammittin carefully in the eyes.

'Er, it is indeed Dean.' Where the hell was this leading to?

'I have been given to understand that you represent Jodhpur. Would I be correct in this assumption?'

'Er, yes, that is correct Dean.'

'And I have been given to understand that Jodhpur are ten to one on favourites to win?'

'Er, are they really Dean? Gosh.'

'Now why do you suppose that would be Rammittin?' The first name usage sent a shiver down Rammittin's spine.

'Er, we have a good team Dean?' He was a little lost here.

'Would it possibly be because we have an extremely good left arm leg spin bowler whose flight, change of speed, googly and "wrong 'un" have all the local batsmen completely bamboozled?'

Rammittin could suddenly feel something very strange about to happen and said absolutely nothing.

'Now if I was a betting man, to win a thousand Rupees I would have to invest in the capital expenditure of ten thousand wouldn't I?'

Rammittin felt it best that a nod would suffice at this juncture.

'But what would happen, let's say, if that bamboozling bowler were a little, shall we say, off colour. And let us surmise that this lead to the other team winning. And somebody put that one thousand rupees on the other team? Wouldn't that give him a return of ten thousand rupees?' A rhetorical question if ever there was one.

Rammittin wanted to see where this was leading up to and again decided on a cautious approach to any answer, which was to say absolutely nothing. He felt that there was a possibility of a better deal coming up. Something better than the previous offer of a holiday cruise in a hold full of cows. Anything was better than that.

The Dean sat back once more and with his hands together in front of him again, looked to the ceiling for inspiration and started again. 'Let's say for example, that this exceptional bowler couldn't cut the mustard. Let's say all his "wrong 'uns" turned into "right 'uns". Let's say all his leg breaks didn't break anything at all. Let's say his slower balls were the norm rather than the exception. Do you see where I'm coming from Rammittin?'

'Er, I think I do Dean,' said Rammittin very slowly, looking straight back at the Dean.

'And let's say that from the proceeds of this ten thousand rupees, somehow your travel itinerary would be upgraded to Business Class on a jumbo jet of,' the Dean hesitated here. 'Of, let's say, Singapore Airlines? I hear their customer service is second to none and the Stewardesses are of above average looks.'

Rammittin was starting to drool here but managed to suppress a dribble from the corner of his mouth.

'And let's say the College managed to come up with some form of certification of your medical studies. Unfortunately the word "Failed" would have to appear somewhere in this certificate, but I'm sure with the judicious use of some correction fluid and a decent colour photocopier no one would be any the wiser once it was hanging on your consultation wall. What would you say to that young Rammittin?'

*   *   *

And so it was that Dr Rammittin Chucknabuttee set off on his voyage of discovery.

Chapter 2. Muddlecombe–cum-Snoring

Dr Rammittin Chucknabuttee, or Dr Rammy as he was now affectionately known, didn't realise he had a vocation in life. Oh, he had a calling. He wanted to get his hands up the front of as many young ladies' vests or down their knickers as possible and felt that a career as a medical practitioner would allow him to achieve his aims and ambitions legally. But this was a basic primeval urge not a vocational calling.

His vocational calling was at Muddlecombe-cum-Snoring.

Muddlecombe–cum-Snoring was a phenomenon. It was twinned with the Lost City of Atlantis, Shangri La, and Brigadoon.

Muddelcombe-cum-Snoring was somewhere in the middle of England between Muddlecombe Magna and Muddlecombe Parva. It was surrounded by gentle rolling hills that had been naturally eroded from an extinct volcano many millions of years ago to form a perfect sinusoidal wave form of the harmonic resonant frequency of all the major air traffic control and communications radio frequency waves. It was also sitting on top of a considerably large iron ore deposit that went down several miles into the earth's crust. This formed a sort of magnetic pole effect whIch fountained out over Muddlecombe

A sort of black hole effect.

Well actually more of a "grey hole" effect, all of which diminished the probability of people actually finding this idyllic little village. So you had the North Pole, the South Pole and the mini middle Muddlecombe Pole. This caused a hole in the clouds with the effect that it never rained during the day and thus giving a constant summer day's effect all the year round. At night when the Ionosphere lowered, the clouds lowered and allowed the rain to feed the crops, grass etc during the prescribed rainy seasons.

If you wanted to look for Muddlecombe you would never find it. It found you. No planes flew over it if they had any sense or a decent compass, and even on Google Earth it was a smudge as if it was the only cloud in the universe. This was why the Air Traffic Centre at West Drayton and the Meteorological Office at Bracknell always overlooked Muddlecombe on the basis that they didn't have a fucking clue that it was there.

As there were no flight paths over Muddlecombe nobody would see it from the air and even if they flew over it all they would see was their compass doing a quick cartwheel and after a tap returning to normal.

The only way to find Muddlecombe-cum-Snoring was to be called there. This was done not on an ad hoc basis as everybody assumed but on strictly sound socio-economic based reasoning.

Captain (newly promoted to Lieutenant Colonel) Creighky O´Riley MC (newly awarded the OBE); (Irish Guards) was introduced to boost the local population with fresh blood which he had gone about with boundless energy. He ended up in a marriage of convenience (he was stony broke and she was a good shag) with Mildred whose grand father "found" Muddlecombe by mistake. A rich Northern Industrialist, he was running away with a young lady from his local bordello trying to escape society's gossip mongers and bumped into Muddlecombe. He died early and his rich mistress married locally, gave birth to Mildred and started up the local school and what passed for the Community College in the evening for adults.

Doe-eyed Mildred, still a good looking woman for her age, was now a school governor and a member of both of the two committees in Muddlecombe: "Mildred's Mafia" as her four lady friends where known; and the Interplanetary Standards and Ethics Committee.

"Mildred's Mafia" consisted of Mildred and Lucinda together with Betty and Fiona. An entirely unelected committee that was formed purely in the interests of gossip.

They had just returned from a holiday in Tenerife which was the watershed for a lot of people's lives in Muddlecombe. Mildred had fallen in love with a one Lieutenant Colonel Chekov Yeboleksi, of the Russian Army (retired), well Russian Intelligence, well Interrogation actually and who had since left the KGB and gone legit. He was now head of the Russian Mafia. It had to be said that he was so besotted with Mildred that he was seriously thinking of joining the normal human race. So much so that he had invested in a little project in the village that was giving the benefits of a higher standard of living to all, well most of the villagers.

This private enterprise was actually part owned by one of Chekov's old employees, a retired hired assassin by the name of Boris (Seven Bellies) Slobovitch who had arrived in Muddlecombe via Primrose Cottage.

Primrose Cottage was a sort of transit and immigration control for Muddlecombe with all new arrivals usually going through this chocolate box picture of an English rose cottage. It had originally belonged to John from London who had discovered it by mistake, as you do, and found the peace, quiet, tranquillity and lack of law enforcement extremely beneficial to his particular line of employment. On his death it had been handed down to his son, John, who like his father enjoyed borrowing things from people and forgetting to give them back.

John had been extremely successful in the property market in Tenerife and had also borrowed some gold bullion from a firm in Heathrow and had with the help of Boris, managed to launder it through the Russian banking system (owned by Chekov) at some considerable profit, a small percentage of which he had passed onto Boris and given him the benefit of the use of Primrose Cottage to lie low whilst things got a bit hot in Tenerife. And we're not talking about the all year round tropical climate there.

Some of this heat had come from two very energetic and attractive undercover Essex CID policewomen who worked under the names of Sharon and Tracey. They had unwittingly bumped into John and subsequently traced Chekov and Boris from Tenerife and with the help of Sidney Sidenose, John's solicitor from Shoreditch, had unwittingly led them to Muddlecombe.

This is where the talents of Dr Rammy had come into play. Here he had obtained full job satisfaction and tried out a few new drugs on the unsuspecting CID ladies. They had to be taken care of for a few hours and who better than our new young doctor in the village to subdue them, well subdue's probably not the right word here. Drugged is probably a better word, and while he was at it he could take advantage of their lack of resistance and fulfil his corporate objectives. It is true to say he had tried the drugs out previously on Boris (a twenty two stone hit man) to treat a severe bout of depression, but this was comparing the same use of drugs on an elephant as on a mouse. But anyway the ladies fortunately couldn't remember much about the episode and Dr Rammy obtained a considerable amount of job satisfaction. As it turned out he and one of the young policewomen were now extremely good friends, well not to put too fine a point on it they were enjoying extremely rewarding companionship together. Isn't it amazing the chances of how two such sexual deviants could be thrown together into such a warm relationship?

All thoughts of him sitting in the Dean's office in Jodhpur had long since vanished and he now had a thriving practice. He had opened up a Breast Clinic in the village. However someone had pointed out the lack of medical terms so he had to change it to Breast *Cancer* Clinic. The same thing, where he felt he could achieve his aims in life and the ladies of Muddlecombe willingly obliged. He was multi-tasking now as well and in the absence of Captain Creighky O´Riley MC (Irish Guards) had taken over the role of introducing new stock into the village population.

Life was extremely pleasant as it should be in a place like Muddlecombe and he was starting up the Muddlecombe Cricket Club. Or the MCC as it was generally known, well generally known in Muddlecombe. Nobody had ever played cricket before but they turned out to be fast learners. The picturesque village green had been taken over and a piece of flat ground had been landscaped into a reasonable pitch. The main trouble being the duck pond. Some of the ducks had suffered concussion from some over zealous batting but had retaliated by hiding the balls below water.

"The Snort and Truffle" pub was strategically placed on the edge of the village green to act as the pavilion with full refreshment facilities available even though a tad more expensive than your normal home made cucumber sandwiches. This is where the fourth member of Mildred's committee came in. Fiona ran the local pub with her husband Brewster Kegworth. Fiona was of Scottish stock and naturally enough was an accountant. She had been called to Muddlecombe in these days of the modern revenue system because she understood those dirty little three letter words such as "VAT" and "TAX".

Brewster Kegworth and Fiona had taken over the "The Snort and Truffle" and managed by some creative accountancy to turn it into a viable business.

Chapter 3. Cricket practice

'You see that piece of wood stuck in ground over there, I will be pleased if you are hitting it with this small round red ball.'

"No problem there," thought the majority of the interested villagers gathered on the village green in Muddlecombe.

'And for every time you are hitting it, I'm going to buy you a pint of the best beer from the lovely Mr Brewster.' Dr Rammy said very slowly turning round to make sure everyone had heard him.

"Bloody Nora, it's Christmas all over again," thought the onlookers, rolling up their shirt sleeves in anticipation and moving towards Dr Rammy.

'But,' Dr Rammy interjected, holding up his hand to stop the tsunami of volunteers. 'Every time you miss that bit of wood, you have to buy *me* a pint of beer.'

This slowed down the cavalry charge considerably, but a few still kept on coming.

'And you have to do it from this distance.' Dr Rammy paced out forty odd paces away from the stump holding a piece of rope and hammered in a little peg every now and then to form a circular boundary round the stump.

The crowd on the village green had increased somewhat by now but the rush of volunteers stuttered.

'Oh arr. 'ere, that's called a stump, ain't it?' called one of the volunteers close by.

'Spot on,' replied Dr Rammy.

'Oh arr. 'ere, and that's sommatt to do with cricket ain't it?'

Dr Rammy could see there was some form of intelligence there after all. 'Now how did you know that?'

'I 'eard that John somebody on the radio talking about them stumps and things and a load of Indians and all that.'

'Well it looks like you're going to have to be the captain then,' continued Dr Rammy.

'Ere, bugger off. You're pulling my pisser!' And everybody had a good laugh.

'Harlot!' somebody shouted from the back.

'What you on about you dozy bugger!'

'It were that John Harlot fella what speaks on the BBC.'

'No it weren't, it were Johnson.'

'What John Johnson?'

'No, Johnson, that fella what does the cricket on the BBC.'

'Oh, that Brian fella with the apple in his mouth?'

'No you pillock, them BBC wallahs is all issued with plums not apples.'

'Well they all sounds a bit posh anyway.'

'Anybody would sound posh to you, you dozy bugger.'

The crowd had intensified and Dr Rammy was getting nowhere. He could see someone at the back standing head and shoulders above everyone else.

'Boris, please to be helping me my friend?' and he waved him over.

'Ere, if you get's him involved and mention beer there won't be much left for us!' The village wag-cum-captain had everyone laughing again.

Boris eventually made it into the throng as Dr Rammy threw him a ball. Boris casually caught it somewhere in his enormous hand, found it and picked it out, throwing it back to Dr Rammy.

'Boris my friend,' Dr Rammy tried putting his arm around his shoulder. 'See these gentlemen here?' he glanced around the gathered party. 'These gentlemen are going to buy you and I a lot of beer.'

'Like buggery we are,' cried out a brave voice from the crowd. 'Ere, give me that ball. I'll show you whose going to buy who all the beers round here!'

'Boris my friend, please to be standing behind that stump over there………….that's it, and every time they throw the ball just catch it and throw it back to me.'

'Da da, yes yes,' (Boris' way of double declutching from Russian into English) 'what is stump please?' Boris enquired scratching his head.

'Oh sorry, that's it over there. That piece of wood sticking up there, that's it my friend. Now just stand behind it and we will be richer by hundreds of pints very quickly.'

The challenge was too much for the villagers and they all rushed to have a go.

Fiona, the landlord's wife and accountant was dragged out of the pub to keep count and she brought out the darts score board and by four thirty Dr Rammy and Boris were up seventy five pints in total. Some of these had to be utilised obviously and so the score line varied from time to time.

There was a little worry in Dr Rammy's mind. Although he was way ahead on the running total, there was one person who was actually in credit on an individual basis.

'Harry,' (or Hercules as he was known in the Interplanetary Standards and Ethic's committee), Harry, you didn't tell me you'd played cricket before?' asked Dr Rammy.

'Don't know nothing about cricket Dr Rammy,' he said with a genuine smile.' But I knows I likes me beer!'

Laughter all round and they were still queuing up to throw the ball. Slowly the deficit was being reduced and the stump was getting hit more often than not.

'Right gentlemen, I think it's time for a tea break.'

'Don't want no bloody tea, what's wrong with Brewster's special draught ale?'

The landlord of the "Snort and Truffle" had been kept busy but was obviously enjoying the day as were all the other villagers who were either partaking in the challenge or watching and giving their friends plenty of advice.

Brewster could see a loss leader here with an end profit eventually and offered everyone partaking free special draught ale. This was extremely well received especially by

Boris who must have lost a couple stone out there in the middle all afternoon. But what's a couple of stone when you've got twenty odd to spare anyway?

Dr Rammy took Boris aside and quietly tried to interrupt his thirst quenching process. You didn't want to get in the way of that!

'Boris my friend, you have been playing a very good game of cricket as what we are calling a wicket keeper.'

Boris managed to interrupt his swallowing process to speak. 'I have?' Another swallow. 'A what?'

After the tea interval they resumed the challenge and by the end of play, so to speak, the scores were virtually even. That is apart from the total amount actually consumed which had been taken into consideration. Dr Rammy actually owed Harry nineteen pints but was able to amortize his costs from his various other creditors. So all in all it was an enjoyable day and Dr Rammy had achieved his objectives and found two useful players, Boris and Harry.

He had also achieved a considerably good fielding side into the bargain, but they were yet to be tested. Batting and bowling were the next objectives.

'Well done lads. We'll see you all again tomorrow then?' said Dr Rammy in the pub later that evening.

'I reckon we'll need a rest day tomorrow,' said a bleary eyed player slurping his beer.

*   *   *

So tomorrow it was.

Only this time there were two bits of wood.

'Ere Harry, look at that. We got two pints a go today. Can't wait.'

'I think Dr Rammy has probably got other ideas.'

'Oh arr, the sneaky bugger.'

Dr Rammy was pacing out the distance between the two stumps and then with his ball of string pacing wide out to the edge of the green and making a boundary.

'What did I say? Look at that, we got to throw the bloody ball from that far out. That ain't fair.'

'Ah, good afternoon gentlemen. Lovely to be seeing you.' Dr Rammy looked up from his boundary walking to hail his players.

'Oh ah? Won't be so bleeding lovely if we don't get any beer and got to buy you bloody beer all evening. I can handle you but I'm buggered if I'm paying for Boris' beer. I doubt if the Bank of England has that sort of collateral.' An aside from a player that most people heard.

Dr Rammy finished off marking the boundary with his pegs and came over to the assembled company. 'Ok boys, you want to be coming over here please?' He led them over to a stump and pointed to the other stump some twenty odd yards down the pitch.

'You reckon you can hit the other stump from here?'

There was a stunned silence as each and everyone looked at each other and started drooling. There was a pregnant pause and someone eventually had the courage to ask the same question in everybody's mind.

'Same deal as before Dr Rammy?' more drooling.

'Same deal as before.'

The drooling was quite clearly intensified as visions of pyramids of beer came to their minds, frothing down from the top of all the chilled beer mugs.

'Bugger me.................'

'Oh, there is a small point I forgot to be mentioning.' The pyramid came crashing down to earth as forlorn faces stared blankly at Dr Rammy.

'You're not allowed to bend your arm and it has to be higher than your shoulder.'

There was another pregnant pause as they all thought about it and the reply wasn't short in coming.

'I knew there were a bloody catch.'

'Oh, arr, but we're still closer to the stump.'

'Oh, arr, and run that bit about the arm past us again Dr Rammy?'

'Well you know when you are throwing ball; your elbow is normally below your shoulder.' He let them think about that as they all practiced throwing. 'Well, in cricket, when you bowl a ball, your elbow must be straight and higher than your shoulder.'

'Oh. Arr, so what you saying is we've got to bowl the bloody ball now, not actually throw it?'

'Yes please.'

Dr Rammy picked up a ball and gently bowled it down the other end of the pitch gently knocking the stump over.

'Same deal?'

'Same deal,' relied Dr Rammy.

'Bugger this; I'm going to have a go at this. I've got a terrible thirst on me standing talking. Let's have that bloody ball.'

And so they all lined up to have a go. As usual Boris was called over to stand behind the stump at the other end and was kept pretty active again and by two thirty they were thirty pints up. But some of them were starting to get the hang of it and come the tea break at four thirty Boris had drunk most of the surplus and it looked fairly even.

All that was except for poor old Harry. Unlike his previous session Harry was slowly going bankrupt in the beer stakes. Dr Rammy had been watching him and was smiling from ear to ear. It was nothing to do with the surplus beer he was owed it was something far more interesting.

Dr Rammy sidled up to Harry as they walked into the pub. 'How's it going then Harry?'

'Bollocks!'

'What is seeming to be the trouble my friend?'

'I don't know what the bloody hell I'm doing wrong but I'm buggered if I can hit that bloody stupid little stump.' He was not a happy bunny. 'Looks like you'll be getting pissed out of your brain on my account. I just can't fathom it out at all.'

'Harry my friend, pleased not to be worrying. You are what we call a swinger.'

'I ain't no swinger. What you getting at. You think I'm queer or sommatt.'

'Harry my friend you are the most precious of bowlers who can swing the ball in flight.'

Harry stopped and looked at Dr Rammy. 'Do what?'

'You can make the ball change direction, and you can make it swing away from the stump or swing into the stump.'

'You're taking the piss.'

'Why else do you think you are missing the stump?'

Harry stood and scratched his head in disbelief. 'Well I'll be buggered. But what about all those beers I owe you?'

'After tea I'll show you how to adjust your bowling to take into account the swing and to change your grip on the ball to change the direction.'

'Well I'll be buggered. I'd best be at it soonest to get me back into the profit margin.'

'You're in the profit margin already in the talent stakes my friend. I'll soon be buying you the beers.'

*   *   *

It was practice morning again and time for the cricket lessons to start. By this time word had got round the village and the crowd had swelled come midday.

'Ere was all this then?'

'I dunno, summat to do with this cricket nonsense.'

'Don't sound like nonsense to me if there's pints of beer involved. You bin down the pub recently?'

'Oh ah, but I can't make head nor tail of the blackboard young Fiona's got rigged up in the bar.'

'Oh ah, well it's this cricket stuff, ain't it?'

'It don't say nothing about cricket on it though, now does it.'

'Oh ah, stands to reason though. It don't have to have "cricket" writ in big words do it? But only them silly buggers what's out there now 'as there names on it so it must it must be summat to do with cricket.'

'I don't understand it all'

'Well from what I can tell, if you can hit that wooden peg out in the middle you get's a pint.'

'So what happens if you miss the bugger?'

'Ah, well then. I reckons then you got to buy some other bugger a pint.'

'I could hit that from Muddlecombe Magna.'

'You couldn't hit Primrose Cottage if you was standing inside it!'

'Put your money where your mouth is.'

'Come on then, let's get on the village green and I'll show you who can hit a bloody stupid little wooden peg,'

And so Fiona's blackboard was kept busy again. And the next day, and the following next day and…………….

*　*　*

'Now then lads,' it was practice morning again. 'This week we're going to make things a little interesting.'

'SAME DEAL?' the cry went out.

'Oh, yes, only this time instead of throwing the ball, some of you will pleased to be hitting the bloody thing.'

'What sort of deal is that then?' There was a lot of head scratching going on in the middle of the village green.

'Well, some of you are going to throw the ball as before, but there's going to be an obstacle in front of the stump.'

'What's that then Dr Rammy, a bloody great brick wall, so as you can get a few more pints in?'

'No, no my friends. One of you will be being the obstacle.'

'Well bugger that. I ain't standing there and let all you other silly buggers throw it at me, not that any of you could hit me on a month of Sundays….'

There was uproar from the assembled players who were eventually silenced by the sight of Dr Rammy coming onto the pitch with a piece of wood in his hand.

'Gentlemen, gentlemen. Please let us be having a piece of decorum.' Dr Rammy shouted. The crowd eventually settled.

'Now, my friends this is what we call a bat. This is what you are going to defend yourself with. This lovely piece of English

Willow will be your salvation. This will make you heroes of your time…..'

'Ere, what's ee going on about the silly old fart. It says "Made in India" on the back.' A loud guffaw came from the assembly.

'Thank you Jack. Most observant. Now you can be the first person, or what we will call you now, "batsman" to use this.'

'I've called 'im a few more things than that.' Came the heckler from the back.'

'I'll bloody show you!' said Jack, striding over to Dr Rammy and grabbing the bat off him. 'Just show me what to do, and I'll wipe the silly grins off their faces.'

'Ok Jack. Now hold the bat like this.'

'Oh, like I does with me thresher.'

'Like 'e does with is cock!' bought the crowd to their knees in laughter. After a few minutes when everybody had got their breath back, Dr Rammy cooled Jack down and showed him the hold and the strokes.

'Right gentlemen. Now then, the deal is this…….'

This silenced the crowd waited with baited breath for the gospel according to Dr Rammy.

'Now the lovely person with the bat stands in front of the stump and guards it with his life while at the other end another person throws the ball at the stump as if his life depended on it……….'

'And a few beers no doubt!'

'Very succinctly said my friend,' replied Dr Rammy. 'Very well said, because if you can hit the stump that the batsman is standing in front of, I will be getting you four pints of beer.'

'Four pints!' the yell went up as everyone tried to get the ball off Dr Rammy.

'Please not to be forgetting the batsman who will be standing in the way when you are throwing the ball, overarm don't forget, and he will be hitting it very hard so as to deny you your beer.'

'Like buggery he will if I've anything to do with it.' This bought a round of cheers.

'But let us not forget that if the batsman can hit the ball over that line of pegs round the green, he will be getting four pints as well.'

This sustained a heavy silence.

'And,' continued Dr Rammy, now having their attention, and like his ancestor before him, knew he had the crowd in the palm of his hand. 'And, if he can hit the ball over that line without it bouncing he will be getting six pints!'

This was where everyone had a certain stunned look on their faces. Some of them were rolling their sleeves up in challenge. Some of them just scratching their heads.

'Six pints?' the sentence rumbled through the crowd. And then repeated. 'Six bloody pints eh?'

'And,' Dr Rammy continued his sermon on the mount. 'And, if anyone can catch the ball after it has been hit he gets two pints, but the person who "bowled" the ball gets two pints as well.'

'Beats the hell out of digging the bloody garden!' This was the generally accepted motion amongst the majority of the crowd. No, it was actually passed unanimously.

'Ok Jack, here's the bat. Now stand in front of the stump, just about a yard in front.

That's it. Now who is going to be the first bowler please?'

The Yukon Gold rush was a mild affair compared to this. But eventually Dr Rammy sorted out a volunteer.

'Now, please to be telling me how you are going to hit the stump with that fine gentleman standing in front of it?'

'Fine gentleman my arse. That's Jack, and I'm going to hurl the bloody ball so fast he'll not know what's hit him.'

'A fine sentiment entirely. But you are hitting Jack, not the stump.'

'If 'ees got any sense 'ee'll get out of the bloody way!'

'You're most correct there my friend, but what if I give him some padding so he won't get hurt.'

'Well that's not fair, that's cheating.'

'No my friend, that's cricket.'

Chapter 4. The Committee meeting

Mildred and Chekov were skipping down the lane from her house, looking lovingly into each others eyes. It was a lovely summer's afternoon, again, and they were in love and the birds were tweeting and everything in their lives was beautiful. A good shag always helps in these matters, when all of a sudden they stopped in their tracks. Chekov pulled Mildred up short and looked towards the village green.

'What's all this Mildred?'

'What's all what darling?' said Mildred looking blissfully into Chekov's eyes.

'What's happening on the green?'

'Oh!' She said, turning to look towards the green. 'Oh that, they're playing cricket darling.'

'Ah,' said Chekov, stopping and staring at the white clothed players. 'I've heard about cricket, but I've never actually seen it.' He stood transfixed and holding Mildred's hand he started walking again.

'Oh, now we mustn't walk over the boundary line. Let's just walk around this way,' and she guided Chekov around the green.

'Isn't that Dr Rammy and, my god that can't be Boris can it?'

'Yes you're right Chekov it is. I know Dr Rammy has started teaching some of the locals but surely Boris can't……………………..'

Just then there was aloud thwack and it came from Boris who had obviously just hit a cricket ball some considerable distance. 'By god he can hit a cricket ball,' continued Mildred in amazement. They watched the ball soar over their heads and splash into the duck pond.

You could see all the players holding their heads in their hands and groaning. 'Oh no, not again Boris,' came the joint groans. Boris was the only one not groaning and had a silly smile on his face just as Dr Rammy went over to him and slapped him on the shoulder.

'That was very good Boris,' said Dr Rammy. 'But now let's see how you get on with the next ball.' Someone produced a new ball, threw it over to Dr Rammy who then skipped down the wicket and bowled again to Boris. Boris skipped down the pitch (you could feel the earth moving when Boris skipped) and tried an enormous swing at the ball only to be left standing and turning round as the ball swerved round his legs to gently knock the bails off the wicket.

'БВАПУ ЬФТ!' bellowed Boris, which roughly translated means "kinnell, that bastard's just bowled me again." Boris' was not a happy bunny now at all and his smile had turned to a face that looked like a bulldog chewing a wasp. He lifted his bat in anger and smacked it down on the pitch with a resounding crack. 'Oh no. Not another new bat,' was the reply from the groaning fielders.

Chekov couldn't contain himself and clapped and laughed at his friend's misfortune. 'Jolly good show old man,' shouted Chekov in a mock posh English accent. Boris turned round to see who was shouting at him and muttered something incomprehensible under his breath, probably in Russian.

'And the same to you Boris,' laughed Chekov and grabbing Mildred they walked off in the direction of the "Snort and Truffle". 'Come on Mildred let's go and have a drink.'

They skipped off to the pub and grabbed a table and chairs outside in the warm sun joining the other spectators. 'Mildred isn't this just heaven? Just so English. A cricket match on a village green. I'm not so sure about Boris though. You must tell me all about this fascinating game.'

'Oh Chekov you are an old romantic but I don't know much about cricket I'm afraid.' Just then Brewster came out of the pub and walked over to Chekov and Mildred.

'Hallo you two love birds, what will it be?'

'Oh, er, I think I'll have a "G and T" please Brewster. What are you having Chekov?' purred Mildred.

'My god, that's it. A "G and T" and a game of cricket on such a beautiful day. What more could you ask for? It's all too perfect for words. Yes please Brewster, we'll have two "G and T"s.' Chekov was completely mesmerised by the atmosphere. He was in love, not only with Mildred but was totally smitten by the Muddlecombe bug. They sat watching the game in bemusement until Brewster arrived with their drinks.

'Thank you Brewster,' said Chekov.

'Brewster,' Chekov continued. 'Tell me about this fascinating game of cricket?'

'Ah, now you've asked the sixty four thousand dollar question.'

'I have?' replied Chekov still a bit bemused.

'To fully understand all the nuances of cricket you have to start learning at the age of seven at boarding school. You have to fully understand the wide range of meteorological variances. You have to understand the differences between the various sub soil strata, the differences of applied top soil strata. Then you need to be able to get into the mind of each grounds man just before the start of each match.' Kegworth had Chekov's full attention.

'You have to understand how the ball swings, how it seams, how it spins, how it turns………………………….'

Chekov interrupted quickly. 'I think it sounds like I need a course at university to even start to understand anything.'

'I'm sorry Chekov. It is a bit bewildering. Now hang on a mo. I think I have an abridged version of the game on a tea towel inside. Just bear with me.' And at that Brewster went back into the pub.

'I wish I hadn't asked now,' said Chekov.

'Oh, you'll come to love it darling. Just sit back and relax and enjoy the game.' Mildred sipped her gin and tonic slowly relaxing in the hot sun.

'It doesn't look like much of a game at the moment. Boris seems to have broken the thing you hit the ball with. I hope he is going to pay for all the breakages.'

'Oh, I'm sure he will. He's a very rich man now and thoroughly enjoying his retirement. Well not exactly retired but at least retired from his horrible old previous employer.'

'Excuse me,' came the quick retort. 'Not so much of the old please!' he teased Mildred.

'Oh, here comes Brewster now.'

'Now then Mr Yeboleksi, man of the world. This should add to your education,' Brewster grinned and winked at Mildred as he handed Chekov the tea towel with the words of wisdom on it.

Chekov picked up the cotton towel and started to read it to himself.

"You have two sides, one out in the field and one in. Each man that's in the side that's in goes out, and when he's out he comes in and the next man goes in until he's out. When they are all out, the side that's out comes in and the side that's been in goes out and tries to get those coming in, out.

Sometimes you get men still in and not out. When a man goes out to go in, the men who are out try to get him out, and when he is out he goes in and the next man in goes out and goes in. There are two men called umpires who stay out all the time and they decide when the men who are in are out.

47

When both sides have been in and all the men have been given out, and both sides have been out twice after all the men have been in, including those who are not out, that is the end of the game!"

There was a stunned silence for several minutes and then Chekov said, 'Mildred can I please have another drink only I think I need it a bit stronger this time.' He downed his gin and tonic and handed it to Mildred with a sort of glazed look on his face.

Mildred got up and taking his glass walked into the pub leaving Chekov staring blankly at nothing in particular. He eventually shook his head and coming back to reality suddenly realised that in all his years in psychological torture he was a mere amateur. There in front of him was the ultimate brainwashing piece of equipment. He could have saved so many hours of sleepless nights trying to extract information from exhausted individuals when all he needed to do was to let them read this and then they would have been putty in his hands. Gibbering idiots ready to disclose anything at his beck and call. Ready to denounce their best friends, wives, girlfriends, lovers, whole government departments. No wonder the British Intelligence Service was so efficient. How many thousands of people had he employed in the Lubyanka KGB Headquarters in Moscow? What a waste!

Mildred returned with their dinks only to find Chekov slowly banging his head on the table and gently crying to himself.

'Are you all right Chekov darling? You look a little upset? Here's your drink, is everything ok?'

Chekov slowly lifted his head from the table as Mildred put the drinks down and put her arms around him, gently smoothing his furrowed brow.

'There there darling I'm sure everything will be alright.'

*   *   *

Mrs Dimmock was, to say the least, a phenomenon. Her husband was as well. So phenomenal that nobody could actually remember who he was. Everyone knew who Mrs Dimmock was, and who Denis Dimmock was, that is after he was born.

But Mr Dimmock remained one of the great rumours of Muddlecombe-cum–Snoring. Some said that he died at the birth of Denis. No one is quite sure if that meant he died giving birth to Denis, or just died when he saw Denis being born.

Rumours had it that it was an immaculate conception. But these rumours were quickly scotched as the villagers didn't want any religious zealots running around flagellating themselves or blowing themselves up. As the local rubbish collection was non existent (the local council being unable to find Muddlecombe) it certainly didn't need any blood or guts to clear up unnecessarily.

Some of the villagers said Mr Dimmock was a travelling salesman, but couldn't remember what he was selling, or where he was travelling from or to.

There was a sort of black cloud hanging over the whole event of Dense's (Denis' nickname for obvious reasons) birth. Very strange, but then everything about Muddlecombe-cum-Snoring was very strange.

As Mrs Dimmock bumbled across the village green the cricket match came to a grinding halt and everybody gave her a respectful salutation. She got to the middle and went over to Boris and gave his bottom a little pinch and quickly skipped out of the way and left him turning a bright shade of purple with all his team mates whistling or giving cat calls.

She made it over to the pub and came and joined Mildred and Chekov. 'Hallo you two young lovers. Still enjoying the lovely afternoon watching these stupid men and their stupid game? Whatever will we be doing here next, eh?'

'Oh, Mar……..oops Mrs Dimmock.' (Mildred nearly forgot her protocol) 'Let the boys enjoy themselves and Chekov is learning all about this delightful game, aren't you darling?'

'It'll be a long time before I even begin to understand it, but my colleague seems to be picking it up fairly quickly.'

'Young Boris? And doesn't he look so smart in those lovely white clothes. I've no doubt I'll have to wash them for him again, but he's enjoying himself so much since he's come here and retired from that ruthless old employer of his.' Mrs Dimmock gave Chekov a wink.

'I see, get at Chekov day today is it?' he laughed and gave Mrs Dimmock a kiss on her cheek.

'Now then, can't stand round here gossiping, things to do, committee meetings to organise. We'll be seeing you later Mildred dear? I hope Boris has tidied up the Cottage.'

'Yes, I'll be over in half an hour. Three o'clock start is it Mrs Dimmock?'

'Spot on Mildred. See you then.' Mrs Dimmock picked up her basket and bumbled over towards Primrose Cottage.

* * *

Gerantinium O'Deighty III, as chairman of the Interplanetary Standards and Ethics Committee had his usual seat at the top of the table. The Cottage was looking prim and proper and the dining room all laid out ready for the committee proceedings.

Nobody knew how long the committee had been in existence. Nobody knew how old Gerantinium was. Nobody knew if they'd actually achieved anything, but it gave the committee members a sort of air of superiority over the other villagers. And recently things had started to happen. Nothing to do with this committee, but as a result of another sort of committee. It was called a company, a limited company to boot which sounded very posh, and it gave the other villagers a sort of air of superiority as everyone was a shareholder, so the airs of superiority evened out. A sort of socialist superiority. But today was just the old ordinary committee meeting which still held it's secrets.

The superiority was at a sort of "thirty fifteen" stage today, as they say at Wimbledon.

Mrs Dimmock was now in full flow laying out the pens and pencils, the drinks, the minutes and one could hear the kettle starting to boil so the coffee should be fairly imminent along with some of Mrs Dimmock's home made cookies.

Gerantinium sat in his usual white robes and as was the way of all people of great wisdom and sagacity; he had left some of his breakfast in his long white beard. He was fussing about arranging everything to his liking and with much "harrumphing" and coughing managed to settle down at long last.

To his right sat Ignatius Cromwell, (or Iggy as he was known in the village) the dour head of politics and religion, he also was doing much "harrumphing" and constantly looking at his watch, he started the coughing routine as well.

Mrs Dimmock dashed out of the room after hearing the kettle boil and several minutes later returned with a tray full of cups of coffee and, after a sigh of relief from Gerantinium, some of her homemade cookies. She poured the coffee and handed out the two cups and then as an afterthought said. 'Oh, I have had apologies from Nostrodamus Macadam, Thor and Harry Hercules.'

'I beg your pardon Mrs D?' queried a startled Gerantinium. What are they apologising for?'

'They said they might be a little bit on the late side.' Mrs Dimmock arranged the biscuits on a plate and handed them round.

'Disgraceful, unheard of, what's the world coming to,' harrumphed Ignatius.

'I must say it's a poor show. What appears to be the problem?' Gerantinium enquired.

'As I understand it, the cricket practice is taking a little bit longer than usual.' Mrs Dimmock looked up from her coffee and biscuit routine.

'That's a damn poor show,' muttered Gerantinium in a purposeful voice to stamp his authority on the proceedings. 'I suppose old Boris has been peppering the poor old ducks again, eh what?' He gave a little giggle but turning to the sour faced Ignatius who gave a little cough and shuffled a few pages about. 'Yes well, anyway…….'

'I thought that at this stage of the meeting it might be of interest to bring in Mrs O'Riley to update us on the new commercial venture in the village.' Mrs Dimmock interjected to save Gerantinium's bacon and to allow for a breather until the other committee members could make an entrance.

'Yes, I think we need to give Mildred and all the people involved in this new project some extremely heartfelt thanks. I don't know about you Ignatius, but I'm enjoying this new fangled inside toilet, and the double glazing is quite something. I don't know quite what we've done to deserve it but I for one am very appreciative.'

Gerantinium looked to Ignatius for a comment. Ignatius straightened himself in the chair and started to mumble something.' Yes, well,' his mumbling died away as Mildred came into the cottage.

'Excuse me gentlemen, I'll just get Mildred settled. Oh, and here comes our other erstwhile members of the committee. My, young Harry Hercules looks a bit hot and bothered. Dr Rammy must be putting them through their paces.' Mrs Dimmock hurried out to the kitchen as the other absentee committee members passed her going into the dining room.

'Mildred darling how are you?' a bit of a daft question as she'd already seen her on the village green, but things were different at the committee meeting in Primrose Cottage. Mrs Dimmock was no longer a bumbling stooped old lady; there was no basket, no shawl, no bonnet, only a smart upright, erudite lady with some considerable charisma and regal bearing. They gave each other a perfunctory kiss and Mildred replied.

'Mary, (what happened to Mrs Dimmock?) thank you for inviting me over. I hope I'm not late?'

'Goodness gracious me Mildred my dear. I doubt if this lot would know time management if it jumped up and bit their what's it's off!' They had a little giggle and Mrs Dimmock continued. 'And what's this you have here my dear? You know how to get round this lot. Now come on in and let's get you started. I thought after the boring minutes etc you could update us with the comings and goings of your little enterprise.'

'Well Fiona thought you might like to see our end of year results so she's done a draft preliminary report that will give you and the villagers some idea of how it's going and I've cooked a little sponge cake for the occasion'

'Splendid, lets go into the committee room shall we.'

'So are we all agreed that those minutes are a correct and true record?' Without looking up Mrs Dimmock signed the minutes and then looking to Mildred quickly moved on. 'Mrs O'Riley has kindly condescended to update us on the new enterprise in the village, so without any further ado I'll hand you over to Mrs O'Riley.'

'And if the chair may interject briefly, I must congratulate you on that fine sponge cake my dear.' Gerantinium had now added Mrs Dimmock's biscuit crumbs together with Mildred's sponge cake crumbs to those of his breakfast in the undergrowth of his beard.

'You're very kind Gerantinium.' Mildred opened up some papers and lifted a sheaf up to read. 'Thank you for asking me to join your prestigious committee. It's a great honour.' (Bullshit always baffles brains) She looked round the assembled members and with her normal doe-eyed expression which immediately had the attention of all the men, and began. 'You will probably all be aware that the Community College is now hosting a small project initiated by our new, or should I say, one of our new members of our community, Boris Slobovitch.'

There were mumblings around the room as to the amount of beer he could consume in an evening in the "Snort and Truffle" which varied from twenty to thirty pints.

Mildred coughed which got the desired effect of silence and continued. 'As you may remember, Mrs Dimmock's young lad and my late, sorry, absent husband, retrieved some considerable amount of stock from Kiev on behalf of Boris. This started the project off in our lapidary evening classes and we subsequently appointed young Dudley as our technical assistant. This all started a year ago and we now have a proper limited company under the name of "Borisky Diamonds".'

There was a short pause while she gathered herself and a ripple of excitement ran through the room. Mrs Dimmock looked on proudly after the mention of her son Denis, or "Dense" as he was normally called.

Mildred shuffled the papers around again. 'Although Boris is the main shareholder, some of you may remember he offered a considerable amount of shares to you in the village at knock down prices in return for your hospitality and kindness in looking after him and his gratitude at the safe return of both Dense and Mr O'Riley. Mr O'Riley hasn't returned yet but we all know he's safe anyway.'

Mrs Dimmock gave Mildred a little sideways look which was acknowledged. Mildred continued. 'So the position is at the end of the first year's trading that we have run into a small profit. I'm sure all you shareholders will by now have received your dividends in some form or another.' She gave Ignatius a sideways glance which started comments around the room to the effect of, 'didn't you buy any shares Iggy old chap?'

'How's your new double glazing Harry?'

'The central heating working alright then Gerry old boy?'

'That inside toilet has saved me a few cold nights eh?'

This caused much tittering and smirking apart from Ignatius who started harrumphing again but was lost for words initially and so settled into a little embarrassed heap with his arms crossed and said. 'Can't we get on with the meeting?'

Mildred waited until the noise had abated and continued. 'So at this moment of time the main shareholder and now President is Boris. A good friend of mine,' Mildred blushed here amidst catcalls from the male element. 'Chekov,' she paused to regain her composure. 'Mr Chekov Yeboleksi has put some considerable capital into the project for the funding of new machinery etc and is now Managing Director. Mr O'Riley and Dense are the two other major shareholders and we now have taken on permanent employees. Fiona is Finance Manager who produced this report. Sharon and Tracey are....'

'The filth!' exploded Gerantinium loudly blowing a considerable amount of detritus from his beard.

'Gerantinium!' Mrs Dimmock interjected quickly. 'Please can we have some order,' as the catcalls and general male chauvinistic motions subsided into muted laughter. 'I think a bit of decorum wouldn't go amiss here Chair!' Mrs Dimmock said sternly.

'Sorry Mrs D.' Gerantinium said sheepishly. 'Please excuse me Mildred, please do continue.'

'As I was saying. Our two CID policewomen are now employed by us on a commission only basis. I understand they are still gainfully employed by Scotland Yard but using this to benefit our increase in sales. Sharon is concentrating on London with some considerable success amongst some of her old underground connections I hear.'

'I hear Dr Rammy is having connections with her as well,' muttered somebody which bought a ripple of subdued mirth. More of your actual dirty laughter.

Mrs Dimmock subdued this even quicker with one of her stern looks. She looked up to Mildred as if to say, "I've put a stop to that nonsense, you may continue now Mildred."

'Meanwhile Tracey is concentrating on the Canary Islands and is finding considerable business in the bespoke jewellery market for the more discerning clientele out there. This also gives us a considerably higher profit margin as well. She is of course in touch with John, the owner of Primrose Cottage and is in liaison with Sidney of course.'

'How is young Sidney these days? Don't see much of him?' queried Gerantinium.

'I think his liaison with Tracey is keeping him busy these days,' confirmed Mildred.

'Dirty lucky bugger,' was a rather loud aside from the floor of the committee.

'Yes well. Anyway, as I was saying,' continued Mildred. 'Sales are good at the moment, but stock is running low so Sidney is following up Boris' initial lead of supplies in Tenerife and hopefully we will have more news soon.'

'What about that fella what keeps coming over and spending a lot of time in the Post Office while Bill is out?' Came the inquisition from Ignatius.

'E's only jealous,' came an aside from the floor. 'Av you seen Betty recently, coooor……….?'

'Dirty lucky bugger,' came another aside.

There was a coughing session from Mrs Dimmock as Mildred re-entered the floor. 'I assume you are talking about Brian, the Director of our largest customer in industrial abrasives.'

'I bet 'e's rubbing Betty up the right way.' More smutty giggles.

'Gentlemen, please,' came a stern warning from Mrs Dimmock. 'You were saying Mildred?'

'The industrial abrasives section is doing extremely well, taking all our low quality stock and increasing our turnover to boot,' Mildred stated in a business like voice, but remembering Brian from Tenerife and his liaison with Betty on their holiday.

Betty had changed from an ugly duckling into a stonking good looking swan since then and the locals had started to go to church just to see her choir practices in their droves, not to sing but just sit and watch. A lot of people thought they were praying, they were, for Betty to bend over again in her low cut dress.

'Well I think that more or less sums up Mildred's little project does it not?' Mrs Dimmock looked up to Mildred to confirm her exit and they both picked up the trays, stopping to let Gerantinium take one last biscuit, and went into the kitchen.

'Well done dear,' said Mrs Dimmock. 'I think you handled that extremely well. I feel we have a very useful new member on our committee. Now, what's happening to Mr O'Riley these days?'

Mildred looked slightly bemused until Mrs Dimmock stepped in to help her out.

'Your husband Mildred?'

'Oh, yes, er wassisname.'

'Creighky?' Mrs Dimmock was trying very hard to help her out now.

'Oh, yes, er, him. Oh yes, well, I don't actually know Mary.' Mildred looked up to Mrs Dimmock as if she would have the answer. And fair enough she did.

'I have a feeling in my blood that he may be coming home in the not too distant future.' Mrs Dimmock's "feelings in her blood" were a safe bet that it was actually going to happen.

'Oh, shit. Oops, sorry. Oh Bugger. Oh double sorry Mary. What I mean to say is ……….'

'Oh shit and oh bugger,' Mrs Dimmock completed the sentence for her.

'Yes, that's it. What am I going to do?'

'Well, to start with I think we need to move Chekov back into Primrose Cottage with Boris and Dudley and then when or, if, Creighky returns, we just need to keep Chekov low and then try and persuade your loving husband to keep his stay here to the minimum.'

'Mary you're a little angel.'

"Yes," thought Mrs Dimmock.

Chapter 5.   Lt Col Creighky O'Riley OBE MC

Creighky O´Riley´s family motto is: "Ferrum aircraft quod multi amotoris vos usquequaque conscendo in sinister," which roughly translates to: "Horses, aircraft and women, you always mount on the left."

This will give you a pretty clear picture of his character as he seems to have kept the family traditions pretty much on course to date.

Apart from the chap whose parachute failed to open at twenty thousand feet and got away with a few bruises and minor fractures, Creighky O´Riley was probably the luckiest man alive.

Born in Northern Ireland he did an apprenticeship at some racing stables south of the border near Dublin, but both his fast growth in height and his fast inability to keep his penis in his pants soon moved him onto greener grass in England one step ahead of several shotgun happy fathers.

He signed up in the Pioneer Corps and went to Korea where his expertise with horses saw him in charge of the ammunition logistics, getting ordnance up to the front. He was given a field commission after all his comrades had been either killed by mines or snipers but somehow he always managed to get through.

It was about then that fame and fortune struck. With his capture of Hill 122 which was subsequently used as a brilliant piece of propaganda. Creighky was immediately promoted to Captain, immediately awarded the Military Cross and immediately honourably discharged after a tour of all recruiting offices back in old Blighty, together with a nice little pension, thank you very much.

Muddlecombe-cum-Snoring was the obvious next posting so to speak and where he met Mildred and they fell in love and got married. It has to be said that the opposition in the village wasn't up to much and Mildred *was* getting a bit desperate.

After another little adventure he ended up wanted for murder in Moscow and from there to Helsinki where he had to lie low at the British Embassy until things calmed down a bit. He was accused of the death of Colonel Svetlana Koffinski, or "the Black Widow" as she was known in the world of the secret service. Responsible for the death of a number of MI6 personnel her demise was celebrated and Creighky was subsequently put on the Birthday's Honours list.

Once everything had died down he was enrolled into the diplomatic service, put on the Army's Reserve listing, once again promoted (honorary) to Lieutenant Colonel and spirited off to join the Botswana British High Commission in the capital, Gaborone as a commercial attaché, military division. Not before a brief trip to London to collect his OBE for his services rendered in helping out MI6.

Is he lucky or what?

*   *   *

The British High Commission in Gaborone, capital of Botswana, is located at one end of the Main Mall at the intersection of Khama Crescent and Queen's Road, with the State House at the other end. Just off Nelson Mandela Drive at the rear of the Government enclave.

The High Commissioner, Sir Reginald Makepeace, was sitting in his office with a brown file on his desk with another file inside it with a red diagonal line across it and the words SECRET marked clearly on the inside. It wasn't marked TOP SECRET as it wasn't of great interest to any foreign body but only of interest to the reader of the file.

The door knocked and he shouted "come in" as Creighky came, closed the door behind him and stared at the High Commissioner's office and all his surroundings. Mostly pictures of the Queen and some black chappie, and some pictures of them both with the person now seated behind the desk.

'Please take a seat Mr O´Riley,' he said pointing to the chair in front of his desk. 'I hope you don't mind me dropping all the Army number rank, medals etc. But I see here it is an *honorary* rank anyway.' He looked up from the folder at Creighky.

'So how's it going? All settled in are we? Sorry I haven't had the chance to go through the old induction process with you, but I hope my under-secretary has been of some use?'

Creighky had been trying to get the secretary under *him* for some time now but without much avail. 'Oh yes, fine girl. Fine girl, most helpful your honour,' he managed to get out.

The High Commissioner was a bit taken aback with the "your honour" bit but carried on anyway.

'Interesting file this of yours. I see we have you here as a sort of lying low procedure. Sorry to hear about Colonel Svetlana Koffinski. I had to cross swords with her once, couldn't of happened to a nicer woman. What's it say about the death. "Coitus interruptus asthmaticus mortalitas."

'Beggin' your pardon your highness,' Creighky jumped in quickly to explain everything. 'But nobody told me she was asthmatic. And there was me thinking this was the start of a fine romance and now they tell me she was interrogating me all the time. No bugger told me that either. So there I was getting' stuck in, so to say, and she's poppin' her clogs………..'

'Yes, I get the picture Mr O´Riley. Please sit down, and I see you got a medal in Korea?' The high Commissioner jumped in even quicker and started to look into the secret file.

'Oh, yes, that was some punch up out there, I can tell you. Them Communist fellas popping off at us without a "by your leave" or "if you please" but we're made of sterner stuff and I gave it back to them with both barrels. Oh they didn't like that much, I can tell you, but there was all this muck and bullets flying about all over the shop……………'

The High Commissioner had been through a lot of "muck and bullets" stories so he let Creighky prattle on while he opened the "Secret " file in front of him which read:

"Second Lieutenant (acting) O´Riley showed incredible bravery or incredible stupidity (the latter was confirmed) in getting ordnance up to the front line. Several times he walked straight through minefields without loss of life to himself or his mules. Later after staying overnight at an Irish Guards mess function he became completely inebriated as was his donkey by the look of things and went charging off towards the enemy lines waving a polo stick. Fortunately his screaming and waving scared the pants of a bunch of new communist recruits who fled their machine gun post as Lt O´Riley crashed into it. Fortunately nobody was hurt and we had captured a strategic hill, No 122, which subsequently lead to further successful operations. While he was in hospital recovering from a bruised buttock and a twisted ankle it was felt this incident could be used to the best propaganda effect. We immediately promoted him, awarded him the Military Cross and shipped him back to the UK for a tour of duty in the recruiting offices prior to his premature release."

The High Commissioner closed the folder and waited for Creighky to slow down before interrupting him.

'Jolly good show old chap. So now where does that leave us? You've got the old uniform all sorted out have you?'

'Oh yes, your honour, all spick and span. Ready for the off as they say at the Down Royal Races in Lisburn.'

'Got all the gongs and swords and things have we?

'Oh, yes, got all the medals and the old sword there. Would not a gun be more useful?

'No, no, we aren't at war here Mr O´Riley. This is a peaceful nation and we are here to promote trade, education, tourism, commercial interests' etc etc, and above all other things, friendship.'

'Right you are there, thank God for that. We don't want any more of them bullets flying about, now do we? And by God am I good at the old friendship bit there your grace.' Mostly with the opposite sex it had to be said.

'Good, well quite. Now if you're all kitted up we have a little ceremonial duty for you to attend to. The sword will be used in the ceremonial sense only if you see my meaning.'

"If you don't see my meaning, and you cock this up you're dead meat" was what the high Commissioner was really trying to say.

'Oh, I like the old ceremonials. Do I get to wear the hat with the old chicken feathers on then?

'Ostrich plumes actually Mr O´Riley. But no, we don't use that any more. The colonial days are long dead and buried.'

'Don't you worry, I've got the old peak cap anyway and them boots, you'll be able to shave in them. I'll have them bulled up sommat beautiful.'

'Good, good, that'll give the locals something to look at. I'm sure your military presence is really what they want. Not a boring old fart like me in a white suit. Just the ticket.'

He turned round and picked up some more bits of paper.

'Now, here's your objective.' He browsed through some official looking invitations. 'These De Beers chappies, sorry, Debswana as it is now called.' He looked up to Creighky to give him a quick explanation. 'De Beers and the local Botswana government have gone into a joint venture…………..'

'The beers, is this some sort of brewery then?' Creighky interrupted thinking things were looking up.

'No, no, De Beers. De Beers, the mining company. Big business out here……'

'Won't I be getting the old ceremonial uniform a wee bit dirty then, having to go down all them dirty coal mines?' Creighky's hopes had been dashed and he didn't really fancy going down any mine shafts, not in his nice new uniform anyway.

'No, no. Diamonds old chap. Diamonds!'

'Oh, the old sparklers is it then?'

'Spot on. And there won't be any going down any mine shafts either. This is purely a social occasion, all you have to do is strut your stuff, look ceremonial and talk to a lot of strangers and there may be a bit of food and drink thrown in I'm sure. How does that grab you?'

'I'm your man. By God that's the ticket. They don't come more social than me, I can tell you that me bucko!

Your "honour" or "your highness" seemed to have gone down the pan. And he'd heard about his social activities from the Helsinki Embassy.

'Yes, good, well that's that then. Now this is all about the inauguration of a new mine somewhere up country, at a place called Jwaneng. They say this is going to be a big one according to these geologist chappies anyway.'

'And will I be getting the old Roller then?'

'Roller, oh you mean Rolls Royce. Good heavens no, we can't run to one of those these days Mr O´Riley. No I'm sorry you'll just have to do with the old Land Rover. You be getting a driver of course.'

'Will that be your nice under- secretary girl then?'

'No, I'm sorry to have to tell you she is far too busy to run you around the countryside. No, you'll have one of our native drivers to get you there and back. Damn good chaps. Treat them nicely Mr O´Riley. Oh and if anybody asks where I am just tell them I have a meeting with a Trade Delegation and offer them my sincere apologies. This is what's called diplomacy now Mr O´Riley.'

'Oh, don't you be worrying yourself on that account there Governor. I'll be the height of diplomacy, just you wait and see.'

'Good, that's the spirit. Now here's all the bumf. If there are any queries, see my under-secretary, she'll sort you out. She's got the dates, hotels, contacts etc all in a nice little presentation for you. And don't forget you are now a representative of Her Majesty's Britannic Government. So you don't have to go round shooting anybody, there's no war, just go and enjoy yourself and try not to get too drunk. Stay in the shade is my motto, and mind out for the cheap South African champagne, try and drink plenty of water.'

'Oh, and don't forget the local greetings. Mma and Rra are marks of respect and thus are more significant than Mr and Mrs. Greeting people politely is one of the first things you must learn to do in Botswana - people get offended if you don't!

The correct form is,"Dumela mma/rra - le kae?" You reply, "Ke teng mma/rra, le kae?"'

'Don't you be worrying yourself your highness? I'm the very sole of discretion and you'll be proud of me. I won' let you down, that's for sure.'

The High Commissioner handed Creighky all the paper work and ushered him out of his office. He went back to his chair behind his desk and sat down with a worried look on his face.

Chapter 6. Mma Xalwo

The Somalis and Ethiopians can trace their heritage back to the Eastern (Ethiopic) Hamitic family of tribes, between the Nubian Nile and the Red Sea. They have been identified with the people of Punt, who were known to the Egyptians of the early dynasties.

They are a race of magnificent physique, tall, active and robust, with fairly regular features, but showing Negro blood in their frequently black complexion and still more in their kinky and even woolly hair. The female of the species being exceptionally beautiful in the eyes of the Europeans.

Xalwo or "ala intee la idhi xalwada iska kala daa", whatever that means in Somali, was no exception. Tall and statuesque with ebony black skin and European features, she stood head and shoulders above her African contemporaries here in Botswana.

Even as a child she had dreamt of becoming a famous model and had pictures of Iman and Shakira her African contemporaries who had found fame and fortune and married to rock or film stars.

She had crossed into Kenya taking a languages degree in Kenyatta University, Nairobi and moved south to more stable climes, looking each time for her knight in shining armour.

And bugger me, there he was.

Everyone in the De Beers offices, (De Beers and the government of Botswana were in discussions re joint ventures at the Orapa, Letlhakane and Damtshaa mines) had been given a programme of the day's events and a list of prominent guests which stated that Her Majesty's Britannic Government was represented by Lieutenant Colonel Creighky O'Riley MC OBE.

And there he was standing close by; you couldn't miss him, resplendent in his uniform, his medals and his ceremonial sword. But it was the boots that did it, and the spurs. He was tall, probably slightly taller than she was, but she *was* wearing high heeled shoes for the occasion. He had that military bearing, probably obtained more with riding horses than parade ground bashing and that certain "swank" when he walked and he was walking towards her right now.

This was it. She was desperate by now but at least he was a handsome specimen. Not quite as young as she would have wished but didn't he look the part? (Just what Mildred had thought at first glance as well?)

As head of the press liaison department she was allowed to be part of the reception committee to welcome distinguished guests. She had been working for De Beers for some time now, visiting all their various mining operations in Orapa, Letlhakane and Damtshaa, reporting on all the good and bad things that happened in the diamond mining industry. Major finds of large diamonds, major disasters and major rescues.

She had rubbed shoulders with the miners on the open-pit mining areas and could see the vast scars that the mining machines had left across the landscape. She knew of the enormous security problem there was of safeguarding any surface diamonds found by the miners, and the enormous lengths the security operations had to go to, to ensure none of these ever got onto the open market.

As well as the miners she had rubbed shoulders with the security personnel, some of whom wanted to rub more than just shoulders with her. And she had seen the way out of her life of poverty as she saw it, and she had manipulated miners, security and office personnel with her womanly wiles to slowly start to collect a small fortune in uncut diamonds.

The problem being that there was no way they could be of any value whilst still in Botswana or surrounding countries with the measures set up by De Beers to check every market place in Southern Africa.

But let's say she could get them to the USA or even the UK or Europe? That's when she looked into the eyes of Lieutenant Colonel Creighky O'Riley MC OBE and realised there was at last a hope for her future.

'Leeoottennant Kollonnell Creyekeee Oh Ryelee?' she said reading his name from the programme and looking straight at him in the eyes through her long flashing eyelashes.

Creighky hadn't failed to notice her among all the other dignitaries, but unusually for him, when she made the first move, he was somewhat taken aback and lost for his normal smooth talking reply.

'Oh, yes, well holy mother of jeysus, you have it there right on the knob, so to speak.' He tried desperately to change his gibberish into something a bit more romantic. 'Well it looks like that in the writing doesn't it? And you could be mistaken for saying that, only the English language is a funny old thing, don't you know.'

Xalwo probably knew more about the English language than Creighky and certainly knew her ranks in most of the world's armies, having fought her way out of Somali with a Kalashnikov in the terrible civil wars there.

'Oh, I am so terribly sorry. Please excuse my ignorance.' With that she lowered her head in supplication. But not before making eye contact again.

'Oh, now don't you go fretting yourself.' Creighky was beginning to regain a bit of composure and the old blarney was about to be brought into full use in the extremely near future.

'Now, excuse *my* ignorance. But wouldn't you be one of them fashion models, and what would a fashion model be knowing about silly old army ranks to be sure. But, I'll tell you anyway just so as you can sleep tonight.' He gave her a little twinkle and a smile. Engaging top gear in blarney, he continued.

'It's pronounced, "left tenant kernel", now how were you to know that? It's a daft old language so it is. But to a lovely lady like yourself, there's no need to be doing with all that military nonsense, you can be calling me

Creighky. And may I know what the queen of the fairies gave you for a name?'

"He's good this boy", thought Xalwo, bowing her head coyly and pushing down the accelerator pedal on the old eyelashes as she replied. 'My name is Miss Xalwo, or Mma Xalwo as they call me here in Botswana. I am the press liaison officer for De Beers or Debswana as it is about to be called, and I am honoured to be allowed to meet such a distinguished guest.'

'Xalwo, that's a beautiful name. It reminds me of the legendary Celtic Queen of Donegal in my home country of Ireland. They said that no man could look at her because of her amazing beauty and she ended up a spinster unable to go with any man and died sad and unhappy. Now we don't want that to happen to *you* now then do we?'

A bit OTT thought Xalwo, but she smiled all the same. 'Mr O´Riley you certainly know how to make a poor woman like me blush under your platitudes. Now then before I turn the colour of the sunset, tell me where did you get all those medals?'

'Don't you be bothering about all that military stuff and nonsense,' Creighky knew there was time enough to impress her with his daring do and his three hour commentary on the Korean War. That would bore the pants off her and then, whey hey!

'Mr O´Riley, I think it is time I introduced you to some of our other distinguished guests. I can't keep you all to myself, now can I?'

With that she grabbed his arm and walked around the enclosure and the marquee introducing him to some of the most boring people he had ever come across. He was too busy trying to look down the front of her dress and his mind was on other undiplomatic matters.

'And this is Rra or *Mr* Krishna Chutnabuttee as you would call him. He is a distinguished member of the Chamber of Commerce for Gaborone, and also the secretary of the BCA ....'

She was interrupted by Creighky.' Just run that by me again darlin'?'

'What?' Xalwo queried.

'The name of this lovely gentleman here?'

'Mr Krishna Chutnabuttee?' Xalwo repeated enquiringly.

Creighky bent down and shook hands with the diminutive gentleman in front of him who was a bit bewildered at having his name mentioned twice.

'Well, it's a small world, and that's no mistake. Would you believe it? We have one of your tribe in our village back home in Blighty. Would you credit that?'

Both Xalwo and the unfortunate Mr Chutnabuttee cringed visibly. But as he was six inches shorter than this buffoon in front of him and at the disadvantage of not having a sword to hand, Mr Chutnabuttee felt that this was probably not the best time to bring up any politically correct discussions.

Mr Chutnabuttee cleared his throat and managed to continue the polite conversation.

'So you say you have another Chutnabuttee in your village?'

'Yes, now what was his name? Young chap, tall good looking fella'. That's it, he just took over from old doctor what's 'is name who died.'

'You say he is a doctor?' enquired Mr Chutnabuttee.

'That's the ticket. Spot on me old mucker. Dr   ……eh ………….Dr Rammy. That's the chap!'

'Dr Rammy,' Mr Chutnabuttee mused a while. 'That wouldn't be Rammittin Chutnabuttee by any chance would it?'

'That's the one, by heavens that'll be your man.'

'Well as you say Mr O´Riley,' (he wasn't going to kowtow to any superior military ranking) 'it is indeed a small world if what you say is true. I have a young nephew by that name who seemed to have disappeared off the face of the earth from his studies at the University College Hospital, Jodhpur and it would be most interesting if indeed he was "your" man as you say.'

'Isn't that incredible?' Creighky looked to Xalwo for confirmation and looked back to Mr Chutnabuttee. 'Well, me bucko, you just leave everything to me and I'll be in touch with the old nephew there and who knows, we may be able to get him out here. What do you say to that my friend.'

Mr Chutnabuttee felt that "my friend" was a step in the right direction from "me bucko" and resigned himself to counting Mr O'Riley or whatever his rank was, as a new acquaintance.' Here is my business card Mr O'Riley. Please to be keeping in touch if you have any news. Oh and it was lovely to see you again Mma Xalwo.'

'The pleasure was all mine, Rra Chutnabuttee.' She felt it best to do a bit of grovelling to try and regain some composure over the tribal incident. 'Come along Mr O'Riley,' (she stressed the words). Dragging Creighky away from the startled Mr Chutnabuttee. 'Let's go and continue our diplomatic tour shall we?' They walked on into the marquee for some refreshments.

'So have you been in diplomacy long then Mr O'Riley?'

'Oh, I can't be doing with all that diplomacy malarkey.'

'Yes, I can see that now.'

'I doubt there's any of the old black stuff around to drink?'

'Black stuff?' enquired Xalwo.

'Yes, the old Dublin stout there, I've got a thirst like the winner of the Curragh.'

'I'm afraid the only black stuff we have here is dynamite.'

'Oh, jeysus, I don't want to be blowing anybody up. I just want a little something to tickle the old tonsils.'

'You'll just have to put up with some of our nice South African Champagne.'

'Champagne! Pish! Do you not have a decent Bushmills or Jamesons?'

'Are they Irish champagnes then?' Xalwo enquired with a twinkle in her eyes. 'Oh, oh, here comes Sir Metumile Kasire.'

'Sir Metal who?'

'Sir Metumile Kasire, the prime minister of Botswana. And we address him as your Excellency.'

'Oh, right you are then.'

'Mma Xalwo, how nice to see you.' Sir Metumile put is arm around Xalwo and gave her a perfunctory kiss on the cheek. 'And who is this fine gentleman with you?' he said standing back and admiring Creighky.

'Rra, your Excellency, may I present Lieutenant Colonel Creighky O'Riley MC OBE. He's from the British High Commission.'

'My God, hasn't he got a shorter name?'

'Creighky's the name your highness. Now don't you be worrying about all that military nonsense.'

'Oh, I'm glad about that. Looks like you've come dressed for battle.'

'Oh, it's the old ceremonials, don't you know. I won't be bothering to kill anybody with the old sword there.'

'That's a relief.'

'And I love those pyjamas your grace. You can't beat a bit of colour there.'

Xalwo was looking for an open cast mine to jump into.

Sir Metumile put his arm around Creighky and laughed out loud. 'I like a man with a sense of humour. And tell me Mr Creighky where did you get all those medals. Rorke's Drift?'

Sir Metumile laughed even louder. Xalwo managed to climb out of the open cast mine and force a titter. He put his arm around Creighky and said, 'Mr Creighky, come on, let's go to the bar, I don't know about you but I could murder a pint of Guinness, how about you my friend? No doubt Mma Xalwo will have some of that South African champagne piss!'

Xalwo managed a black look at the two men walking arm in arm towards the refreshment marquee.

'God now you're talking. Don't tell me you've actually got some of the black stuff here then?'

'I'm sorry my friend, another joke. No I'm afraid the only black stuff we have out here is ....'

'Dynamite.' Interrupted Creighky. 'Yes don't tell me.'

'Oh, you're learning quickly. No, I wish that we did have some of the old liquid gold. It takes me back to my halcyon days at Trinity College Dublin when I was studying politics........'

'Dublin. Now that's a terrible place and all, with that Leeson Street,' Creighky said as they purposefully made it to the bar. 'How many bars are there in that street? I never got to counting in the end.'

'Oh, yes. A beautiful city Dublin. But Oh, those hangovers. Oh, and by the way, how is my friend Reginald. Working hard as usual?'

'Reginald?' Creighky looked bemused.

'Sir Reginald Makepeace,' continued Sir Metumile.

'The British High Commissioner,' hissed Xalwo as she elbowed Creighky.

'Oh, the boss? Oh yes, up to his arse in them trade delegations don't you know. A good man that. Works too hard. Needs to get out a lot more.'

Xalwo looked around for another open cast mine.

'Mr Creighky, I like you, you speak your mind. You're like a breath of fresh air round here. Now what are you going to drink. Looks like it's South African piss or South African piss.'

'Why don't we try some of that South African stuff then me bucko? I don't suppose they'll be having any pint glasses?'

Xalwo was losing the will to live but managed to get hold of a champagne flute in order to uphold some sort of decorum.

Fat chance!

*   *   *

'Come in.' The High Commissioner called across his office. 'Good afternoon Mr O'Riley. Recovered from your little trip up to Jwaneng then have we?'

'Oh, the trip back was a wee bit on the old bumpy side. I seem to be a wee bit off colour, so to say.'

'I don't suppose that would have anything to do with a hangover would it Mr O'Riley?'

'Ah, right you are there your Excellency. That would be the reason no doubt. You've hit the nail on the head there.'

'And I've just had a call from another gentleman who has the same affliction. Now who do you suppose that would be?'

'Ah you have me there. No wait a minute. That'll be old Metal what's 'is name. Sorry, Sir Metal thingy. Oh bejeysus, it's all coming back to me now. Wasn't, sorry, isn't he a big wig in the old government or something?'

'Oh, they don't come any bigger wigs than Sir Metal thingy as you call him. He's the prime minister of Botswana which is where you are right now if you can remember that far back.'

'Oh shit. Oh I'm sorry, what I meant was ……………..'

'Oh shit is spot on I think for this occasion. I'm just going through the driver's report of last night. Very interesting: he says that when the police arrived at the Mokala Lodge Hotel at 3 o'clock in the morning following a complaint from a resident of unruly noises, they were met by a scene of two gentlemen and a lady dancing round a sword singing Molly Malone.'

'Oh shit.'

'Shall I go on?' a rhetorical question if ever there was.

Creighky had his head in his hands in front of the High Commissioner.

'The gentlemen in question started making loud shushing noises and the lady together with a large member of the entourage cordoned the police off into a corner and after a few minutes discussion managed to come to an agreed solution. The police went over and shook hands with both the prime minister and then yourself and everybody went quietly off to bed or wherever the police go to at 3 o'clock in the morning.'

'I suppose an apology is out of the question your highness?'

'Lt Col Creighky O'Riley MC OBE, an apology is right out of the question. What I forgot to mention is that His Excellency Sir Metumile Kasire said that I was working far too hard and needed to get out more.'

'Now there's a thing, did he now?'

'And asked me over with my good lady for a weekend at his private hunting lodge up country.'

'Did he bejeysus? Well he's that sort of fella. I found him most agreeable as well don't you know.'

'So it's me who should be apologising to you, or rather I should be thanking you for your own unusual diplomatic approach to the prime minister which has put me in a position to talk directly to him on his own. Something I've been trying to do for the last 12 months since I arrived.'

'There you go then. If there's anything else I can do for you, now don't you be afraid to be asking me.'

'I'm glad you said that Mr Creighky because the situation is that I was due to go back to the UK that weekend to deliver some important papers of a delicate matter that have come into my possession recently. I'm damned if I'm going to give up an offer like a weekend with the prime minister, so as we are rather short staffed perhaps you could help me out on this matter and pop over in my place.'

*   *   *

'Hallo, is that de Beers Head office? Oh it is good. Could you put me through to a Miss, sorry, Mma Xalwo please? I think she works in some office that deals with the press and all that malarkey.'

'Hallo yes. What? Oh who is calling, it's me. I mean it's Lieutenant Colonel O'Riley from the British High Commission.'

'Hallo yes. Is it Creighky? How did you know my name? Oh it's you Xalwo. How the devil are you now?'

'Not feeling too good eh? Yes, I know the feeling.'

'Listen, when can I see you again?'

'Never?'

'Oh, now don't be like that.'

'Not until the hangover goes?'

'Oh, right you are then.'

'This weekend?'

'That would be great.'

'Do what?'

'Can I get the whole weekend off?'

'No problem for this weekend I wouldn't think. I've got the old man eating out of me hand.'

'Go where?'

'Up to a safari lodge up country?'

'Have to hire a car?'

'Jeysus that would be something else. Will we be seeing the old lions and tigers then? Do I need to take the old sword with me?'

'No. They got people with guns to look after you eh?'

'Will I be getting a decent Irish whisky, none of that South African…… ?'

'You'll make sure of that. God, that'll be a blessed relief.'

'Good, I'll organise the old car then and see you on Friday.'

Creighky put the phone down and jumped punching his fist in the air shouting, 'Yes, you little beauty. Whey hey!'

Whatever that meant.

*　*　*

Xalwo put the phone down and said quietly to herself, 'got you sucker! Let's proceed with Plan A.'

*　*　*

'Now that was something else. What a weekend. I've never seen so many of them wild animals and that. And all the wild things coming down to the lake at night and the sunsets and all that fresh air. Jeysus I've never slept so much in me life.'

Some thanks to a bottle of Bushmills every night with a little something the local Witch Doctor had given Xalwo (Melatonin) to aid restful nights and contain his libido within manageable bounds. God he was a handful, but she managed to maintain her composure just long enough before he dropped off to coma land.

'I'm glad you enjoyed it Creighky my dear.' Plan A was going to plan so to speak. He was very nearly eating out of her hand. She patted his thigh as he drove up to her apartment.

'That sure was one big zoo. I never saw any zoo keepers, now did you?'

'Creighky, that wasn't a zoo that was a game reserve.'

'But how the hell do they feed all them animals. There must have been hundreds of them wild beasts or whatever you call them.'

'It's a natural park. The animals are in their natural environment. They survive on the natural food cycle.'

'I never saw anyone riding round on a bicycle dishing out the old pork chops there.'

Xalwo laughed. She wasn't quite sure if Creighky was having her on or not. 'Creighky, you make me laugh. It's natures way of ensuring that it's the survival of the fittest. Dog eats dog.'

'Now you don't have to tell me about that. Sure wasn't I in Korea where the buggers eat dog there.'

'No, you dozy bugger. The survival of the fittest ensures that each class of animal is safeguarded to promote it's strongest lineage to maintain it's heritage. But the weakest serve a purpose in supplying sustenance for the strongest. Now you'd better pull over here.' She pointed to a parking space in front of a tall apartment block.

'I tell you what my princess (Creighky still hadn't achieved *his* plan A yet so a bit of flattery wouldn't go amiss here and there.) why don't we do that again next weekend and you can teach me some more all about wild animals and their mating habits?'

Creighky gave her a long lingering look, and then jumped in quickly. 'Oh shit. I forgot. I've got to go back to Blighty next weekend.'

'You have to go away next weekend'? Implored Xalwo as if her poor heart was broken.

'Wouldn't you now it. I've got to go and do a bit of courier work for old Reggie there. But I won't be long.'

'Oh Creighky dear, what am I going to do without you?' her tongue couldn't' get much further into her cheek. 'What sort of courier work?'

'That's the rub. I don't know the details but it's sort of hush-hush. The old diplomatic bag and all that.'

Xalwo's brain went into overdrive. Looked like Plan B was going to come into action a bit sooner than expected.

'Creighky darling, why don't you come up for a quick cup of coffee? There's plenty of time to hand the car back.'

Creighky's brain was going into overdrive as well. Looked like Plan A could be in action at long last.

'There's a cracking idea, I've a thirst on me like one of them wild beasts.'

He parked the car and Xalwo showed him up the lift into her apartment. 'You just sit yourself down there and I'll get the coffee on. Will instant be ok big boy?'

"The more instant the better," thought Creighky to himself. 'Ah, sure that'll do nicely princess.'

She came through with the coffee, put it down on the coffee table in front of the sofa and beckoned Creighky to come closer to her.

'Now then Creighky, I want you to do me a great big favour. Do you think you're up for it?'

"Jeysus, am I up for it? I'm gagging for it," he thought but the words came out somewhat differently. 'Princess, you know I'd walk over burning coals and crawl over broken glass to do whatever your little heart desires.'

'I take it that's a yes then.'

'Hey, you're a right little tease so you are. Now then, what can I do for you? I'll do anything as long as it doesn't cost me any money or make me thirsty.'

'Good. Now I have a little trinket that I picked up in the course of work shall we say, that needs to be somewhere near London to be of any value.'

Creighky looked at her blankly with only *his* Plan A in mind.

'And to be of any value,' she looked Creighky in the eyes to see if the lights were on and got a brief second of recognition. 'To be of any value, it has to bypass all these silly little taxes, import, export, VAT etc etc.'

She got hold of Creighky's hand which triggered off a few "below the waist" brain cells. 'Now let's say somebody was going to the UK with a diplomatic bag, which does away with all those taxes, how grateful do you think a person would………….'

Then lights suddenly came on and Creighky was there in a flash.

'I'm your man. By God, I'm your man. Isn't that just what I'll be doing next weekend? Jeysus! Are a lucky woman? Are you one lucky son of a gun? Xalwo, couldn't I be doing that for you. Just like you said.'

'Creighky, you're a darling. Could you really?' She gave him a big hug and out again before his roaming hands started on their lustful way. 'You great big handsome beast. Now you'd best get the hire car back and I'll pop over after work and we'll meet somewhere before you leave.'

She lifted him up and ushered him purposefully out of the apartment and into the lift before any of his adrenalin could really get going. With a big kiss she waved him goodbye. He got down to the reception floor and was just about to get in the car when the thought struck him that he hadn't had any coffee. Or any Plan A either.

*   *   *

Two days later Creighky was back in her apartment after she had finished work.

'Now here you are Creighky darling. Here's my little trinket which is all your responsibility now.' She handed over a small velvet bag with a drawstring and continued as he looked at it.' Now you have power of attorney to place this in a safe deposit box. The bank details are all there. This has been witnessed and authorised by a public notary whose office is here in Gaborone with it's head office is in London. All you have to do is sign here.'

She gave the paper to Creighky and wrapped herself around him as she passed him the pen to sign. 'That's all there is to it big boy.'

'What's in it for me gorgeous?' Creighky enquired thinking of Plan A.

'You just sign there darling and wait and see when it's all over. You'll get your reward don't you worry.' She turned his face to hers and gave him a big wet slobbery kiss.

Poor Creighky's brain cells connected to above and below the waist line were going into warp speed together with his imagination as Xalwo gently guided his hand onto the paper and smoothed his furrowed brow as he signed the document.

'There now. That wasn't so painful now was it?'

That's all she knew. There was a terrible pain growing in his groinal area.

'So all you have to do is to pop into the branch of the bank here.' She pointed out the address in London. 'They will ask you for some form of identification, that'll be your passport, and they will initiate a safe deposit box for you. Place the bag in it as you are watching and after it's all locked away, they will give you the key and when you bring it back to me, off we go and celebrate with a nice long weekend up country in a nice safari lodge with lots of Irish whisky.'

"Bugger the whisky!" thought Creighky. The pain in his groinal area was getting worse.

'Now all you have to do is pop that little bag into *your* diplomatic bag and the job's done. Here's a little spending money for your trouble. Now don't you go spending all that on whisky?'

'Xalwo, would I be after doing that? Don't you worry your little head over anything now?'

Xalwo tore off a copy from the document and gave it to Creighky. 'Here's your copy to show to the bank, but I will fax them a copy anyway and nothing could be simpler, now could it?'

'I don't suppose there's a drop of Bushmills in this beautiful apartment of yours is there? I've a terrible thirst coming on.' For the word "thirst" one should read: "a terrible pain in the groinal area!"

'Don't you remember big boy, you drunk it all last weekend.' For that one should read: "you just go home now before you start trying to get your hands down into my knickers!"

Chapter 7. The Hero's return

Mildred raped him.

Well he was going to be away for some time in the foreseeable future and in the meantime she felt it best to take advantage of the present.

They both lay naked, flat on their backs, Mildred gently caressing a limp hand by her side as Chekov stared, eyes wide open to an indiscriminate spot focussed somewhere between the bed and the ceiling. He was covered in a fine film of perspiration with an incongruous smile spread over the width of his face.

After some considerable length of time, Mildred managed to try some form of conversation.

'He's coming back.'

Chekov's facial muscles tried strenuously to rearrange themselves back into the normal audio mode and eventually came up with,

' Er?'

'He's coming back!'

' Er.'

'Wassisname.'

' Er.'

'You know……….'

` Er.'

'Thingamajig.'

` Er.'

'My husband.'

` Er!'

'Creighky.'

'Crikey!'

'That's the one.'

'БВАПУ ЬФТ!' which is a Russian swear word, roughly translated meaning "Kinnell".

Chekov started to try and sit up.

Mildred pushed him back down.

'Not right now.'

'Oh'

'Not today.'

'Oh.'

'Mrs Dimmock reckoned he'd be coming back fairly soon though.'

'Oh shit.'

'So you'll have to pop back to Primrose Cottage for a while.'

'Oh shit.'

'Yes, that does mean living with Boris.'

'Oh shit.'

They just lay there for some considerable time contemplating the logistics of Creighky's return, then Mildred raped him again.

It wasn't a very big rape though this time.

*   *   *

'Hang on I'm coming,' said Mildred rushing to the front door. She opened it only to be brushed aside by Creighky.

'Hallo me darling. It's me, the hero returns, give us a big kiss you old shagbag!'

'Er, oh, yes, hallo, we've been expecting you. Look Creighky, I've got a meeting on at the Community College right now. I've made your bed up in the spare room. Why don't you pop down to the "Snort", I'm sure Brewster will knock you up some crisps or something. Must dash, see you. Oh, and how long will you be staying?'

'Just the weekend,' replied Creighky and with that Mildred grabbed her coat and handbag and squeezing past Creighky made it to the front door before he could gather his wits about him and closed the door behind her escaping out into the front path.

"Well," thought Creighky, "looks like there's no Plan A here then either."

"I'll be getting some craic down at the old "Snort" then," he thought and he went upstairs and unpacked.

*   *   *

Creighky strode down the lane to the "Snort and Truffle" with an air of assurance of a man who had a stonking good tale to tell everyone. After all he'd been away for well over a year now and everybody had missed his tales of daring do in Kiev, Moscow, Helsinki and now Africa. Boy, were they in for some stories. Would they be glad to see him!

It had been over a year now since he left Muddlecombe for Kiev on a trip to collect Boris' pension funds with Mrs Dimmock's son Dense. Little did he know the "pension funds" were diamonds Boris had secreted away from his boss, Chekov, for his old age. And now Boris was the chairman of the new company with his old boss as the MD and major capital shareholder. And Creighky and Dense were the other shareholders. It's a funny old world that's for sure.

So Creighky walked into the pub and was duly greeted with reverence.

'Creighky you old bugger. You been away then?'

'Hallo you old sod. You're looking well for a man in your condition.'

'I remember the face, can't put a name to it though.'

'Bugger me it's old what' is name.'

'That's kind of you Creighky, mines a pint of Brewster's best bitter.'

Then he saw the barmaid, Blossom Deecup. The last time he saw her he got a left hook to the nose a right elbow to the solar plexus and a knee to the nuts. That was after he had his hand half way down the back of her jeans.

'Blossom darling, you're lookin' as beautiful as ever.'

'And you are?'

Brewster the landlord was looking on watching the proceedings of Creighky's entrance and noticing a sharp halt to the profit margins. 'Blossom, why don't you get this nice man a pint of the dark stuff? Whoever he is!'

This brought a round of laughter to the pub as Brewster winked at Blossom.

'Brewster, God bless you, you're a saint so you are.'

'I'll put it on the tab then shall I sir.' This brought another round of giggling. There was a long pause and Brewster felt someone had to say it.

'Welcome back Creighky.'

Now it may seem strange that nobody had mentioned or had the temerity to ask Creighky where he had been for the last twelve months, and nobody had asked him what he had been doing. Although half the villagers may be inbred they weren't daft. Having to put up with his Korean muck and bullets story every night for the past few years it would have taken someone incredibly stupid to start off another round of boring anecdotes.

Oh,oh, and in he came.

Every time Boris entered the pub it was like a total eclipse of the sun. As soon as he had managed to get his large frame through the door it was like the sun rising on a brand new day again.

'Creighky my friend, where have you been!'

Oh shit. The whole pub cringed as Boris rumbled over to Creighky and gave him a great big hug. Putting him down, Creighky took a deep breath to rearrange his rib cage, and after managing to get some air back into his lungs he completed a whole sentence.

'Boris!'

'Da da, yes, yes,' this was Boris' way of double declutching from Russian into English. 'Creighky my friend, I worry for you muchly when I hear you with Black Widow, then my friend Dense tell me all about you and I hear you go to Buckingham Palace to get medal.'

The truth of the matter is that Creighky did go down to Buck House to get his OBE as did Dense, but Creighky was in a political limbo land at the time being on the wanted list for the murder of the Black Widow, Colonel Svetlana Koffinski, an ex KGB double agent who had been promoted sideways into the FSB in Kiev.

Well it wasn't actually murder as they discovered later, more your actual manslaughter.

Well more your actual woman slaughter to be precise.

Well not actually slaughter per se, more your actual shagged to death. Not that Creighky knew anything about it and she didn't realise it until it was too late anyway and didn't know much about it either. Things started going tits up during an asthma attack in the middle of frenzied lovemaking.

That's probably where the saying came from as that's how they found her the next day. A tad on the cold side too. And Creighky and Dense managed to escape to the British Embassy in Helsinki where Creighky had to stay until secreted out for the day for his medal and back and then out to Africa to lie low until the Russians either found out about the "cock up" or forgot about him.

'But I don't see you back here then I hear you out in Africa. I worry for you much and I have to thank you much for you bringing my pension fund back to me and …………………'

'Boris can we talk about this pension fund bit please,' interrupted Creighky.

'Da da, yes yes,' Boris continued.

'Me and me old bucko Dense were under the impression that it was the old Post Office savings, not your actual wee bits of glass.'

'Da da, yes yes,' Boris started again. 'I have trouble to get home to Kiev as FSB watching me and brother there, so he tell me of plan, but I forget to tell you of plan in case you get tortured.'

'Oh. That's very decent of you old man,' said Creighky with just a hint of sarcasm in his voice.

"Da da, yes yes,' Boris continued.' Yes I know I am bastard but I very sorry and now I give you shares in company and now I buy you drink.'

'Now you're talking. I'll have the same again my friend,' Creighky finished his pint and offered it back to Brewster behind the bar.

'So please be telling me of how you escape Kiev my friend?'

Oh, no, the groan went round the pub and the drinks started to be taken outside in the sun as Dr Rammy's cricket practice came to an end. It was another beautiful summer's evening in Muddlecombe as the sun set and a load of extremely thirsty cricketers were swiftly approaching the pub only to be put off by waving arms telling them of the arrival of Creighky and some more bullshit. So a volunteer was sent in to get hold of the bar staff for an outside order.

Several hours later, Brewster could see the profit margins zooming up nicely as Boris and Creighky reduced his stock levels considerably, and that with the cricket team outside as well.

Fiona and Dr Rammy were in deep conversation in front of her double entry blackboard when Creighky took a keen interest of these proceedings and stared interrogating Boris.

'Borish, my friend. I can't help notishing that you are wearing white.' One could see where the bar stock was going quite clearly. 'And whash all that gobbly dee gook the beautiful Fiona ish writing on that board.' Creighky had inbuilt flattery for any woman or blarney as they called it back in Ireland.

'Da da, yes yes,' the instant lowering of bar stock levels didn't seem to make any difference to Boris as he continued.

'I am cricketeer my friend, is that not so Dr Rammy,' he shouted across the bar.

'What was that Boris?' Dr Rammy was rudely interrupted from his in-depth discussion with Fiona on the vagaries of the day's order of play and the credits and debits of the team players.

'I am cricketeer!' Boris shouted back.

'You are that Boris my friend and ………..oh, hallo Creighky, I didn't see you there.' He had hoped he could get away without bumping into him.

'Yes, our very own Boris is a damn fine cricketeer, and he is causing me much debiting in cricketing finance terms. Another twenty two pints up again today you old bugger.'

This puzzled Creighky who shook his head and then suddenly a spark of memory kicked in that was relevant to Dr Rammy.

'Rammy me old mucker, I bumped into one of your lot out in Boshwanaland.'

'You did what?'

'One of your lot, one of your tribe, you know, the old Chucking butties gang. Hang on there a tick, he gave me a card, I've got it here somewhere.'

With that Creighky proceeded in what could only be described as a good imitation of a circus clown act but eventually came up with the card.

'There you are, I told you show. Here what's it shay here, you read it me old mucker.' And with that he fell off the bar stool, which was long overdue, and Boris and Dr Rammy picked both him and the card off the floor.

Dr Rammy investigated the card and suddenly exploded, 'bugger me it's my old uncle Krishna. You met uncle Krishna?' a bit of a daft question to ask Creighky in his current state but heigh-ho, let's give it a go.

'Unka who?' yes it was a stupid thing to try until Dr Rammy investigated the card further.

'Mr Krishna Chutnabuttee, President of the Gaborone Chamber of Commerce and, listen to this, Secretary of the Botswana Cricket Association. Well where did you meet him Creighky?'

'At a pish-up!' Creighky was quite clear on that matter, although it wasn't a piss-up at the time it quite clearly ended up as one.

'With my mate old shir metal thingy, prime minishter of Boshwanaland.

'Who?'

Dr Rammy and the rest of the audience were a little unclear on what they had just heard and knowing Creighky it was more than not a little bit of exaggeration. But in his current state they doubted if he had any brain cells left to make anything up other than the truth.

'Did you just say the prime minister of Botswana?' Dr Rammy said it but on behalf of the entire assembled crowd who were now engrossed in the ensuing inquisition.

'My old mate metal wassisname. No, no I beg your parding, *shir* metal thingy. 'You mushn't forget the *shir*.' Creighky slurred but he wasn't quite sure who he was slurring at.

'The prime minister of Botswana?'

'Yesh, whatever you just shaid. Me old mate from Trinity College Dublin and Leeshon Shtreet.'

Creighky did a double take to try and focus on those nearest him to ascertain that his words were being fully understood and believed.

There was an uneasy silence around the pub until Creighky started looking towards Fiona's blackboard and after gaining a reasonable focussing length tried another bit of conversation again.

'Whashthat!'

'Oh, oh, are you going to try and explain it to him or will I.' Dr Rammy looked forlornly at Fiona.

'Let me handle this,' she said quietly in reply.

'It's a blackboard!'

At which point Creighky fell off his stool again but permanently this time.

*   *   *

Mildred was relieved to get the call from Fiona at the pub telling her Creighky was being brought home knowing that no further proceedings would accrue from the evening and she could go to bed in the safe knowledge that no molestation would occur.

Once the getting him upstairs bit had been accomplished with the help of Boris and Dr Rammy, she took his shoes off and drew the line at taking anything else off. But her eyes were drawn to a velvet bag on the table top next to his bed. The type of bag she had seen many times in the packaging and despatch department of the jewellery project.

Her interest was immediately aroused and knowing there would be no further interruptions, she picked it up and was staring open mouthed at an extremely large bit of glass. She could not dare to think it would be a diamond so she put it back in the bag and took it through to her room knowing full well Creighky would not be surfacing until very late the next day.

*   *   *

The loud knocking on the front door woke Chekov and putting on his dressing gown he looked outside to see Mildred.

Opening the door he pulled her in only after ascertaining nobody was around. He looked at his watch and said, 'what's the matter Mildred, it's only seven o'clock in the morning. You'd better come inside quickly.'

He hoped she hadn't come here to rape him again. He was still exhausted from the last session.

Without a word she took the bag out and showed him the bit of glass.

'БВАПУ ЪФТ!' which roughly translates to "Kinnell" that's a big bugger.

'Where did you find that?'

'In Creighky's room, is that a diamond?'

'I, I don't know. What are you going to do about it?'

I don't know, what do you suggest? I'll have to put it back fairly soon before he wakes up.'

A pregnant pause ensued until Chekov stopped scratching his head and said, 'We'd best let Dudley have a look at it.'

'A bit smartish,' confirmed Mildred. 'Is he still sleeping here with Boris and you?'

'Yes, he's upstairs, but had a bit of a thrash last night at the "Snort".'

'As did everyone else by the sounds of things,' replied Mildred. 'Do you think you can wake him?'

'We'll have to give it a go.'

So half an hour later a bemused Dudley was sitting down in the kitchen of Primrose Cottage with a large mug of hot black coffee, wondering what the hell was going on.

'Dudley, we're awfully sorry to get you out of bed at this time but something very important has come up,' Mildred tried the softly

softly approach. 'Dudley, will you have a look at this for us please?'

'Oi'll give it a go lowk.' Dudley came from a part of the country called the Black Country where they appeared to speak a different language from everybody else, but Mildred pushed on anyway as she undid the velvet bag and rolled the item in front of the bewildered Dudley.

This was of the very few times that anybody had ever seen Dudley lost for words, in whatever language. But not for too long.

'Bugger me!' Both Mildred and Chekov were ok on this bit so far.

'Well oi'll be buggered.' More or less ok with that as they both sat waiting for the next words of wisdom.

'Bludey norrah!' there seemed to be some pattern emerging here.

All that was to follow was some considerable shaking of the head until, 'we'd best get down to the lab bludey quickly.' No problem with that as they picked up the item in question and waited for Dudley and Chekov to get dressed and set off for the Community College.

'You got the keys Mildred?' enquired Chekov.

'Oh, yes, I was expecting something like this to happen.'

They quickly opened up the school and allowed Dudley to open up his restricted area for diamond cutting. He sat down and reaching for his large magnifying glass quickly set about examining the stone. It was some while before any recognisable sentence was forthcoming other than a similar conversation they had already had in the cottage. The stone was now on the electronic scales and this stimulated a full sentence at last.

'Bludey norrah! Yowl never believe this. That's got to be over twenty carats at least!'

'And it is a diamond?' Chekov wanted some form of confirmation.

'Too fooking troo, that's a bludey dowmond awrite, a fooking big bugger! Just look at the bludey colour, and the clarity of it! Get a decent coot on that fooker and it'll be worth a bludey fortune oi'll bet!'

'I take it that's a yes then?' enquired Mildred sheepishly. 'What do we do now?'

'God knows,' didn't help matters from Chekov.

'I've got an idea,' said Mildred.

*   *   *

'Here's your breakfast darling.' Mildred had a tray of fresh orange juice, coffee with toast and marmalade ready for Creighky to wake up.

It took a bit of time but eventually his eyes slowly opened and he managed some words.

'Jeysus fucking Christ, where the hell am I?' Not the most romantic greeting but Mildred had patience and stamina if nothing else.

'Oh it's you Mildred,' some more evidence of recognition. 'My head feels like I've got a gang of navvies working on it.'

'Now don't you bother about that, here's some pills. Drink them down now like a good boy,' and she watched as he tried to get up on one elbow but had to be helped and Mildred held the glass for him.

'My goodness gracious, what's this. Oh Creighky you haven't bought me a little present have you?' she said as she reached across and picked up the velvet bag.

'Jeysus Christ! God no Mildred. What I meant to say was that I forgot your present. That's for her, her ………..' Creighky was now fully upright and stuttering very badly. He continued trying to pick up the thread. 'That's for her Highness's Britannic Government property. I've to pop down to London tomorrow and pop in to the Foreign Office and deposit that in a safe keeping so to say.' "Phew I think I got away with that," thought Creighky.

"You lying bastard," thought Mildred, but as quick as a flash came out with, 'I'd love a day out in London darling.'

'I'd love for you to come sweetheart,' the euphemisms were flying about all over the place. 'But I've got to spend a lot of time at the boring old Foreign Office and I doubt they'd let you in without the old security clearance there. And then I've to get to Heathrow and on the old plane back to Jo'berg don't you know. So I doubt if we'd have an awful lot of time together sweetest."

'Never mind, some other day eh?' Mildred put the bag back and walked out of his room. 'Shit, now what do I do.'

*   *   *

It was time for the weekly meeting of Mildred's mafia at Muddlecombe Hall, the home of Lucinda D'Arcy Landacre. A supposedly whist drive but it was gossip driven with the help of a few bottles of wine and Lucinda's generosity in the kitchen. Or more probably one of her servant's generosity with their culinary skills. Mildred, Betty, Fiona and Lucinda sat round the expansive lounge of Muddlecombe hall and after the initial time allotted for greeting and the first glass of wine got down to the nitty-gritty.

'So the old man's back then Mildred?'

'Back and gone.'

'Coorr, that was quick.'

'Thank God!' Mildred got them all laughing.

'Did you get him to bed all right?' Fiona queried having seen Creighky being carried out of the pub.

'Well, Boris and Dr Rammy did. I wasn't going to touch him.'

'That's not a very nice way to treat your beloved.' Betty asked.

'You don't know how I treat my beloved,' replied Mildred giving Betty a big wink.

'You dirty bitch. But I don't suppose we will get to find out will we?'

'Nosy buggers. Oh, and you'll never guess what I found in Mr O´Riley´s possession after he'd been put to bed.'

'Mildred really, I thought you said you didn't touch him?' Lucinda was getting interested now.

'Oh, no. but he did leave something by the side of the bed.'

'Go on Mildred,' the assembled audience replied in anticipation.

'A little bag with something inside it.'

'And……..'

'A bloody great diamond.'

'No!'

'Yes. So I takes it down to Primrose Cottage while he's still comatose and drags Chekov out of bed………….'

'For God's sake Mildred can't you leave the poor chap alone?' Betty chirped in.

'For God's sake Betty can't *you* get your brain above the waistline? No, I showed it to him……'

'Dirty cow!'

'Fiona really! No I showed the diamond to him and he drags poor Dudley out of bed and off we goes to the school and opens up his lab and he nearly has an orgasm. Whatever one of those is.'

That had the place in hysterics.

'More wine girls?' Lucinda being the perfect hostess had noticed a sharp evaporation and filled up the glasses.

'So what did Dudley say?' The questioning was getting intense now.

'I don't know. Something about a lot of carrots. But he was impressed anyway?'

'So where did Creighky get this from?'

'I don't know. I took it back and woke him up thinking it was a present for me and he stuttered about it being something to do with the government and off he goes down to London and buggers off back to wherever he came from.'

'Where did he come from?'

'Well, that's the sixty four thousand dollar question. I don't know.'

'Mildred, you really must be more careful with your men.' Lucinda said with some seriousness which was totally missed.

'Doesn't he work in Africa?' Betty asked.

'Yes, he was talking about some country in South Africa in the pub the other night,' Fiona put her penny's worth in. 'I think it was called something like Bottle wander land or something.'

'Isn't that near Rhodesia?' Betty enquired.

'They`ve done away with that place haven't they? Isn't that Zambezi land or something now?' Fiona asked.

'No, that's Zambia.' Lucinda added as Mildred listened disinterestedly.

'I know who will know. Young Dr Rammy.' Fiona brightened up.

'No, he's from India, not Africa.'

'Yes, I know he's from India but Creighky gave him a card the other night in the pub, just before he fell over, which had the name of someone he'd met out there who might be related to Dr Rammy.'

* * *

'Hallo, is that Mr Krishna Chutnabuttee?' The gathered audience in the "Snort" were breathless waiting for Dr Rammy to get the connection using Fiona's phone.

'Yes I can wait, will he be long? He's on the other line in his office.' Dr Rammy kept them all up to date.

'Hallo. Mr Chutnabuttee. Mr Krishna Chutnabuttee…………?'

'My names Rammittin Chutnabuttee……………….'

'Doctor Rammittin Chutnabuttee………'

'Yes……………'

'Yes……………'

'Yes, uncle it's me………….'

'Yes, *doctor* Rammittin…………..'

'Well, it's a bit of a long story…………..'

'I'm in England…………………..'

'In a lovely little village called Muddlecombe-cum-Snoring……………'

'Yes, I have my own practice here…………..'

The audience were getting a bit restless here with several arm gesticulations and waving signs imploring him to get a move on.

'Yes, I'm very well……………..'

'No, I'm not married……………'

More gesticulations, with Dr Rammy holding his hand in front of the phone explaining that he had to get the family rituals out of the way first.

'Yes, I'm still playing cricket………….'

'Who for………?'

'The Muddlecombe Cricket Club……..'

'The who…….?

'Uncle are you there………………?'

'It's a terrible line…………..'

'I am having a lot of crackling on the line………………..?

'Hallo, oh you're there uncle……………'

'Yes, that's right…………'

'MCC?'

'Yes, the MCC……………..'

'You what………?'

Fiona, Lucinda, Betty, Mildred, Brewster and Blossom were all pulling their hair out by now.

'You want me to do what…….?'

'Come out there and play……………'

'It's a bit inconvenient right now uncle, but I am giving it my earnest consideration…………………..'

'Look uncle what I'm really phoning up about is …………….'

The audience all breathed a sigh of relief.

'Yes I see on your card that you are big chief of cricket in Botswana………..'

'Yes uncle, but can I be asking if you are meeting someone called Creighky O'Riley…………..''

'Hurray!' whispered the assembled crowd.

'Captain,' hissed Mildred.

'Captain Creighky O'Riley………..''

'No, he's been promoted now,' interrupted Brewster who had to sit through the whole episode the other night as requested by Boris. He's a Lieutenant now. No, sorry, Lieutenant Colonel.'

Dr Rammy put his hand over the phone again. 'Are we all quite sure on his bloody rank now please?'

'Yes, Lieutenant Colonel.'

'He's a Lieutenant Colonel uncle………….'

'Yes, in the Army……………….'

'He's not actually in the Army,' whispered Mildred in a slightly embarrassed tone.

Dr Rammy covered the phone again.

'Pleased to be telling me what the bloody hell he *is* in!'

'I think it's something to do with diplomats,' winced Mildred.

'Yes, I'm still here uncle.. …………..'

'Yes, we think he is being in the diplomatic army…….'

'The diplomatic *Corps*,' hissed Brewster.

'Sorry, the diplomatic corps………..'

'Is he a big stupid bugger with a sword………….?'

Dr Rammy covered the phone again.

'He's got the big stupid bit right,' confirmed Mildred. 'I'm not so sure about the sword.'

'We're not sure about the sword bit there uncle………………'

'He was in ceremonial dress………'

'At an official function…………………'

'With a who……?'

'Mister who……?'

'Oh, a Mamma ……………?'

'Mamma salvo……..?'

Mildred's ears picked up as did the rest of the audience.

'She works for who……………….?'

'Beers………..?'

'Oh, sorry, *The* beers………..?'

'Oh, sorry. *Dee* beers……'

'What do they do uncle………..?'

'Mining………..'

'What sort of mining, coal…….?'

'Diamonds…………….???????'

'Did you just say diamonds uncle?'

Chapter 8. Chekov goes to Africa

So she raped him again.

Well, it had been four days since she'd had him last and he was buggering off to Africa now for god knows how long, so what's a girl supposed to do?

Chekov lay there with glazed eyes and that stupid grin across his face trying to get some brain cells working but like Samson after Delilah had given him the old short back and sides, he was, not to put too fine a point on it, fucked.

*　*　*

Mildred rushed back to see Chekov after Dr Rammy's phone call to his uncle and gave him a verbatim account of the call. Well, not quite verbatim but a pretty good account by all means.

This had jerked Chekov into action and within minutes he was back in the pub and had Dr Rammy in full consultation.

Chekov checked the business card for addresses etc and got Dr Rammy to phone Uncle Krishna back to confirm some details.

'Uncle, I have a gentleman here who would like to go through some of the details with you if you are not minding please?'

'Yes uncle, but can I what.........?'

'Confirm who I am playing cricket for..........?

'Is it the MCC......?

'Yes that's right uncle, now can I hand you over to my friend Mr Chekov...........'

'He sounds Russian...........''

'Yes, he is Russian.............'

'Uncle, it's OK, he speaks very good English, probably better than you or I......'

'I'm not being cheeky uncle.........'

'You can't spank me any more uncle, I'm bigger than you now.............'

'OK, OK, here's Mr Chekov.............'

With that Dr Rammy handed over the phone to Chekov, wiped his brow and quickly ordered a pint from Brewster.

'Hallo, yes, it's Chekov Yeboleksi here Mr Chutnabuttee..............'

'I am speaking English...........'

'That's my name; anyway I would just like to ask you some brief questions. Firstly can we confirm that our mutual friend Creighky O'Riley has been in the company of...............'

'The big stupid bugger with the sword.....?

Brewster quickly jumped in here and nodded his head up and down to give Chekov the answer he was looking for.

'Yes, that is correct Mr Chutnabuttee. Now was he with any one ......?'

'Yes, a young lady........'

'That would be a Miss..................'

'Miss Salvo……………?'

'Mma Salvo, good. And she worked for….?'

'……….De Beers……………..?'

'Good, and that's the big diamond mining company……………..?'

'She's their liaison officer…………?'

'Is she now,…………………?'

'That beautiful………?'

'And where would this lovely lady work…..?'

'No, not who does she work for. Where does she work? Where would their offices be………….?'

'Just around the corner from you………..?'

'And where would that be………………?'

'In the Main Mall,……………?'

'And that is in …………..?'

'The capital, which would be…………..?'

'Ah, yes. Gaborone and that is in which country…?'

'Botswana. That's lovely Mr Chutnabuttee. Can I thank you for your help? I may like to talk to you again……………..'

'Yes it's lovely weather here thank you……………?'

'And you what…………………?'

'You want me to do what……….?'

'Kick his arse and get him out there to play cricket…………?'

Chekov put the phone down and wiped *his* brow as well.

'Brewster I think I need a large vodka please?'

*   *   *

'Mildred darling I have a plan.'

He then contacted some of his friends at the Russian Embassy. Well, if being the retired head of KGB Interrogation didn't stand for something in these days what did?

And so he booked a flight out to Gaborone via Johannesburg and booked a room in the Gaborone Sun Hotel and off he jetted leaving his distraught lover Mildred all on her own.

Well, this would give them both time to recuperate. And boy! Did Chekov need it?

So with unglazed eyes and his grin now fully back into the normal position Chekov flew off to Africa.

*   *   *

The flight out to Johannesburg was uneventful if a bit tedious but the connection into Botswana reminded him of the old days in Russia with some fairly antiquated aircraft. But he made it OK and after clearing customs and immigration, was welcomed by a member of the Russian Embassy who drove him to his hotel not before giving him a brown envelope.

This information only confirmed what he already thought after Dr Rammy's conversation with his uncle and so after a good night's sleep he got a taxi into the centre of Gaborone and got out at the shopping centre in the Main Mall.

The Chutnabuttee Emporium wasn't hard to find.

'Good morning, is Mr Krishna Chutnabuttee in please?'

'Yes, can I please be asking who is asking?' enquired a very pleasant lady all doled up in a beautiful sari.

'Mr Chekov Yeboleksi. We spoke last week with his nephew Dr Rammittin from England.'

'Oh. Young Rammy? Oh how pleased we were to hear he is alright. He is doctor in your town?'

'Well not exactly a town but yes he is our doctor, although I haven't had the pleasure.'

'You haven't had the pleasure?'

'Well, what I mean is I haven't been ill enough to visit his practice, but I hear he is well liked by our villagers.'

'Please excuse my manners. I am so overcome with joy that I am forgetting to take you to see Mr Krishna. He is in office. Please to be coming this way Mr Cockoff.'

'Chekov.'

'Please to be accepting my apologies. Krishna!' The shout nearly deafened Chekov as a medium sized gentleman appeared from behind a rack of stores.

'Mr?' the lady stopped to make sure she had got the name right but was interrupted by Chekov.

'Yeboleksi, Chekov Yeboleksi.'

'He is talking with young Rammy in England,' confirmed the lady.

'Oh, goodness gracious, you are here already?' stuttered Krishna. 'Oh, please, please to be coming into my office. Can I get you a cup of tea? Dupinda, why don't you get us both a nice cup of the lovely Darjeeling?'

'Thank you Mr Krishna, but I won't be keeping you long. I just wanted to talk about our mutual friend Mr Creighky O'Riley.'

'Oh, that big stupid bugger with the sword?'

'Yes, that's the one. Now can you tell me where you met him?'

'Yes. It was at opening ceremony of new De Beers mine up at Jwaneng. I am Chairman of Chamber of Commerce and get to go to posh functions with all big wigs.'

'And what was Mr O'Riley doing there?'

'He is from British High Commission and prancing round like big cock......'

'Like a what?' Chekov was a bit taken a back.

'Like bloody big chicken and swinging his sword like bloody Errol Flynn and Mma Xalwo wrapped all around him.'

'Ah, that is the Mma Salvo we talked about?'

Mr Chutnabuttee moved around the office and closed the door. 'Damn fine woman, her name is Xalwo, she is Somali. A bit too tall for me,' he gave Chekov a wink. 'But beautiful woman. Works for De Beers. In charge of press people and social functions. Legs up to bloody ceiling!'

Chekov was beginning to get the picture. 'And how did she get on with Mr O'Riley?'

'Oh, she all over him, like bloody rash. Then she goes off with him and Sir Metumile Kasire.'

'Who the hell is he?'

'He is big white chief, only he is big black chief really.'

Chekov was losing the plot here so went back on track. 'Mr Chutnabuttee, can you tell me more about Mr O'Riley and Mma who..........?'

'Mma Xalwo. Spelt with "X" and then an "A", an "L", a "W" and an "O" of course.'

'Of course,' continued confused Chekov. 'But how do you feel their relationship was going?'

'Oh, I see them together in town, and they make a fine couple. But I'm not knowing if he is getting leg over.'

'No, quite,' said Chekov a bit shocked.

'Now, Mr Cockoff............'

'Chekov!'

'Oh, I am very rude. But please to be telling me all about my lovely nephew and his cricket?'

'Mr Krishna, I'm afraid I know nothing about cricket. I am from Kiev but worked in Russia for a long time, so cricket is all very strange to me.'

'But he is playing for a damn fine team?'

'That's as maybe Mr Krishna. I do sometimes watch them practicing but can't tell you any more about them.'

'Mr Chekov. Please I am putting cards on the table.' Mr Chutnabuttee sat down on the office table and looked up at Chekov.

'I am Secretary of the cricket association here in Botswana, and we are in, how you say, chicken and egg position. You know. We are very young but are desperate to play fine teams like young Rammy is playing for.'

Chekov was a bit confused over the chicken and egg bit but let Mr Chutnabuttee carry on.

'It would send a powerful message to the other world cricket countries to see us playing a team with such prestige as you are having in your fine city.'

Chekov had never heard of Muddlecombe being called a city before, but humoured him. 'Mr Chutnabuttee, I don't know what I can do, but I promise to talk to Dr Rammittin when I get back.'

'Oh, what lovely words, "Doctor Rammittin." You don't know how proud that makes me feel when I hear that.'

'Now, Mr Chutnabuttee, before I take my leave, can you please tell me where I can find Mma, er Xalwo?'

'That's right. Mma Xalwo.'

'Where can I find her office?'

*   *   *

It wasn't far to the De Beers' head office on the Main Mall so he had a pleasant walk in the mid morning sun and entered the lobby of the office and walked up to reception.

'Please, may I talk with Mma Xalwo?'

'Is she in De Beers Botswana, Debswana Diamond Company or Diamond Trading Company Botswana?' A prim bespectacled receptionist enquired

'I understand she is in the media centre.'

'I'll see if I can contact her. Who shall I say is calling?'

Chekov pulled out the envelope he was given from the Russian Embassy and pulled out a business card which he gave to the receptionist.

'Mr Chekov Yeebol.......??

'Yeboleksi'

'Hold the line; I'll see if she is available.'

'Mma who?'

'Mma Xalwo, that's spelt with an "X".'

'Hallo, is that Mma Xalwo?'

'It is, oh, good, I have a gentleman in reception for you............'

'No, he is not a tall stupid Irishman. He's a Mr Chekov Yebo,...Yeb...olek...si, and he's from the Embassy of the Russian Federation....................'

'She'll come right down Mr Yebol........'

'Thank you,' Chekov quickly interrupted to save the poor girl any more embarrassment. He waited a few minutes before he saw a tall, well dressed black lady descend the stairs down to the reception area.

"Yes, I can see what Krishna said about the legs now," he thought as he stood up and walked towards her.

'You must be Miss Xalwo?'

'Yes, I am. And you are..?

'My name is Chekov Yeboleksi.' He gave her his card.

'My, what does the Russian cultural attaché want with little old De Beers?'

'Miss Xalwo,' he guided her away from the bat ears of the receptionist to a quiet corner of the marbled floor entrance.

She eyed him up and down. "Mm," she thought. "Tall and really quite handsome for his age." The sallow skin and the dark rims under the eyes together with the grey hair at the temples gave him an air of sophistication and reminded her of Omar Shariff. (As it did Mildred)

The dark rims below the eyes had been accentuated recently thanks to Mildred as well.

'Miss Xalwo, I'm afraid the Embassy of the Russian Federation does not have an interest in De Beers. I have a personal interest in you.'

'You are a very forward gentleman indeed.' Miss Xalwo gave him a little frown.

'I'm sorry; my English is not very good. No, I don't mean that sort of personal interest.'

"Oh, that's a shame," she thought, but let him carry on.

'Miss Xalwo, I have an idea concerning a certain Mr Creighky O'Riley and diamonds that I feel could be to your advantage.'

This took her by surprise but she quickly regained her composure.

'Mr Yebol,......??

'Yeboleksi, but please call me Chekov.'

'Yes, right. Well, Chekov, do you not want to talk to our retail department?'

Chekov hadn't been in the interrogation business for twenty years not to notice her hesitation.

'No, Miss Xalwo.' His dark eyes looked intensely and deeply into hers and in a slow deliberate voice he replied. 'I do not wish to see your retail department. But what I have to say is best said privately, and may I suggest we discuss this in a more relaxed atmosphere with some food and drink.'

And without giving her time to reply, carried on. 'Perhaps you could recommend a good restaurant for tonight?'

'Mr Yebol…, Chekov, you certainly know how to twist a girl's arm.' Quickly thinking for an expensive place she came up with, 'Why don't we do the Bull and Bush, you'll like that.'

'I look forward to that. Can we meet there at, say eight o'clock?'

*   *   *

Chekov returned to the Embassy of the Russian Federation and got them to book a table for him and so he prepared his plan for the night.

*   *   *

'Thank you for coming Miss Xalwo, I hope you don't feel I'm being too forward, but I've taken the liberty of ordering some champagne.'

"Not that South African………………Holy shit! Moët! Where the hell did he get that from?" She thought as the waiter dropped the silver ice bucket down and proceeded to open the bottle.

Chekov noticed the opening of the pupils of her eyes and proceeded. 'And some Royal Beluga Caviar. I hope you don't think me too presumptuous?'

There was a slight hesitation in her voice as she tried to reply. The words "holy shit" eventually translated to '…….er, no, I like it when men are presumptuous, especially with champagne and caviar.'

Chekov, with years of interrogation experience always went for the "good cop, bad cop" routine wherever possible, and with some years experience in London, found that the best approach for the English was politeness, good manners, and high tea at the Ritz.

Failing that he could always fall back on the old "testicles in the vice" routine which seldom failed, not really appropriate for the current interviewee, so tonight he was doing it English style. He had noticed the surprise of the champagne which had cost him an arm and a leg, and felt he could proceed with the rest of the routine.

They made small talk about the weather and the menu while the dinks were duly consumed.

'Miss Xalwo, you may be wondering why I have asked you here tonight.' She just looked at him without changing her expression. 'You no doubt gather that I am not a cultural attaché of the Russian Embassy……….'

'Yes, I thought I smelt a whiff of the old KGB,' she replied stone faced.

'You are a very astute young lady, as well as beautiful and intelligent.' She let the compliment ride over her head.

Chekov continued, unabashed. 'You are correct in thinking I was in the KGB, but times have changed and we must move forward with them.' He sipped his drink, allowing her to take in this information.

'I now have found religion.'

That hit the spot as she nearly choked on her champagne. 'I find that hard to believe Mr Yeb, yebol……..'

'Please call me Chekov.' He had another drink to push the point further. 'I have found the religion of private enterprise together with profit.'

Xalwo finished spluttering and raised her glass. 'I'll drink to that.'

'I now have considerable business interests worldwide, but the one I want to cultivate most is in England. He produced his business card and gave it to her.

'Managing Director of Borisky Diamonds,' she read aloud without flinching. 'Head office, Muddlecombe-cum-Snoring.'

'So, you see we have a common interest, not only in goods but also in people, would you not agree?'

Xalwo looked him straight in the eyes but said nothing.

Chekov had another drink and continued. 'Let me put it another way. A certain gentleman who just happens to work for the British High Commission not a million miles away from here, returned home, to Muddlecombe,' he paused again looking Xalwo straight in the eyes. 'A certain tall stupid Irishman,' he paused again but getting no response from Xalwo carried on. 'Who got very drunk and left an item lying about only to be found by his wife…..'

'His wife!' Spluttered Xalwo.

Not only did this catch her off guard but Chekov as well. 'He did tell you about his wife didn't he?'

Xalwo could see plans A, B and C going right down the pan. 'Er, well, actually he did overlook that bit.'

'Ah,' Chekov had to stop and think about this and had another drink as did Xalwo. 'Now that *is* interesting.'

'Yes, it is, isn't it?' said Xalwo very pensively looking down to contemplate things. Things were going into pear-shaped mode at this instant.

Nothing was said for several seconds as *both* parties went into contemplating mode.

'Another bottle of champagne?' was all that Chekov could think of right now.

'Yes, I think that would be a good idea,' replied Xalwo.

'Miss Xalwo, I think it is time we both put our cards on the table, don't you?'

'Fire away,' was the instant reply.

'As MD for this little company, it is my duty to ensure all products purchased are done efficiently to ensure maximum profits.' He had another pensive moment and carried on. 'The item in question was a product that we would like to purchase and it is my duty to find out where it came from.'

Xalwo looked at him again but without comment.

'Would I be correct in the assumption that it came from you?'

'It might have done.'

'Good, that sorts that out.' Chekov said with some authority. 'Now all we have to do is to find out if this supplier,' he looked up at her. 'If this supplier can fulfil our corporate needs on a continuing basis.'

Again Xalwo said nothing.

'The question is obviously price but I wonder if there are any other benefits we could offer?'

Xalwo looked at Chekov again but this time just the hint of a smile was forthcoming.

Chekov picked this up immediately.

'Chekov, I may call you Chekov?'

'Fire away.'

Xalwo picked up her champagne flute and swirled it around while waiting to put the right words in the correct order. Chekov responded by swirling his drink similarly whilst continuing to look her straight in the eyes waiting for the right response.

'Let us assume, rightly or wrongly that the products in question are available to you at a price that favours both our interests.' Mma Xalwo said with some deliberation.

Chekov just nodded as she continued.

'There is a logistics problem of getting this item from the current owner to the new owner under the assumption again that full recompense can be made within the legalities of the world trade.'

Chekov was starting to lose the plot here a bit, but kept quiet if a bit bemused.

Xalwo picked up on this and continued on another tack. 'Basically what I'm saying is that a lot of distance and frontiers have to be crossed and certain formalities have to be bypassed for a cost effective solution.'

'Ah, yes, I think I'm with you on that Miss Xalwo,' Chekov having had similar experiences with some of his own trading products. Like drugs and gold bullion to name but a few.

'The first problem is that the goods have to be in a Western country to capitalise on their worth. Actually that is only one of many problems which will occur in moving them to that part of the world.'

'Like getting them out of this country?' Chekov was fully up to speed now.

'And getting them past the security network in situ,' added Mma Xalwo to make things a bit more complicated.

'Ah, yes,' confirmed Chekov retreating into a contemplating mood. 'I think this needs a lot of thinking about,' he said because he couldn't think of anything else to say. 'Would you like some more champagne?'

'That seems like a good idea,' replied Mma Xalwo who couldn't think of anything to say either.

'Ah, but,' started Chekov, 'how did Creighky get the item out of the country?'

'Diplomatic bag,' said Xalwo dismally. 'There aren't a lot of those about either.' Brightening up she carried on. 'I see the item reached it's destination then.'

'Oh, yes, we felt it best not to interrupt the process to call too much attention to ourselves.' He paused there and then continued with a fresh glass of champagne. 'It was very big wasn't it? Our man reckoned on 22 carats.'

'26 actually,' said Xalwo matter of factually, as if one talks about bloody great diamonds like that every day.

'Yes, I feel our calibration may be a bit overdue on the electronic scales.'

'That was when Mrs O'Riley found the item?'

'Yes,' Chekov paused and then picked up on something he had noticed earlier. 'So, how did you get on with our Lt Col O'Riley then?'

'Well, we were getting on quite nicely thank you.'

'But now you've found out he is married?'

'Yes, that sort of buggers up Plan B,' Xalwo let slip, with a considerable amount of champagne inside her by now.

'Plan B being?' Chekov jumped in quickly using all his skills as an interrogator.

'You know, the old grab'em and stuff'em and get a passport……'

'……..trick,' Chekov finished the sentence off for her.

'Whoops,' slurred Xalwo. 'The old cat's out of the bag now,' she said looking up from her drinking position.

'That's very interesting,' Chekov continued looking up for inspiration. 'Very interesting indeed.' He continued. 'So the old get 'em married quickly trick was Plan B then?' Not looking to her for any confirmation.

'Was,' slurred a reply. She was now looking very miserable indeed.

'I don't see why we can't carry on with Plan B.'

That stumped her as she nearly spilled her drink. 'I beg your pardon?' she said looking up now.

'Don't Mr O'Riley and Mrs O'Riley have to get divorced first?' A simple question but one that obviously had to be answered.

'Exactly!' Chekov had brightened up considerably.

'Won't Mrs O'Riley have something to say about all this?' Another simple question she felt.

'I think she will be considerably relieved.'

'Oh.' That was a simple answer to her question which shut her up.

The evening progressed with some lovely food to sober them up a bit and they talked about this and that until Chekov asked her how she met Creighky.

'Oh, it was at the opening of the new mine along at Jwaneng. It was a sort of garden party. I organised it and invited the High Commissioner but he couldn't make it so they sent the cavalry instead.'

'The cavalry?'

'Oh, yes, he turned up in full military gear, medals, a sword and all. Poor Mr Chutnabuttee, our Chamber of Commerce man was most upset by his bad manners and …….'

'Ah, yes, the Chutnabuttee Emporium man. Yes, I bumped into him, but all he was interested in was this stupid game of cricket.'

'Isn't he related to one of your villagers or something?'

'Yes, our Dr Rammy………………….'

Chekov stopped and looked as if he had seen a ghost or something had just crawled down the front of his underpants.

'Good God!'

Xalwo sat up straight as did Chekov but said nothing in amazement. She looked to Chekov to finish the sentence with an open mouth. Nothing came out for several seconds until, 'Of course!' Chekov said out loud. 'My dear young lady I think I have found the answer to our prayers.'

'You have?' Hoping he would reveal all.

'Yes. Now, shall we have another drink?'

'Well, I suppose I could manage another Moët if you twisted my arm.'

They finished the meal and as Chekov was paying the bill she asked him if he wanted to go back to her place for some coffee which was badly needed. After all she was none the wiser and still had made no agreement re the trading of her commodities. There was the small matter of new Plans A, B and C.

'That's very kind of you Miss Xalwo, but I've had a long day and I need an early night as there are lots of things I have to do tomorrow.'

'Yes, you poor thing you must be exhausted and probably jet lagged as well.' She leant over and patted his arm.

Not only was he jet lagged but shag lagged as well. The last thing he wanted was to be asked up to a beautiful lady's apartment to demonstrate his shortcomings, as it were.

'But we will be talking again won't we?' The long eyelashes came into action once more.

'Oh, you can be sure of that. But first I have to discus a little logistics matter with a mutual friend of ours. And when you next see Mr O'Riley, our meeting must be kept a secret.'

* * *

'Mr Chutnabuttee, how nice to see you again.'

'Oh. It's Mr Tick off.'

'Chekov.'

'Oh, I am so sorry. I am not speaking Russian very well.'

'That's alright; I don't speak Gujurati very well either.'

'Oh, Mr Chekov, you are taking the piss now, but please to be coming in and can I offer you a nice cup of the old Darjeeling?'

'Mr Chutnabuttee, that would be lovely.'

'Good.' He gave his wife a shout across the shop floor and Chekov and himself settled down in his office.

'Now, what can I be doing the pleasure of Mr Chekov?'

Chekov made himself comfortable and eventually started. 'Mr Chutnabuttee, tell me about this game of cricket.'

'Cricket, cricket! Oh my god, you are wanting me to tell you about cricket, have you got a couple of hours?'

'Mr Chutnabuttee, may I call you Krishna, I have all the time in the world.'

Mr Chutnabuttee relaxed and prepared himself for a long sermon.

'Oh, what a wondrous game. No one can explain all the various ins and outings of the game. All the beautiful nuances, all the variations of flight of the ball, all the various weather conditions that can affect it. All the variety of different woods used to make the cricket bat……………..'

Chekov quickly interrupted. He had all the time in the world but not that long. 'And what about young Dr Rammy?'

'Oh, goodness gracious me! That boy is charmed. He is so talented; it does not surprise me he is now playing for your most reverend team.'

Chekov couldn't quite comprehend this but let it pass.

Chutnabuttee continued. 'When he was only six years old he was playing with his balls.' Chekov wasn't quite sure on that one either.

'When he was ten, he was googling and then he had the audacity to do the "wrong one", now can you believe that?'

Chekov couldn't make head or tail of anything but carried on the conversation. 'No, it is hard to believe isn't it?'

'By the time he was at top school, he was playing for Rajasthan region, a mere boy of thirteen. And knocking over timber of many great men.'

Chekov felt now was the time to wind the bait in slowly having laid the trap.

'And you would like to see him play out here?'

'Oh, dear Mr Chekov, you don't know how proud I would be to see that boy again.'

'He's quite a big man now, and a practicing Doctor to boot.'

'Oh, I am forgetting, he is much professional now. But I bet he is still damn fine man on cricket pitch.'

'Oh yes, he has them hard at it. I don't think his team have been beaten yet.' A pretty safe bet as they hadn't played anyone yet.

'Oh, to see him leading a team like the MCC out on our modest land would bring tears to my eyes.'

'So you think bringing the team over here would help?'

'Mr Chekov, I am secretary to Botswana Cricket Association. We are small fries in big world of international cricket. If I could see your team playing out here, just think what that would mean. Don't you see? Other world teams would come running to bash our door down for competitions and we could raise much money for improving our cricket. And we could be recognised internationally and have test matches and a new pavilion and ………..'

Mr Chutnabuttee looked to the heavens with raised hands and swooned as he ran out of superlatives.

Thankfully Chekov was there to bring him down to earth. 'So, how would you finance a trip for Dr Rammy and his friends over here?'

'Oh, Mr Chekov, I am being carried away and forgetting mundane matters. That is a good question. Please let us have a cup of tea first,' he beckoned his wife in with a tray and they started to relax and enjoy the Darjeeling. 'Dupinda darling, can we get some lovely biscuits for my honourable guest here?'

They sat for a while in deep thought until Mr Chutnabuttee started.' I must have discussions with our committee and talk money with them.'

'Will that take long?' Chekov was hoping to have this all wrapped up within the next few days.

'Oh, I hope not. I will have extremely extraordinary meeting tomorrow and we must bash out some ideas.'

'What about sponsorship?'

'Oh gosh, what bloody marvellous idea, why am I not thinking of that. I am so excited.'

'Say some company, well known internationally, like De Beers for example?'

'Mr Chekov, you are being like a breath of fresh wind.' Mr Chutnabuttee stood up from behind his desk and shouted to his wife. 'Dupinda, I am going out, pleased to be looking after fortress.' He turned to Chekov and said excitedly. 'Mr Chekov my friend, I have much to do. Please be excusing me. I have to round up committee and then I have to go to De Beers. Oh, my gosh, so many things to do. And where can I be getting in touch with you my dear friend?'

'I am staying at the Gaborone Sun Hotel.'

'Good, I will be leaving messages there for you. Oh my gosh, I can't believe this is all happening. Oh, Mr Chekov, I am not knowing where to thank you enough.'

'Krishna my friend, it hasn't happened yet, but I'm sure you will make it happen.'

'Oh, you can be betting bottom ruppee on that.'

Mr Chutnabuttee rushed out of the office putting his jacket on and at the same time Chekov slowly finished his tea. 'Dupinda, can I borrow your telephone please?'

Chekov took out his diary and found the number he wanted and dialled it out.

'Miss Xalwo? Hi, it's Chekov here. I think now is the time to do some serious talking.'

'Yes, that's right.'

'Where would you like to meet up?'

'The same place?'

'But not so much champagne?'

'There's no pleasing you ladies is there.'

'Oh, and by the way. You be getting a Mr Chutnabuttee calling on you.'

'About what?'

'Something to do with sponsorship.'

'Sponsoring what?'

'Some sort of sport. I think it's called cricket.'

'Why?'

'I'll tell you all about it tonight.'

*   *   *

'Good evening Mma Xalwo, it's nice to have you back again.' The head waiter showed her to her seat with Chekov waiting for her at the table.

They made themselves comfortable and studied the menu, ordered the wine and sat down to a pleasant evening of eating and drinking.

'So tell me about Mr Chutnabuttee.' She felt she should start the ball rolling.

'I'll tell you about cutting your overheads, shall I?'

'Whatever.'

'They are both related and this is where you come in not only as a supplier but as a sponsor.'

'Me?'

140

'Not you personally, but your company. The famous De Beers Corporation who must surely want to promote an activity that would help promote the country of their domicile.'

'Would they?'

'Oh, yes, and then that would save our little company considerable overheads in logistics.'

'Would it?' Xalwo wasn't quite sure where this was leading up to.

'Mr Chutnabuttee will be calling on you or someone in your company to raise money for sponsorship for a cricket match.'

'Will he?'

'A cricket match between this country and the cricket team from my village.'

'Would he?' Xalwo was losing the plot here but continued. 'And why would he want to do that.'

'Ah, yes, I was afraid you were going to ask that question.' Chekov sipped some wine before giving considerable consideration to his reply.

'Do you know, I really haven't got a fucking clue!'

Xalwo nearly choked on her wine and was eventually brought out of spasm by some hearty back slapping from Chekov.

The hovering waiters slowly faded away into the background as Xalwo regained full use of her facilities. However she was still obviously having problems with the oral facilities.

'Ah, er, I, er, I am not quite sure I heard you right there.'

'This Chutnabuttee gentleman has a nephew who is our local doctor and he wants him to bring his village team out here to play against the national team.'

'Why?'

'Don't ask me. Something to do with promoting his cricket association on a world wide basis. Why he has picked our village team I can't for the love of me understand'

'I'm sorry, but somewhere along the line I've lost the plot.'

'Yes, I'm not quite sure I have the plot either, but it just so happens to fit in with my plot. But there are some small details I haven't mentioned yet, but first of all I need to hear from you what assets you can bring to this venture.'

Xalwo took another drink of wine, this time very slowly. She put the glass down and folded her arms on the table and looked straight at Chekov.

'Now then we're getting down to the nitty-gritty are we?'

'Yes please.'

'Ok.' She gathered her thoughts and continued. 'I have considerable assets but they are of no use whatsoever within the geographical bounds of this continent.'

'I understand that,' replied Chekov, keeping eye contact with her.

'As long as that is understood, I can realistically offer you assets worth in the region of one million dollars.'

Chekov did a little cough, had another drink and sat back in his chair with his eyebrows at a considerably higher altitude than previously. A little sideways movement of the head confirmed a positive response to Mma Xalwo's statement.

Chekov was trying to translate "Holy Shit" into something a little bit more sophisticated.

'Good!' He thought that would do for the time being.

Xalwo said nothing.

'And how do you propose to demonstrate these assets to me?'

'I don't propose to demonstrate these assets to you until you demonstrate some US Dollars to me.'

'OK.' Chekov was speechless again. "Fifteen all" was the expression he was thinking of.

'OK, er, good,' it was a start. Xalwo was still saying nothing.

'Right, I need to think about the logistics of this,' he said, trying to give himself time to gather his thoughts as she said nothing again. He had never realised that *he* would be at the other end of the interrogation process.

'I think now is a good time to take advantage of this restaurant's fine cuisine, don't you?'

Xalwo said nothing other than picking up her serviette whilst still looking Chekov straight in the eye. She knew she had him by the balls and was enjoying it, so why not enjoy the food as well.

Chekov could now feel how his past "customers" had felt and didn't like the feeling that much at all. But after the main course ideas started to come to him and he gingerly put forward his plan to Xalwo.

'Right, this is how I see things as they stand. You have what I want, and you are not prepared to display these things until you have some form of commitment from me, am I right?'

'So far.'

'Ok. Now I feel I, or should I say my company and myself have a lot more to offer you other than purely monetary gain.'

Xalwo again said nothing.

'One of the beautiful things about our company is our location. It is in, how can I best describe it? It is in a free trading zone.'

He stopped there to get some form of reaction which did eventually come in the form of raised eyebrows.

'When I say free trading zone, I mean free from any authorities. Free from the encumbrances of the legal system.'

'Tell me more.' Xalwo started to look interested.

'I feel the best way to wet your appetite is to introduce you to our community.'

'And how do you propose to do that?'

'Well, why don't you come back to our humble village and let's talk about further incentives.'

'And how do you propose to do that?'

'I'll pay the fare. And why don't you talk to your friend Mr O'Riley and get a visitors visa while I sort out the travel bit. But I feel it's not in our best interests just yet to tell him about us and your visit to our village. How does that sound?'

'Interesting.'

'Good, I feel we have an extremely long and prosperous future ahead of us.'

'Oh, and by the way. Mr Chutnabuttee has been talking to our marketing department about this cricket thing.'

'Has he now? That's interesting.'

'Isn't it just. But I'm still at a loss as to how this can benefit our little venture.'

'Ah, well, all will be explained in the fullness of time. I would ask you for a favour though please?'

'As long as it doesn't involve any expense or pain.'

'Oh, no. Just a few words with your marketing department to point out how important Mr Chutnabuttee's quest is to both your company and your country.'

'And to our little venture?'

'It is extremely important to our little venture, but I don't think we need to mention that do you?'

* * *

'Krishna my friend, how are you this lovely morning?' Chekov was trying out his charm technique.

'Oh, Mr Chekov, I am exceedingly excellent. And how might you be?'

'All the better for seeing you.'

'Please to be coming in. A cup of the old Darjeeling?'

'That's very kind of you, but I won't keep you. Just to let you know I will be returning to the UK in a few days time.'

145

'Oh, goodness gracious, I am just about to be calling you. I have been talking to many people and have been making many roads. The chairman of my committee is having talks with the lovely De Beers company to finalise details of getting lovely money for lovely cricket match. I should be hearing from him by early bird.'

'Well done Krishna, you *have* been working hard. Now then, have any dates been agreed yet?'

'No, not yet, but our season starts soon and we are feeling that some choosing of team is necessary and some practice is much needed to play against such a fine team as yours.'

'Well, I'm sure the game will be played on a friendly basis. So we are looking at sometime next month?' Chekov was at a loss as to why all this fuss was over such a simple game of cricket. But, as everybody kept telling him, he didn't understand the nuances of the game.

'So, can we confirm then that the expenses for the cricket team to come out here will be covered by your Association? Albeit to be confirmed by your chairman?'

'Oh, I hope so, and we will be having such a famous time and Botswana Cricket Association will be most honoured. I am wondering if Denis or Trevor will be playing?'

Chekov couldn't actually remember seeing much of Dense at the practices and certainly didn't know any Trevor, but he persevered. 'I don't know who is playing I'm afraid.'

He left off there as Mr Chutnabuttee went into some sort of rapture. 'Oh, my goodness, imagine Denis Compton and Trevor Bailey playing out here. Oh, I am so excited.'

'Oh, and perhaps wouldn't it be in your interests to mention this to the British High Commissioner, don't you think?'

'Goodness gracious me, you are having bright light in your brain. Yes, by golly, it would be of much interest to my friend Sir Reginald. He is great cricket lover; he will be tickled lots of colours when I am telling him.'

'Oh, and I don't think you need to mention me in that conversation, but you could mention Mr O'Riley if you like as he comes from the same village as well, and he did start the communications with your nephew Dr Rammittin.'

'That big stupid Irishman with the sword?'

*   *   *

'Lt Col Crikey O'Riley OBE MC, you never fail to surprise me. I didn't know you were an aficionado of cricket?'

'Oh, right you are there your honour. I'm not all that sure I know that myself.'

'Don't be modest man! Getting the MCC to come and play over here is some feat I can tell you, and old Rra Chutnabuttee tells me his nephew, your local doctor, is playing for them, and all down to you, you sly dog. Your friend Sir Metumile Kasire will be *most* impressed'

'Is that so, well there you go, as I said, if you ever wants anything doing, I'm your man, so I am.'

Crikey had a sort of vacant but happy look about him. "Perhaps all would be revealed later" he thought to himself as he was about to leave.

'Now, while we're at it you *could* help me out. As you know we're a bit understaffed here so could I ask you to look after the logistics of the visitors when they get here?'

'Oh, I've done old logistics there,' said Creighky. "Or was it geometry?" he wondered.

'Well then, that's it all sorted then. Have a word with the transport department and my PA and she'll help you out with the accommodation side and have a natter with old Rra Chutnabuttee about the itinerary and Bob's your uncle. Tickety-boo. All yours old chap. Give me a bell if you have any queries then, OK?'

Creighky's expression of vacant but happy was seriously veering towards the vacant side of things as he left Sir Reginald's office in a state of complete bewilderment. No change there then.

*   *   *

Thomas Lord who played for the White Conduit Cricket Club at Islington, moved to Dorset Fields in Marylebone to set up a new private cricket ground at the impatience of the nobility with the ever growing crowds and subsequently moved to St John's Wood in

1814, the now home of the Marylebone Cricket Club.

At the same time as a rather large gentleman with a beard was belting hell out of anything anybody could throw at him at Muddlecombe, the statue of another large gentlemen with a beard, who was also known to have dispensed with several cricket balls in his time, W G Grace, was standing in the Coronation Garden at the Lords cricket ground in North London. At the bar in the Long Room, two people were talking.

'Pinky old chap, ah, there you are. How's it going?'

'Botham's just got another ton.'

'Jolly good show old man, 'nother Pimms old boy?'

'No thanks Pongo. Best not, got the old memsahib waiting for me. We've got guests tonight.'

'Gosh, best not upset the old memsahib then eh? Look, I've just had a telephone call from that young South African lad, what's' is name, bollocks or something?'

'Pollocks.'

'That's the fella. Wants to know if we've got any spare itinerary for the MCC for a few games in the near future.'

'What's he after then?'

'Well, he knows we're going down to the jolly old antipodes in a couple of months and they've got some slots in their schedule, probably want a bit of revenue injection shouldn't doubt.'

'Well the boys could do with a bit of sunshine and practice before they get stuck into those bloody Aussies and those bloody awful tins of cold beer.'

'So I'll give him a buzz back then old chap?'

'Yes, why not? See what the deal is, see if we can get discount on accommodation, travel etc and perhaps a little something revenue wise for the old MCC , eh, old man?'

'Wizard prang old chap, what a spiffing idea. Talk to you tomorrow then at the committee meeting.'

'Oh, and lets keep the publicity down for this eh? Let the chaps have a bit of peace and quiet while they're practicing, eh, old boy?'

'A nod's as good as a wink to a blind horse, old chap,' said Pongo tapping the side of his nose.

Pinky went away with a puzzled expression on his face, and then suddenly stopped. 'Ooopps, pardon me old chap. Still can't control the old farts, don't you know?' He bent his knees, straightened for a second then walked away a tad embarrassed, but then put his nose in the air and muttered, '28 guineas an ounce straight from gay Paree.'

*   *   *

'Hallo Pongo old boy, how the devil are you these days?'

'Oh, fair to middling don't you know...' He put the phone over his shoulder and looked desperately at his secretary and held his hands open.

His secretary muttered, 'Sir Reginald Makepeace, calling from long distance somewhere in Africa.

'Makers old boy, how lovely to hear from you. What the blazes are you doing these days, still at the old Foreign Office then?'

'Yes, they sent me out of the way down here in Botswana.'

'Where the bloody hell's that old boy?'

'South Africa.'

'Ah, that would explain why you couldn't make it for the Old Boys reunion then?'

'Yes, sorry about that Pongo, how did it go?'

'Oh, you know, got a bit squiffy, but there's not many of us left nowadays, glad to hear you're still alive. Some of the silly buggers thought you'd popped off as well.'

'Ah, no, can't help you there old chap.'

'Jolly good show, you hang on in there.'

'Listen, Pongo, the reason I'm ringing is that a little birdie has told me that your lot might be coming out our way soon, any truth in that old boy?'

'Bugger me, I've heard of the early bird getting the worm, must have been up bloody early that's all I can say.'

'I take it that's a yes then, will you be coming out with them?'

'No, sorry old boy can't make it. Not in the budget.'

'Oh, that's a bit of a bummer, well anyway, can't stay, give my regards to the memsahib. She ok?'

'No improvement there I'm afraid old chap.'

'Pongo, you are a wag. Talk soon.'

"By Christ those boys at the FO are on top notch with their intelligence," muttered Pongo to himself, as he walked back to the bar scratching his head.

*   *   *

`Hello, is that the BBC?'

'Oh, good. Can you help me please?'

'Oh, yes, I'm Sir Reginald Makepeace.'

'I would like to speak to the DG if possible please. Can you tell him I'm calling from South Africa and only want a quick word.'

'Yes, I can hold for a bit.'

'You can, oh that would be splendid.'

'Hallo, hallo, is that Sir William?'

'Bill you old bugger, it's Makers here, how the devil are you.'

'Reggy Makepeace, Sir Reggy now.'

'I'm in South Africa, actually in a place called Botswana. I'm still in the jolly old FO, the High Commissioner in Gaborone.'

'No, not a lot of people have heard of it.'

'Well, actually, I've just been talking to old Pongo at the MCC and he tells me his lot are coming down our way for a game of cricket. Sort of off the cuff warm up match prior to the Aussies. Strictly on the QT you understand.'

'How's Pongo? Well you know old Pongo, hasn't changed a bit, still a bit of a silly arse, anyway, the locals down here are jumping up and down, happy as sand boys over this cricket match. Would put them on the map so to speak. And I was wondering if you had anybody spare who could come down and do a broadcast here, that would really put the icing on the cake for these boys, I can tell you. It might just put a few house points on the old CV for me as well.'

'Yes Botswana, in a couple of month's time.'

'Yes OK, I'll get my secretary to liaise with your PA and we'll take it from there.'

'That's fantastic old boy. I owe you one. Lovely to talk to you again, regards to the lovely wife.'

'Sheila? No improvement there I'm afraid old chap.'

'Ha ha.'

Chapter 9. An extra
ordinary AGM

'Hallo, Mildred? Hallo, its Chekov here,' he shouted down the phone in the cool air-conditioned proximity of his hotel room on Gaborone.

'Yes, it's me. How are you?

There was a slight pause and then, 'Yes, I'm still in Africa. You're what?'

'Oh, missing me. Yes gorgeous, I'm missing you to.

'Mildred dear, I want you to do something for me please?'

'What's it worth? You little minx. I'll show you what it's worth when I get back.'

'I'll be back soon, but first of all I want you to set up an AGM.'

'Do what, set up an AGM, an Annual General Meeting.'

'What's one of those?'

'I just want to set up a meeting with all the people involved in our little diamond enterprise.'

'When?'

'Well, it will have to be in……..,' Chekov got out his diary and looked at it for a few seconds.

'It will have to be in two weeks time, at the weekend.'

'Yes, I know it's a bit short notice. Do you want all the sales staff as well, you know the two "ladies",' Mildred spelled out the word ladies with some annunciation. 'Sharon and Tracey?'

'Yes, especially them.'

'Well Tracey's in Tenerife.'

'Well explain it to her that it's very important. I'll explain it in detail as soon as I can. But I've found a very useful benefactor who could save us a lot of money and help the old profits.'

'Oh, he sounds interesting.'

'It's a she actually.'

'Oh, yes,' Mildred said very slowly inferring all sorts of innuendos. 'How old is she?'

'Younger than you,' Chekov said with a smile on his face starting to enjoy Mildred's obvious discomfort.

'Oh, yes, and I suppose she's extremely ugly?'

'Oh, yes, nearly as ugly as you.' Chekov was laughing by this time.

'Bitch!'

'Rich bitch, with lots of collateral,' continued Chekov in some state of arousal now, thinking of his last moments with Mildred. 'And do you know who she has the hots for my little chickadee?'

'I'll kill her,' retorted Mildred. She carried on. 'And where does she keep the dog and the white stick?'

'She doesn't have a white stick. She is carrying a candle for a certain Mr O'Riley if you please.'

There was a stunned silence at the other end of the line.

'I thought that might interest you.'

Another silence until Mildred recovered and started. 'Boy, she must be blind.'

'Oh, she's not blind at all, she's a very intelligent woman who we need to come on board on our company, and Mr O'Riley can make her a very happy "British Citizen."' Chekov stressed the British Citizen bit and waited for Mildred to pick up the thread of the conversation.

'Listen, Mildred dear, just think about that. But first we need to get her in front of our personnel to explain our company thinking.'

'Our company thinking is to make money as I understand it?'

'Precisely, but she needs a lot of money to pay for her "stock" shall we say, and I think I have a way of persuading her how not to upset our cash flow situation.'

'You just keep your persuading hands off her.'

'You can trust me sweetheart.'

'Don't you sweetheart me buster. Just wait till I get you home you dirty old man.'

'Can't wait. Talk later, but let's get that meeting organised first eh?'

'Leave that with me big boy!'

Chekov put the phone down in a pool of sweat and collapsed onto his bed. Mildred had even managed to rape him over the phone!

*   *   *

'Miss Xalwo my dear, how nice to see you again.'

'Cut the crap big boy!' stereo ear bashing thought Chekov after his conversation with Mildred. He had since asked to see Xalwo again at their favourite restaurant.

'Champagne?'

'Oh, you know how to get round a girl don't you?'

They waited while the waiter poured the champagne and then relaxed after a few sips.

'So, what's new?' Miss Xalwo was the first to get into the nitty-gritty.

'Right, thank you for coming here tonight. I would just like to update you on the situation with regard to our proposed joint project.'

'Fire away,' she sat back and relaxed with the large crystal champagne flute in her hand.

'Ok,' Chekov was preparing himself for the charm offensive. 'I have arranged for an extraordinary annual general meeting of our company and we would like to invite you to be at that meeting.'

'No strings attached?'

'No strings attached.' But Chekov knew once she was in the rarefied atmosphere of Muddlecombe-cum-Snoring he would have his evil way with her. Well, only in as much as company incentives so to speak.

'I have set a tentative date in two weeks time which I hope is not too intrusive into your busy schedule out here. All our directors and sales staff will be there including our export staff so that you can ask as many questions as you like. I have asked our company accountant to be present with all our current trading figures and last years balance sheets as well.'

'My, you have been busy?'

'I'm afraid I've have to take a flier on the dates which will be over the weekend, but I hope we can organise some relaxation time for you as well. Now all I need is confirmation that these proceedings are suitable to you my dear.'

'I will just have to check with my diary,' as she opened up her handbag and pulled out her little black book. 'Yes it looks ok so far. I might have to fend off old "pushy paws" for a few days.'

'Pushy paws?'

'Our old friend Mr O'Riley.'

'Well, I'm sorry to have to break up such a fine romance but I can assure you, you will not regret it.' Chekov got out his diary now and continued. 'Might I suggest that we take the early flight on the Thursday which will get us into Heathrow late that night? Then you can have all day Friday to recuperate and be ready for the AGM on the Saturday.'

'That sounds ok so far.'

'I feel you may need to stay a while longer after the weekend to tie up any loose ends and to talk with our staff. So I would recommend the return flight on the Thursday, which means you will need to be away for a week.'

*　*　*

'Brewster my friend, can I introduce you to Miss Xalwo. This is our landlord of the local hostelry, Mr Brewster Kegworth.'

'Nice to meet you Brewster,' said Xalwo as she let him put her baggage into his Range Rover.

'Should I say, Mma Xalwo?' Brewster said whilst lifting her luggage.

'Hmmm. You may indeed. You certainly know how to make a girl feel at home.'

'Oh, we may be country bumpkins but some of us have travelled a bit. Welcome to England and soon the village of Muddlecombe will welcome you too.' Brewster gave Chekov a little wink as they got in the car and drove out of the one way systems around a rain-soaked Heathrow, up the long road to the welcoming arms of peace, tranquillity and, with a bit luck, prosperity.

*　*　*

Xalwo woke with the tapping at her door and Fiona bringing her breakfast.

'I'm sorry to wake you but I thought you'd best have some breakfast before it's supper time.' Fiona always was a wicked little tease.

Xalwo rubbed her eyes and eventually got the old oral muscles working.

'What time is it?' She managed at last.

'Let's just call this brunch time shall we?' the satire was getting through to Xalwo but she felt a great desire *not* to know the time. Suffice it to say it was obviously round about somewhere between breakfast and dinner time. Who's counting? She had never felt so relaxed in her life. She briefly remembered the flight, the journey up and Brewster introducing her to his wife as she went straight to bed in his lovely old English Pub.

The breakfast was mouth watering, with fresh orange juice and a lightly cooked meal, toast and home made marmalade, just enough to get her juices going and get her into the "getting out of bed" mode.

She had a strange feeling of euphoria as she made her way downstairs to be met by Brewster and a beautiful middle aged lady hanging from Chekov. He came over to her pulling this delightful lady after him and greeted her.

'Good morning Xalwo. I hope you slept well. May I introduce you to Mrs Mildred O'Riley?'

Xalwo was lost for words but not for too long before Mildred came over and kissed her on both cheeks. 'Welcome to Muddlecombe, Mma Xalwo. Come outside of this den of iniquity and let's show you around our humble village.' She grabbed Xalwo's hand and guided her outside into a blaze of sunshine.

Xalwo stopped and blinked at the beautiful setting outside the pub as Mildred said, 'I hear you've met old what's 'is name. I can never remember his name.'

Xalwo felt no malice in this statement; she in fact felt a certain kindred spirit and smiled at Mildred.

'Old pushy paws!'

'That's him,' replied Mildred and they both laughed out loud.

'I think the old Muddlecombe magic is starting to cast it's spell,' said Chekov to Brewster, a few paces behind the ladies as they both walked out onto the village green.

'Duck!'

'Oh, no. Boris is at it again.' They all took evasive action as Boris smacked a cricket ball into the duck pond once more.

'I forgot to mention the dangerous side to our village,' said Chekov, catching the ladies up and directing them off the cricket pitch.

Xalwo just stood still and just took a deep breath as she took in the peace and tranquillity of the scenery, once the ball had been rescued from the duck sanctuary.

*   *   *

'Good morning everyone,' Mildred addressed the assembled company all now sitting comfortably in the dining room of Primrose Cottage. It always puzzled Mildred that no matter how many people you shoved into the cottage, it always seemed to have plenty of room. But that was by the way.

'Welcome to our extraordinary annual general meeting of Borisky Diamonds. I would like to also extend a warm welcome to Mma,' Mildred checked on the pronunciation. 'Mma Xalwo from Botswana whom you all met yesterday. We hope you are fully rested after your journey from Africa.' Mildred looked over to Xalwo who smiled and taking that as a cue that she was well rested, she continued.

'As company secretary, I feel it unnecessary to go over the last minutes and bore you all, so I now hand you over to our esteemed Managing Director, Mr Chekov Yeboleksi.' Mildred gave him a little pat on the backside as he stood up and smiled back at Mildred.

'Thank you Mrs O'Riley.'

'You're welcome,' came a quick response from Mildred who had just finished rubbing her hand down the back of Chekov's trousers.

A roll of tittering fell over the room, but Chekov managed to gain some control and straightened himself as he continued.

'The reason I have asked for this meeting is to let you all meet our esteemed lady guest here,' he looked across at Xalwo. 'To give her some idea of how our little business is run and in the hope that she may want to join our venture in some form or another.' Chekov paused and continued looking again at Xalwo.

'*Mma* Xalwo, have I at last got it right?' a nod from Xalwo let him continue. 'Mma Xalwo has access to considerable amount of stock which could benefit our organisation. All we have to do is to persuade her to let us have some of that stock.' Chekov paused again.

'Obviously she is not a charity, but neither are we, so we must decide between us the most cost effective solution of moving her stock into our small organisation.'

Chekov looked down to some papers and then started. 'I feel it best to get the nasty finance details out of the way, so to start with I would like to call upon our lovely Finance Director to give us a brief history of our trading and I'm sure Mma Xalwo will want to ask questions?' Chekov turned to Fiona and back to Xalwo as Fiona started to shuffle a load more papers.

'Thank you Chekov,' Fiona started and opening her papers continued. 'We have been trading now for just over a year and our first trading figures have been extremely promising. It's not often a company goes into profit in the first year, but we managed it, and have paid out handsome dividends to our shareholders at the same time.'

'Could I ask what your dividend yield was Fiona please?' Xalwo asked quickly.

'Yes, I have done some ratios here and worked out some figures and it comes out as approximately 203% after tax.'

'Yield?' asked Xalwo incredulously.

'Yes, yield,' confirmed Fiona.

'203%,' Xalwo spluttered out.

'Yes to the nearest point of a percentage.' Fiona said quite noncommittally.

The silence in the room was deafening as Xalwo collected her thoughts and her heartbeat and slowly got her breath back again.

' The reason being,' Fiona felt it best to give some sort of argument as to why they were making such money, 'the reason being is that we don't have any fixed costs. No fixed assets. All our manufacturing equipment comes from the Educational Trust for the Community college. Thank you Mildred.' Fiona gave Mildred a little smile which no doubt would be explained to Mma Xalwo later. 'We don't pay out any salaries, everybody is a shareholder and gets dividends and the sales department, as will be explained later are on commission only. We don't own any property, company cars etc etc. We have the odd expense here and there, like getting you over here but we don't have to put you up in any big grand hotel. I am also looking at setting up an offshore investment corporation in Panama due to it's favourable tax laws, in order to maximise our shares. Of course every shareholder in this venture will automatically become a shareholder in this new bank. But I digress.....'

'Er, thank you Fiona, I'll, er, let you carry on, er,,,,,,,,,,,' Xalwo was in no state to put a reasonable sentence together at this point of the proceedings and Chekov felt it best to have a little rest now.

Chekov was watching these proceedings like a hawk and things were going exactly as planned. 'Perhaps we could give Fiona a breather now and go into our sales department projections. Thank you Fiona.' Chekov shuffled some of his papers around and then looked towards the two suntanned ladies in mini skirts sitting smoking in the corner. 'Can I introduce you to our sales department, Sharon and Tracey?

'Sharon runs our UK sales and Tracey is our export expert, although she only concentrates on the Canary Islands for the time being. How's it going girls?'

'Smashing thank you big boy,' Sharon took the gum out of her mouth and winked at Chekov. Chekov tried to withhold a blush remembering his brief encounter with the two ladies a long time ago whilst he was working in Tenerife.

'I should explain that both Sharon and Tracey are full time employees of Scotland Yard, or the police to you and me Mma Xalwo.' Chekov felt he had to say something to hide his embarrassment.

Xalwo looked disbelievingly at the two girls but said nothing. This was the strangest board meeting she had ever been to and she'd been to some weird meetings in Somali that were held at the point of a Kalashnikov.

She nodded and let them carry on.

'So how are the UK Sales going Sharon?'

'Smashing. Yer, as Chekov said we're still in with the Yard but,' she looked over to Xalwo and continued. 'But we gets paid on a commission basis on the diamonds so as to complement our meagre wages from the old bill. And very nice too, thank you very much.'

'So what's the forecast looking like for this year then Sharon?' Chekov wasn't expecting a full blown bookings and billings forecast spreadsheet but had hoped for something a bit more concrete than "smashing".

'Yer, like I said, it's going smashing.' Chekov held his head in his hands as Sharon continued.

'Well, we starts off with some old friends of ours down the smoke, who owed us a few favours and we shows them our stuff. Well they was all over us like a bloody rash. And the ones who didn't want anything, well we was all over *them* like a rash until they saw the light, so to speak.'

Sharon gave everybody a broad wink and carried on.

'"Sharon darlin' I want some more of that" they keeps telling us and so we asked them what they was doing with it and they takes us round to their shops in the East End. Then after a few months we gets the nod from some of the big boys and bugger me we ends up in Bond Street. The old certification's a bit dodgy but we get's that all sorted out and they can't get enough of us. They never had it so good, we can double their mark up and they can afford to pay some of the rents in town now with their profits. Old Sidney has done us good too, He's introduced us to some of his kosher friends and we're really into the big time now. We had that Ratner geezer sniffing round, but we told him to bugger off, didn't want no bleeding common or garden high street rubbish. We got our standards ain't we Tracey?'

Tracey gave Sharon the nod and they looked to Chekov who looked to Xalwo who was still in a state of shock.

Chekov felt it best to try Sharon a bit further.

'And what's your prognosis for the next twelve months Sharon?'

'I ain't got no prognosis, but I tell you what, I could double our sales if we had the stock, and then some more. Bleeding hell we haven't even started on Birmingham or Liverpool or even Glasgow, not that I fancy going up there at this time of year. I tell you what, give me some more stock and I'll soon be driving that nice red Ferrari I saw in Park Lane last week, eh Tracey?' Sharon winked over to Tracey who confirmed the years forecast figures.

'So it's going well then ladies?' Chekov threw his tuppence into the ring for what it was worth. Things were getting better by the moment as he looked over to Xalwo.

'And how about you Tracey? I would like to thank Tracey for coming back here from Tenerife at such short notice.'

Tracey took the floor.

'No probs there Chekov. Come back business class with all the toffs, bleeding lovely, free drinks, the lot. Met a nice geezer and be seeing a bit more of him I hope.' Tracey looked across to Sharon and exchanged winks.

'Yer, well like Sharon says, we're chuffed to bits since we bumped into your little game. Never 'ad it so good, some geezer said. Well, it all started when we was after Boris, cor, 'ee didn't 'arf give us the old run around on the old day job. But then we bumped into John, the geezer what owns this drum. And he's up to his arse in villainy, what with the old gold bullion stuff and that. Anyway we 'as a little chat with him and he puts us onto some other geezers what are running a jewellery chain and Bob's yer uncle. It's the same with them. Can't get enough at our prices. Gets the old audit certificate sorted out and off we go. But get a load of this. They wants a lot of bespoke stuff, that's special made gear, for the retired old tarts out there. Dripping with gold and soft as shit. Begging your pardon miss. Anyway, we puts it to Dudley, and bless his soul he comes up trumps.'

'Dudley's our cutter, helped by our staff at the Community College.' interrupted Chekov, turning to Xalwo. 'We'll see him later, but the trouble is nobody can understand his Black Country accent. Sorry Tracey, you were saying?'

'Well, this bespoke stuff's going like shit off a shovel. Sorry miss, slip of the old tongue again. But the punters will pay anything. I ain't pushing through the sales that Sharon is doing, but by Christ, the old profit margins is beautiful, and my commission is worked out on margins as well, so we're all doing very nicely thank you very much. I think I'll have the silver Ferrari, eh Sharon?'

Xalwo was getting the drift of things by now and after a long silence she managed to get her breath back and started asking questions.

'Can I ask you young ladies a question?' she said getting her brain back into the normality mode.

'Fire away darling,' Sharon spoke for them both.

'Erm, exactly how do you correlate your current position with your permanent position, in the police I believe you said?' Xalwo couldn't believe she was asking this question, but there was this nagging doubt in her mind about this situation. There was a nagging doubt in her mind about the whole bloody set up.

'Do what?' Sharon was again the representative for both her and Tracey.

'I think what Mma Xalwo is trying to say is how do you manage to hold down two jobs?' Chekov felt it best to simplify matters.

'Well, that's the beauty of it.' Tracey was in the chair now. 'When we starts off in Tenerife we was on the gold bullion case and stumbles over young Boris here, who leads us to John. Well John is a bit of a naughty lad, as are most of the geezers living in Tenerife, so we put it to him what we wanted and what could he give us back in return.'

'I'm sorry, I'm a bit lost here,' said Xalwo.

'Well, what I mean is that we told him we had suspicions about the gold bullion but needed to send some sort of fall guy back to England to keep our bosses happy. And in return could he help us out with the old Boris diamonds lark a bit. Well John and Boris are old buddies and there ain't nothing John would stop at to help Boris out. So he drops us a few choice names of some of the small fish in the pond and we use our talents to overcome their shyness and Bob's yer uncle.'

'And then John helps you out with the diamonds?' Xalwo was slowly getting the picture.

'That's it girl. John don't hold with drugs you see, being of the old school so we gets all the druggies and drop outs and them some more, and that leads to all sorts of interesting things that not only keeps our bosses in the Yard happy, but the Inland Revenue is tickled pink with us as well. Our bosses is happy, we're happy and John can relax for a while. Well, we've got to look after John. If it weren't for him where would we all be? No nice little cottage in the country, eh?'

The silence said it all. Exactly, no Primrose Cottage. The thought was too much to contemplate. Xalwo was trying to get her head round the set up, trying to make head or tale of the whole situation.

'I think now would be a good time as any to stop for a break.' Chekov broke the silence with some welcome news. 'I've asked Mrs Dimmock to help us with the catering and I know Mildred has added some of her specialities as well, so lets adjourn for half an hour shall we?' A rhetorical question if there ever was.

Poor Xalwo just sat there with a glazed look over her face until Mildred took her arm. 'You haven't met Mrs "D" yet have you? She's an absolute little gem. Come on, let's go into the kitchen.'

Xalwo at last managed to get the brain functioning back to some semblance of normality and walked with Mildred into the kitchen.

Then a very strange thing happened.

As Xalwo entered the kitchen, Mrs Dimmock stopped what she was doing and curtsied in front of Xalwo, taking her hand and kissing it, uttering a strange phrase. 'Selam teanaste'lle'n Itegue. Dehna neh?'

Xalwo, not for the first time today, was dumbstruck. Not only was she speechless but it looked like she was bloodless. All the blood had drained from her body and she was a paler shade of white, which is quite something when you started out as a darker shade of black.

Mrs Dimmock took her and guided her over to a kitchen stool and sat her down. Mildred was beside herself.

'What the bloody hell is going on Mrs D, sorry Mary?' Mildred hissed.

'All I said was welcome home princess and I hope you are alright. In Amharic of course.'

'Of course,' confirmed Mildred, who couldn't believe it. 'Why would you say that?'

'Well, what else could I say?'

Mildred shrugged her shoulders and continued as if everything was quite normal. 'Silly me, what else *could* you say?' Mildred gave a very strange look indeed but was ignored by Mrs Dimmock.

'Exactly,' continued Mrs Dimmock sternly and who by now had poured a nice cup of tea for Xalwo and was getting her to drink it down.

Some colour eventually returned to Xalwo's cheeks and there was evidence of a pulse at last. Then as the colour returned a small tear rolled lazily down her cheek.

She looked into Mrs Dimmock's eyes and said. 'The last time anyone said something like that to me was thirty years ago when I was a small girl, being smuggled out of the palace and being told that I must never tell anyone of my royal blood upon pain of death. I have travelled a long way to hear what you have just said.' Xalwo wiped the tear away and then looked into Mrs Dimmock's eyes again.

'How did you know?'

'Old Gerantinium and your great grand uncle Haile Selassie were buddies a long time a go. They shared a common lineage going back to the Solomonic dynasty in the 13th century. It's a religious thing you know,' Mrs Dimmock said matter of factly.

'I feel as if a hundred tons of hardship, pain and suffering have been lifted off my shoulders all of a sudden. Where the hell am I? Is this some sort of paradise, have I died and gone to heaven?'

'No, my dear, you're in Muddlecombe,' Mrs Dimmock confirmed bringing everyone down to earth. 'Now, we'd best get the tea and cakes out to the meeting or I shall be getting the sack.'

Xalwo, Mildred and Mrs Dimmock got all the food and drink ready and walked back to the dining room. As Mildred passed Chekov she gave him a big wink. Chekov wasn't quite sure what all that was about, whether it was his lucky night or whether something of cataclysmic proportions had just happened in the kitchen. He was right on both accounts.

The second session involved lots of legal documents flying about all over the place: memorandums and articles of association; companies house registration; balance sheets; trading figures, all very boring but necessary and Xalwo was now a different person. Although she was still having difficulty in understanding their trading modus operandi, she was now starting to enjoy the cut and thrust of the boardroom politics and feeling considerably more relaxed. She felt she was getting to know the personalities involved and the benefits each of them had to offer in making this little operation run like clockwork.

At four o'clock they called for close of day operations as Boris had to go for cricket practice, which was obviously a far higher priority than discussing high finance and strategic planning.

They all adjourned to the pub and sat outside taking in the clean fresh smell of the new mown hay and the smell of the drains in the duck pond.

'We must really prioritise those bloody drains,' said Chekov as the drinks arrived on the garden tables under the parasols. 'Thank you Brewster,' Chekov replied handing round the drinks.

'How's it going Mma Xalwo?' Brewster asked out of curiosity.

'Brewster, my friend, can I drink this extremely large gin and tonic first before I answer your questions?'

'Of course you can my dear. It's obviously going well then,' he concluded and left them to enjoy their refreshments.

Chekov and Mildred looked at each other and felt it best to continue where Brewster had left off, to say nothing until Xalwo had time to reflect on the days happening. They sat in the evening sun watching the cricket practice, letting the alcohol swarm over their brain cells to deaden the pain. Only Xalwo was the one in pain, well not so much pain as confusion, a normal occurrence in Muddlecombe.

Chekov was actually enjoying his drink; his project was going to plan as it were. The more Xalwo fell under the magic of the Muddlecombe spell the easier it would be to negotiate a cost effective solution in obtaining her stock. However he was still a bit puzzled as to the happenings in the kitchen when Mildred had signalled some form of incident.

They watched as Mrs Dimmock, obviously having finished tidying up the cottage, came out, closed the front door, pulled the key out and after going through the low garden gate, walked out onto the village green. She walked straight though the cricket practice, bringing everything to a grinding halt, stopping briefly to pop the keys into Boris' pocket, giving his bottom a little tweak, and with a little sidestep out of the way of any backlash, walked off wiggling her backside at Boris. She walked off the pitch with a wicked backward glance onto the lane up to her home.

This bought a round of applause to everyone except Boris who was now a lovely shade of crimson.

Everyone knew exactly what he was going to do with the next ball, and sure enough…………………..duck!'

The official air raid warning now over, everyone returned to some form of semblance. Xalwo finished her gin and tonic and after another prolonged silence said, 'just who is that woman?'

After an even longer period of silence, Mildred felt it only right and proper to answer. 'Ah, yes, well, that's a bloody good question.'

Chekov felt he had something to say, so after another lengthy silence added, 'Ah, yes, now that *is* a bloody good question.'

Xalwo looked from one to the other with a blank expression expecting some form of reply, or even some form of intelligence.

No chance.

That is until Chekov came up with, 'anybody want another drink?' he got a very stern look from both the ladies as if to say, "What a bloody stupid question, is Hitler anti-Semitic?"

He nodded and got up and went inside the pub as Mildred turned to Xalwo and said. 'Nobody is very sure who or what she is, but all we know is that she seems to know what's going to happen a long time before it actually does happen. I'm what they call a newcomer here. Although I was born and bred here, my mother wasn't but she started up the community college where we now help Dudley with the diamonds. Mrs D doesn't seem to have aged since I've known her. Come to think of it neither do any of the other villagers.'

Xalwo interrupted, 'it's all very strange, but then again it's not a bad sort of strange. I feel so relaxed here, so tranquil, so……'

Mildred finished it for her. 'So at home?'

'Well, er, well, that's it. THAT IS IT! You've hit the nail right on the head.' I've only been here two days and I feel as if I've been here all my life.'

'Weird isn't it,' confirmed Mildred as they both looked blankly out onto the cricket pitch.

'Hallo, anyone in?' Chekov brought them back down to ground with the arrival of the drinks. 'You two looked miles away?'

'We were discussing Mrs Dimmock.'

'Ah, yes, well, that would explain it. Anyway, get this lot down you. Now don't forget Mildred has knocked up a little something for you tonight Xalwo, so we'll be dining at chez O'Riley tonight.'

'Can't wait,' said Xalwo.'

'Good, that's it settled then,' as if there was a glut of Michelin star restaurants to choose from. 'See you at seven, we'll come over to the pub and pick you up.' Mildred rose and gave Xalwo a kiss on the cheek and grabbed Chekov steering him off home rather rapidly.

"She's sex mad," thought Chekov as he was raced away to Mildred's cottage. Once they were out of hearing range Mildred said in a very loud whisper, 'you'll never believe what just happened in Primrose Cottage?'

'I think quite a lot happened at our meeting,' said Chekov not fully understanding Mildred's excited question.

'I caught them at it.'

'You caught who at it?' Chekov had a pained expression on his face.

'Xalwo and Mrs D.'

'The little scallywags. What were they doing, pinching the biscuits?' A hint of sarcasm popped up.

'No, they were talking……..'

'No, they weren't………?' another hint of sarcasm was interjected before Mildred could finish her sentence.

'They were talking in a foreign language, Amharic.'

'Am, who?' Chekov wasn't quite sure where this was leading or where it had come from even.

'Xalwo is only some sort of bleeding royal princess and of course old Mrs D and her great uncle, some highly somebody or other, were great pals. Well not actually Mrs D's but old Gerantinium……….'

'That'll be old Haile Selassie………….'

'Don't tell me you know him as well?' Mildred was distraught.

'Not me per se, but I did sort of know a man or two who helped him leave the country as it were.'

'As it were?' Mildred wasn't sure what to say, so just tried to keep the conversation ticking over. She wasn't going to introduce modern history into the curriculum at this specific moment on such a lovely romantic evening.

Mildred was getting as nearly confused as Mma Xalwo.

*   *   *

'Mildred, that was a lovely meal. I can't remember the last time I had home cooking. And I can't believe I'm sitting here with the wife of a man I'm currently seeing.'

'Well, I was married very young and I have to say there wasn't a lot to pick from here in Muddlecombe. I think it must have been the boots and the spurs that did it.'

'Kinky,' said Xalwo with raised eyebrows and a smile.

'You don't know the half of it my dear. Just you wait. Well I wasn't into that and then Blossom Deecup from the "Snort" appeared on the scene including anything else in a skirt. That is excluding Scotsmen.'

'Shame,' came a snide remark.

'And then of course this gentle, loving and kind man appeared on the horizon in Tenerife and it's all downhill from there,' said Mildred laughing and giving Chekov a great big hug and a kiss.

Chekov hadn't gone too deeply into his chequered past yet with Mildred. He felt talking about his time in the Interrogation section of the KGB and how he had risen rapidly in the ranks thanks to his grasp of testicles as part of his interrogation system which was not really appropriate at this moment of time.

'So you see my dear Xalwo, he's all yours,' Mildred said very softly with a great big grin all over her face. 'You have my deepest sympathy.'

'And this is where our little plan comes in very nicely,' said Chekov interrupting the ladies.

'What plan?' said Xalwo.

'Ah, well all will be revealed but first we must discuss our commercial relationship.'

'Ah, yes, I suppose we had better get down to the nitty-gritty,' sighed Xalwo.

'So after our little board meeting today, what do you think of it so far?'

'I'm impressed. I don't know how anybody *couldn't* be involved with such a profitable and cost effective organisation.'

'Good, that's a start. Now let's see where you can fit into all this.' Chekov took a deep breath. 'As you will have noticed we have a lot of shareholders and not a lot of salaried people.'

'Yes, I wondered about that. But then you did pay out a large dividend to your shareholders.'

'Well spotted Xalwo.' Chekov continued. 'So this is what we intend to offer to you.' Chekov gave a little cough, had a drink of wine and continued with everybody in rapt attention.

'We want your stock and there are two ways of allowing you to part with it. One, cash. Two, shares. Let us consider the latter first and the benefits this will entail for you.'

'I'm listening,' said Xalwo who had a drink as well.

'Whichever way we go, be it cash or shares, your stock will be valued against the Rapaport Diamond Trade Report prices and offered accordingly against that registry, in US dollars. OK?'

'That sounds fair so far.' Xalwo replied.

'Of course they will not actually be entered onto the registry you understand, but there will *be* certification, but let's not go into that just yet.'

Xalwo looked puzzled.

'Moving on, so, if we offer you shares you will then become a shareholder and be given a dividend according to your share of the company at the time of dividend issue. We have just had our last issue last month so you will have to wait a few months until the next issue.'

'Ok, with you so far,' said Xalwo.

'And then of course you will become a director of the company and it's my guess that you will probably be the majority shareholder and therefore be given an executive directorship.'

'Sounds good so far,' she replied.

'Now all we have to do is to agree terms and then we need to see your stock.' Chekov sat back now and awaited Xalwo's response.

'Ok, well as you know I have a limited amount of stock in the UK, delivered to my bank safe deposit in London by old "pushy paws" himself. Now as to the rest, it is in Botswana and I'd be interested in how you intend to get it out of there?' It was her turn to sit back and listen and have another drink while she was at it.

'We have another plan for that as well, Plan A.' Chekov smiled at Xalwo.

'You have been busy planning haven't you?'

'Yes, but I don't want to go into too many details so far, and as I said, all will be revealed. But before you go back we need a quiet word with Dr Rammy before he sets off on his cricket tour.'

Xalwo looked a little puzzled but let Chekov continue.

'However the second Plan, Plan B, which came out of *your* idea, first discussed initially in the restaurant in Gaborone, which just so happens to coincide with *my* plans, or should I say, *our* plans,' he gave a quick look to Mildred who positively purred. 'They need to be timed to perfection. The third party involved must not be made aware of anything and we must all meet together at precisely the same time and place to make sure this project is a success.' Mildred looked into Chekov's eyes and gave him a little squeeze in excitement.

'Anyway, young lovers, it's time for my bed. I am a bit jet lagged. We've still got a lot to talk about and I only have one day left. So can you please excuse me, I'm off to bed. Goodnight.'

Xalwo left feeling extremely relaxed and contented.

Chapter 10. Botswana XI
versus MCC

'Good afternoon ladies and gentlemen, well here we are on a lovely sunny day here in the capital of Botswana, Gaborone, at the Gaborone Cricket club on the outskirts of the city. This is John Harlot here, reporting to you for the BBC overseas programme and hoping you all at home are listening to this match with interest.

It is the first time Botswana have hosted any major cricket international team and they have high expectations of showing off their young players with a few helpings of experience thrown in from some old neighbours in South Africa.

I talked to the Secretary of the Botswana cricket Association a Mr Krishna Chutnabuttee who is excited at the opportunity to get Botswana on the international scene.

Quite by coincidence he has his nephew, a Dr Rammittin Chutnabuttee playing for the opposition, the visitors from England, our own MCC. I haven't had a chance to ask Dr Rammittin which county he plays for in England just yet and I have not had a chance to talk to the teams just yet but I have just been handed the team lists:

and……………………………………………………………..glanc ing………..down…………………..through the list of the MCC,…………………I can't seem to find……….any…………………..names that come immediately to mind, Slobovitch appears to be opening the batting with the captain, Dr Chutnabuttee. Oh well, anyway here goes and as the sides come out into the middle it appears that the MCC have won the toss and have decided to bat.

Well listeners, as I said it is a lovely day here in Gaborone as ,,,,,,,,,,,, ah yes I can see the fielding team coming out now with the two umpires and, my goodness here come the batsmen, and isn't he a big one. I assume this must be Slobovitch who I can only describe as a sort of large version of W G Grace, an extremely larger version, and that must be Dr Rammittin Chutnabuttee. A slightly built young Asian man with his turban, quite a good-looker ladies, I must warn you, ha, ha, ha.

Ok, well the batsmen are now out in the middle of the crease and Slobovitch is standing right in the middle of the pitch obviously surveying the field, only he isn't looking around much. The umpire asks him if he needs a guard to which Mr Slobovitch just laughs. Ah hang on a mo, Dr Chutnabuttee is walking up to his fellow batsman and they are having a little discussion.'

"Niet, niet, no, no," says Slobovitch but he is still standing in the middle of the pitch. The bowler is now marking his run out and then coming back to the umpire talking to him about something. I think what he is saying is that he can't see past the batsman to the wicket. The umpire is now consulting with the batsman and Dr Chutnabuttee is involved and, well Slobovitch is quite obviously quite happy where he is. The bowler isn't as he can't see a jolly thing. Well, this is jolly exciting I must say. I can't remember a batsman taking such a guard as this before. He is as I have said an extremely large gentleman and it must be very difficult for the bowler to see where he's aiming at, but the umpire shrugs his shoulders and the bowler throws his arms up in the air and walks back to his marker.

Ok, well ladies and gentlemen here we go. A famous cricket match for this small African country and oh, what's happening now. The wicket keeper is throwing up his arms. It would appear he can't see the bowler now. Oh dear, this is going to be a long day.

Ok, now the umpire has told everyone to get on with the game and the bowler is now walking back to his crease. Well, let's hope we can start a cricket match. Ok, so this young right arm fast bowler is now running down to bowl and ………………..oooofff! Oh, my goodness, I bet that hurt. Dear oh dear. Well listeners the problem of the bowler is quite clearly that as he can't see the stumps he must try and get the batsman to relinquish his position in the middle of the pitch and has done just that by bowling straight at him, hitting him amidships so to speak. Straight in his stomach, well one of them.

After all that Slobovitch does not feel overly concerned. He has found the ball and extracted it from his folds and thrown it back to the bowler. Can you believe that? The bowler is trying to kill him and he virtually is saying have another go old chap.

And so the bowler walks back to his mark and after much scratching of the head starts his run up again. And he comes in to bowl now and…………..oh, no, oh dear oh dear, oh goodness gracious. Well I suppose if one must stand in the middle of the pitch one must take one's punishment, another whizzer, straight into the solar plexus. Boy, I bet that hurt.

Poor Slobovitch looks around his person for the ball and once again extracts it and throws it back to the bowler. Well, well, what an incredible start to an international game of cricket.

The poor bowler is scratching his head but now suddenly starts to smile. He doesn't go back to his mark but stands by the umpire ready to bowl. He looks at the umpire and the umpire looks at him and offers him to bowl, and he does, oh what beauty, he has lobbed it straight over the batsman's head into the arms of the wicket keeper who slowly knocks the bails off and with a lovely smile on his face looks to the umpire and in unison with the bowler they ask the inevitable question: "Owzat!"

As the fielding team jump about in hysteria, the only people not jumping up and down are the two umpires and the two batsmen; the umpire gently lifts his arms up and extends them signalling a wide.

Oh my gosh, oh dear oh dear, the fielding team are not happy about that at all, they are all running to the umpire shouting at him and jumping up and down in disbelief.

The umpire stands his ground and does not move a muscle and eventually each fielder returns to his position as their captain realises the futility of it and disperses them back to their respective parts of the field. He collects the ball and throws it back to his bowler who starts his weary way back to his mark.

He starts his run up again but with obvious added zest and once more, oh dear, oh dear not again, how much punishment can this poor man take. Slobovitch retrieves the ball from his folds and throws it back to the bowler.

Well listeners I can honestly say I have never seen anything like this before, I don't now where this is going, I don't know where all this is going to lead to, I really don't.

So here we go again, the bowler is shaking his head as he walks back to start his run up, and he's off again on his demolition run and, bowls and,……………………..oh dear, oh my goodness, I don't believe it, I have never seen anything like this before, what a game of cricket! Slobovitch has quite clearly got the range of the ball by now and has dispatched it, he has smashed the b,……………..ball, he has hit the ball off into the horizon. It's still travelling, to somewhere in Africa. Oh my goodness, this is unbelievable, the poor bowler is on his knees hitting the pitch with his fists as Dr

Chutnabuttee walks up and shakes Slobovitch by the hand.

Well, well, what a game. What will happen next?

Well the umpire signals a six and they have found a new ball and he has shown it to all concerned including Mr Slobovitch who doesn't seem that concerned at all.

The bowler takes it and starts to polish it anew. He looks at Slobovitch quite clearly as if saying this is war. Slobovitch is totally unphased by all this and just stands in the middle of the pitch gently swaying his bat to and fro ready for the next delivery.

And the young fast bowler starts off again, this time there is a spring in his step as he hurls the ball down to the ………….oh dear, oh dear, oh dear.

The ball is off on another trajectory to outer space as Slobovitch gives it an all mighty swing and connects right in the middle of the bat. The crowd are on their feet, they have never seem anything like this, neither have I, the power of the man is incredible, but then I suppose with his weight behind the bat the law of an equal and opposite force as described in the laws of physics would explain it all.

The poor bowler grabs his hat from the umpire and storms off only to be told to come back as his wide means there is another ball left in the over, if they can find another ball that is.

The captain walks over to his bowler and tries to counsel him and motivate him into some renewed energy. Someone has found a ball throws it to the bowler and he walks back to his mark.

I would not like to be a batsman at this point of the procedures as the bowler starts his run up only after scraping the ground with his boots like an enraged bull, for surely that is his state of mind right now. And he hurls the ball and nearly hurls himself with it as well and,…………………….oh, no,no,no,oh no, oh goodness gracious, oh dear oh dear. Well can you believe it? Well I suppose so; anything is possible in this game. Slobovitch is smiling like a Cheshire cat as he watches the ball disappear into oblivion after another almighty swing of the bat and a true connection made in the middle, the only problem being that he has broken his bat.

Well, eighteen off the over, I am sorry, of course, no, there is the one extra for the wide, nineteen off the over, and what an over. I've never seen anything like it and hate to think what is going to happen now that Slobovitch has got his eye in. I presume they have enough bats for him. The chap at the other end, Dr Chutnabuttee hasn't moved from his crease all this time, just leaning on his bat with a large smile on his face. Quite clearly he knows he is not needed to do any running between the wickets.

But now he must face the bowling and oh. What's happening now? Oh I see, another batsman is coming onto the field. Yes I see it now, Mr Slobovitch is quite clearly only needed to hit the ball over the boundary and not expected to do any running between the wicket so he now has a runner.

Ok, now all is settled and the other bowler is now starting his run up and bowls. Well, there's a change, Dr Chutnabuttee just plays a nice straight forward defensive shot and lets the fielders return the ball to the bowler.'

'Only the two runs off that over so we are now back to see what Slobovitch will be doing. The bowler is talking to his captain and is bowling from way outside his crease to get round the monumental Mr Slobovitch. But although it hits the wicket, the umpire has signalled a no-ball which he quite obviously has to do.'

'Well, what a fascinating day this has been so far, and oh, what is happening now, Slobovitch is walking off the pitch towards the pavilion. His captain runs up to him and is starting to say something to him, but Slobovitch just lifts his right arm up and down to his mouth indicating quite clearly that he is thirsty. Well, now what happens?

Both the umpires are conferring and have asked Dr Chutnabuttee over and are having a long discussion with him. The captain shrugs his shoulders and calls to the pavilion, and, here comes, ah, oh, it's not our friend Slobovitch, it's a new batsman by the look of things.

Well, what's all this about, oh, I've just been handed a note from one of our staff and, oh, would you believe it, our friend Slobovitch is now down in the scorer's book as "retired, thirsty."

Incredible, what a game, I've no doubt the poor Slobovitch is exhausted after that innings although he didn't have to do any running between the wickets but at least he made a decent score and it's probably just as well for the poor home team, to give them a breather and to save money on new balls! And new bats as well!'

*   *   *

'Well good afternoon ladies and gentlemen and welcome back to the Gaborone cricket club on this second session of this memorable cricket match here in sunny Gaborone in Botswana. Well what a first innings from the visitors the MCC, with a score of two hundred and thirty five runs.

A fine innings from Slobovitch with a score of eighty four. That's ten sixes and six fours, not a single single, pardon the pun, in his score. Then their captain, Dr Chutnabuttee with a nice seventy five and a few cameos after they had perished to take the score up to two hundred and thirty five. All this in only thirty two overs, that's an average of nearly seven runs an over which is quite unheard of in this type of innings.

Well now they have had a break and the local team are coming out to bat. Dr Chutnabuttee is to open the bowling and we've been given to understand he is a slow left arm leg spin bowler.

Well the new batsmen have all taken their stands at the crease and the opening batsman for Botswana has taken a guard and the umpire signals the start of the second session.'

'Well that was an interesting over from Dr Chutnabuttee. What a mixture of deliveries that had the batsmen completely baffled but they managed to survive and a maiden over has duly been recorded.

Now we have a new bowler at the club house end, a certain Harry Hercules who apparently is a fast right arm over the wicket bowler. He has measured out his run up and awaits the umpires go ahead. And he starts his run up and bowls.

Oh, my goodness, wow, incredible, what a ball. That was fast alright but it swung so much the poor wicket keeper didn't have a chance to stop it and it goes to the boundary for four byes. Well Botswana are up and running on the score board. Boy that was a sizzler.

It is interesting to see the MCC have six slips in a very deep position and one can see why if the ball is going to swing that much.

Well here goes Hercules again and he comes up to bowl and oh, my gosh, that just flew down the leg side and poor Slobovitch the wicket-keeper just looked on in amazement as it went down the leg side for another wide and four byes again. Well Botswana are scoring at the same fast rate as the MCC but they haven't touched the ball yet.

So here comes Hercules again and he hurls the ball down at a furious rate and all the batsman can do is wave his bat in the general direction of the ball as it curls past everybody but is stopped by a quick thinking long on who throws the ball back to the wicket keeper saving a few runs this time. So another run is added to the score.

And so the bowler picks the ball up again and starts his run and comes in to bowl. And he throws himself and the ball down at a frightening speed and, oh my gosh, goodness gracious me, this time the batsman touched it but too late he only snicked it and it was caught at slips for a fantastic wicket and everybody is jumping up and down celebrating their first wicket. Poor Hercules is buried under a mass of bodies as the bemused batsman walks off in bewilderment shaking his head. He didn't really know what hit him it was so fast and it must have swung a good two yards virtually from leg to the on side after it had bounced off the pitch at a ferocious speed.

So Botswana are nine for one, what will happen next? What an incredible game of cricket as the next batsman comes out.'

'Well at last someone has mastered the MCC bowling and the score is slowly increasing and now Botswana are forty six for one and seem to be on top. Dr Chutnabuttee has closed down one end with his spin bowling but at the other end they have managed to get the bat onto the ball and score a few runs together with a lot of byes from some wayward fast bowling. A couple of nice boundaries and the scoreboard is ticking over nicely as Hercules comes in furiously to bowl and a nice drive from the batsman sends the ball racing towards the boundary as they start a leisurely run for at least three runs…………oh my goodness, oh this is fantastic, what a throw. Well have you ever seen anything like this? The batsman quite obviously went for the extra run as the ball was nearly to the boundary when the fielder just picked up the ball and hurled it straight onto the stumps!

The wicket keeper just got out of the way and pointed to the stumps as the ball came flying straight in as if the wicket keeper knew that it was going to be a direct hit! I can't believe it! What a throw from the other end of the field, absolutely incredible! Slobovitch is not the most mobile of wicket keepers it has to be said, in actual fact he doesn't move at all and one can see now why he doesn't need to move if they can hit the stumps from that distance!

Well, the fielding side are delirious; they are jumping up and down slapping everybody on the back and running up to their captain and doing some sort of ritual, raising their right arms up and down to their mouths as if they have a glass in their hands, very strange.'

*   *   *

'My dear nephew, can I be having a word with you please in your large ear?' Krishna had dragged Dr Rammy outside.

'Of course uncle, wasn't that some cricket match? Unbelievable, didn't ever think our boys could ever play like that. Fantastic!'

'Not fantastic!' Krishna was not a happy man.

'Oh, come on uncle, the best side won you must agree?'

'It was not being the best side; it was not being the bloody MCC!'

'What you on about?'

'You are not being the MCC, you are not being the bloody Marylebone Cricket Club. Where are Trevor and Denis and Freddy and Godfrey and…..' Krishna was starting to splutter in fury.

Before Dr Rammy could answer Krishna started to splutter again. 'Where are the Edrich brothers, where are the bloody Bedser twins, where are all the bloody cricket players from Marylebone?' Krishna was about to blow a fuse.

'I don't know,' said Dr Rammy shrugging his shoulders.

'Why don't you know?'

'We are coming from Muddlecombe, not Marylebone.'

'Then please be telling me what the blinking hell you are doing here?'

'You asked us here.'

'No I didn't.'

'Yes you did.'

'No I didn't, I asked for the MCC!'

'And we are the MCC.' Dr Rammy was starting to see the funny side of this now.

'You are not being the bloody MCC, you are ……..' Krishna was about to go into nuclear overload when Dr Rammy answered the question for him.

'……………………..the MCC.' Dr Rammy said ever so slowly and smiling.

'You, you, you, you are not ………..'
Krishna was just about to pop. 'Where are all
the bloody people coming from Marylebone?'
    'Actually they don't come from
Marylebone……………..' Dr Rammy said before he
was interrupted again.
    'You are not the bloody MCC……………………
………………you are not…………
……..………..you are just not………
…………………………. playing cricket!'

*   *   *

Fortunately Dr Rammy had put in a
contingency plan just in case they actually won.
Not that he could ever have dreamed of such a
win. But one should never underestimate the
motivational powers of a pint of beer!
    So after the match he got out his
briefcase and took out the file with the player's
alcoholic debit and credit accounts. It would
have been a lot easier to calculate the results
had it not been for the whole team jumping up
and down screaming for drinks. In a short time
he realised that if he didn't get some drinks in
soon he would be facing a lynching squad of his
fellow dry throated colleagues.
    He quickly bought a round for everyone
and then sat down to do the calculations as a
hush descended at the bar at the Gaborone
cricket club whilst his team started to swallow
their beer. He had to be quick.
    "84 pints of beer for Boris," Dr Rammy
quickly calculated. That should shut him up for
a couple of days and then he worked out all the

other equations. The problem was that everyone got a win bonus at the end, but he still had the kitty left over from the practices at home. However it wasn't looking good. He may have to dig into the contingency account after all. What the hell, the boys deserved it.

'Dr Rammy, can I introduce you to Sir Reginald Makepeace, he's the sort of British boss out here,' Creighky looked from Sir Reginald to Dr Rammy

'British High Commissioner. Nice to meet you young man. I bet your uncle is jolly proud of you. I bet he can't stop talking about you.'

"I bet he has now" thought Dr Rammy.

'Fantastic match, well done. Now I hope my colleague here Mr O'Riley is looking after you alright?'

'Oh, yes, old Creighky is doing a great job.'

'And what have you got planned after this Mr O'Riley?'

'Ah, the old logistics is it? Right you are then, well they have a couple of nights here in Gaborone and then we're off up to Francistown for a game sponsored by the old De Beers lot. And a night there and after that I thought they would like to go on the old safari there up the Okinawa delta.'

'Okavango delta.' Sir Reginald interrupted.

'That's the one. My god it's beautiful up there, so it is, with all them lions and tigers running around like they was at home in your front garden. I thought the boys would like that.'

'Good show O'Riley, jolly good show. I'm sure they'll enjoy that, although I doubt if they'll see many tigers.'

*   *   *

At the Lords cricket ground in North London in the Long Room, someone answered the telephone

'Hallo. MCC, Long Room.'

'Hallo, that you Pongo?'

'Yes?'

'It's me, Makers. Sir Reginald Makepeace from Gaborone.'

'Oh, yes, hallo Makers. How the devil are you old boy?'

'Damn fine Pongo, damn fine. Just watched a cracking game of cricket. Your boys put up a damn fine show. Haven't had so much fun since they debagged the Head Prefect.'

'Good show old sport…………'

'Golly, you've got some stonking good new boys in there, I'll say. That Russian chappie, by the left, he couldn't half hit that ball. Lost three bloody balls thanks to him. Mind you he must be knocking on a bit but the old bugger retired thirsty. What do you say about that old sport? I think he just wanted to give our local boys a bit of a rest from running all over the park all day. And that young doctor chappie, damn incredible bowler. Had 'em tied up in knots, and that Hercules? A tad on the wayward side but my god he'd put the fear of Christ up 'em I can tell you. Damn fine show all round. Give my regards to the memsahib, must dash. Toodle loo.'

198

'Pinky, old chap. It's going well then?'

'What the bloody hell you on about old boy?'

'Our boys out in Africa?'

'What the blazes are you twittering on about Pongo?'

'You know, our lads in South Africa.'

'Our lads in South Africa are getting stuffed. Those yapi bastards have found some young fresh faced kid who's hurling the bloody ball down at over ninety miles an hour. He's gone through us like a red hot knife through butter.'

'Ah, has he now. How strange?' Pongo went into deep uncontrollable confusion. 'And we haven't got any Russians playing for us then? Or any doctors or a Hercules'?'

'Pongo old chap I think you've lost it completely. What in hell's name are you talking about? I think you need a stiff drink, 'cause I bloody well do.'

Chapter 11. A dastardly plot unfolds, slowly.

Pieter Van de Nitwit or Piet as he was known could trace his ancestors back to the people first called the Grensboere, then the Voortrekkers, then Boers, then Afrikaaners. They had taken part in the "Groot Trek". Starting in 1835, when more than 10,000 Boers, the Voortrekkers, left the Cape Colony with their families and went north and north-east. The colonial aspirations of the Premier of the Cape Colony, Sir Cecil Rhodes, together with the help of Lord Kitchener had driven the Boers out of their lands and dispersed them throughout the northern part of what is now known as South Africa.

The hatred of the British was still festering in Piet's subconscious mind which was not exactly overloaded with intelligence. To say he was as intelligent as bait would instigate litigation from the fishing industry, he certainly wouldn't have passed any GCE'or whatever the local education authority were handing out.

There were certainly no NVQs on offer even though they hadn't been invented yet.

His ancestors where pretty NVQless as well, as they followed the great Trek in their ox wagons but took a wrong turning and ended up in Botswana instead of Natal.

The one thing Piet did have was the propensity for hard work, no matter where. He had even dismissed his ancestral separatist ideas and worked with the blacks underground but had difficulty keeping up with *their* capacity for hard work and so had ended up on the surface doing menial jobs that no one else would do. He was very proud of his latrines and this didn't go unnoticed by personnel who promoted him into the kitchens, cleaning all the utensils and crockery and helping with the vegetables, potato peeling etc.

He was working there when the garden party took place for the opening of the new mines at Jwaneng. He had watched the beauty of Mma Xalwo for many years as she worked around the mines. He watched her in all her beauty at the garden party and had then seen this big stupid bugger with a sword dash all his romantic hopes. The uniform was a dead give away to his nationality, British. Piet spat the name into the soup tureen.

When Piet finished his day job he had a siesta and then did his other job which was a night watchman, which just so happened to be at the Mokala Lodge Hotel. He was on duty that night when the Prime Minister, Mma Xalwo and the big stupid bugger with the sword started their prancing about. It was Piet who called the police into believing that the bastard British bugger would be dragged away screaming to prison. But it was not to be and his hatred festered on.

At some weekends when he was allowed to leave the Jwaneng workers settlement, he took all his hard earned money back to his family in Gaborone where his parents would have a big pot of potjie on the go in their nice apartment block with his brother and sister. His brother, Jacobus, was the intelligent one and had a nice cushy job driving taxis whilst his sister was a cleaner by both day and night in various offices.

The family lived just above the poverty level but comfortably and the two brothers played rugby at weekends for the local team who needed a bit of weight at numbers 4 and 5 in the scrum. They fitted the parts beautifully, big and stupid. Then after the match they would have a braai at the clubhouse and get very drunk and start remembering the good old days when their ancestors got slaughtered by the British and it wasn't long before "the big stupid bugger with the sword's" name cropped up and he got the blame for the majority of the Boers bad luck.

In their drunken haze a plot began to unfold that would not only get the revenge they, their family and their ancestors would want but also gain them some wealth at the same time.

Kidnapping.

*   *   *

'Pass me another Castle bru?'

'Ok.'

Jacobus took the bottle of beer and put it into his mouth ripping the bottle top of with his teeth and spitting it out onto the floor.

Big and stupid, but dangerous.

'So, how we gonna do this kidnapping then bru?'

Piet looked to his elder brother and started to think. 'Christ min, you're the bloody brains.' Piet wanted nothing to do with this thinking bit.

'Christ min, it was you're bloody idea.'

'Yeah, well,' Piet looked like he was going to have to get this thinking thing going after all. 'Yeah, well, I just thought, you know, just write a note and put it in the door,'

'Isn't there something missing like getting hold of the bloke first?'

'Yeah, well, I was coming to that.'

'And who is going to do the writing?'

'Christ min, you've got a bloody certificate.'

'That's allowing me to drive a bloody taxi round Gaborone not write a bloody book.'

'Now, there's an idea!'

'Where?'

'Your taxi.'

'What about my taxi?'

'You could pick him up in your taxi.'

There was a long silence when the brain cells started to accelerate up to the warp speed of a slug.

'Yeah.' Jacobus had never thought of that. 'Good thinking there bru. Yeah, brilliant.'

*   *   *

Creighky had just come out of the High Commission to get a sandwich and for a bit of fresh air.

Jacobus leaned out of the window of his taxi. 'Hey mister, do you want a taxi?'

'No thanks.'

'Oh.'

And Creighky walked on back to work, leaving poor Jacobus in a state of disbelief. He couldn't understand why he didn't want a taxi. So he waited until after lunch until Creighky had finished work.

*   *   *

Creighky finished work; well his definition of work and anybody else's differed considerably. He just went round chatting up the young female secretaries, so he wasn't exactly exhausted when he strode out into the sunshine looking forward to a walk in the open air to work up an appetite for his evening meal.

'Hey mister, do you want a taxi?'

'No thanks.'

'Oh.'

Poor Jacobus had waited all day for this, ignoring the pleading public desperate for taxis. Never mind, he was a patient man if nothing else. Tomorrow was another day.

*   *   *

Another boring frustrating day. Everybody except "the big stupid bugger with the sword" wanted a taxi.

It was getting late and Jacobus was about to give up hope when out strode Creighky.

'Hey mister, do you want a taxi?'

'Now that's what I call service. Right you are me old sunshine. Now just you be waiting a second there me bucko, ah, here she comes now. I got us a taxi princess!' Creighky shouted to a young girl coming out of the High Commission entrance. One of the young secretaries had succumbed to his charm.

'Now you just jump in there me darling and I'll whisk you off for a magical evening fit for a queen.' The young girl slid across the back seat of the taxi as Creighky joined her and let the driver close the door.

'The Old Bull and Bush there me old matey. Say, haven't I seen you before, do you have a permanent booking for the High Commission?'

'Oh, no Sir, no I haven't been here before, just a coincidence.'

'Oh,' said Creighky and got down to the business of pouring his charm all over the poor innocent victim.

Poor Jacobus didn't know what to do. He'd got his man and a bloody woman as well. That wasn't in the plan so he just dropped them off at the restaurant.

*　　*　　*

'Nobody said it was going to be easy bru. Maybe we'd better think up another plan.'

'Just pass me another bloody Castle mate.' Jacobus opened it and swallowed most of it in one gulp. 'Listen Piet, if that bugger doesn't want a taxi, how the hell am I supposed to get him into it, short of bashing him over the head with me bloody knoblekerry and dragging him into the bloody taxi in front of all those people in the Mall?'

'Ah, you've got me there bru.'

'I've got you there have I? And how the bloody hell am I suppose to make a living at the same time waiting just for this big stupid bugger all day long?'

'Ah, you've got me there again bru.'

'Just pass me another bloody Castle!'

They sat looking at each other for some considerable time until Piet had a brilliant idea.

'Why don't we wait until it's dark?'

Jacobus sat drinking his beer for another long time and then, 'Bloody brilliant why didn't I think of that!'

'There you go then.'

'Bloody brilliant,' repeated Jacobus.

*   *   *

The next evening Jacobus did his daily runs and then went out later on at night but returned fairly quickly. And in a strange mood.

'Piet?'

'Yes bru, you're back awful quick?'

'Yes, and do you know why?'

'Ah, you've got me there bru.'

'The big stupid bugger with the sword finishes work before it gets dark!'

'So?'

'So, there's no bugger left at the High Commission once it's gets dark is there?'

'Bloody hell, they've got it cushy haven't they? Ah, what about the security people?'

'What about the security people?'

'They must work at night?'

'They probably do. But the big fucking stupid bugger with the sword doesn't!' Jacobus was shouting now.

'Ah.'

There was a pregnant pause before Jacobus broke the silence with, 'just pass me a bloody Castle!'

There was another awfully long pregnant pause whilst they both considered the benefits of the Castle brewery products.

'I know……..'

'Yes, what do you know?' Jacobus held his breath.

'What about if we picked him up from where he lives?'

'You mean bang him over the head and drag him into the taxi outside where he lives at night when it's dark and there's nobody around to see us?'

'Hey bru, that's a fantastic idea!'

Jacobus preened himself with pride. But as they say, pride comes before a fall.

'Er, just one little thing bru. Where the fuck does he live?'

'Ah, you've got me there bru.'

'Pass me another Castle.'

More pregnant pauses.

'Any rugby on the tele?'

'Why don't we…………….?' Piet's little eyes lit up at the sudden realisation to all their problems.

'Why don't we what?' Jacobus looked impatiently at his brother.

'Why don't we ask someone where he lives?'

'Bloody brilliant bru. Bloody brilliant,' Jacobus concluded. But suddenly he started to frown.

'Who?'

'Ah, you've got me there bru.'

Charles Darwin would probably have shot himself had he seen some of the end results of all this evolutionary progress he had forecasted.

'Why don't we……………..? Piet had come up with another fantastic idea.

Jacobus yawned. 'Go on then. Why don't we what?'

'Why don't we ask at the High Commission?'

Jacobus was going to say "brilliant" but though better of it. 'Er, yes, why don't we?' He felt there must be a reason why they couldn't but for his life he couldn't think of any.

'Do you want another Castle bru?' Piet interjected before he got his brilliant idea shot down in flames.

'Now that's a good idea.'

*   *   *

Jacobus got up early the next day and did a few calls first before he passed the High Commission. He stopped, parked up outside and walked purposefully into reception.

'Good morning sir, can I help you?' asked a polite young receptionist.

Jacobus spun round wondering who she was addressing, never having been called sir in his life before. He suddenly realised she was addressing him and walked up to the desk.

'Yes, actually you probably can.' He cleared his throat and began to speak in his best Sunday school English.

'Can you tell me where the big stu…………….' Jacobus suddenly stopped dead in his tracks. He turned a bright crimson, muttered something under his breath that sounded like "bullocks", turned and ran out of reception leaving a very confused receptionist who looked up and watched in amazement as he nearly collided with the glass doors and jumped into his taxi outside. He drove off leaving a considerable amount of tyre rubber on the street outside.

He arrived back at their apartment in a state of some distress and dashed up the stairs letting himself in only after a considerable battle with a bunch of keys.

'Piet, you stupid bastard, you forgot to tell me his name!' He stood there shaking.

'Ah, you've got me there bru,' said Piet slowly gazing in bewilderment at the sight of a large trembling heap of humanity in front of him. 'Can I get you a Castle?'

*   *   *

Two days later, having slowly recovered from his state of distress, Jacobus dropped a fare off at one of the cities drinking holes only to watch a big stupid drunk come swaying out of the pub.

'Do you want a taxi mister?'

'Well, hallo there me bucko. Well aren't you a bleshing in dishguishe, hic. I think you'd besht take me home before I, hic, before I,……….'

The big stupid drunk leant against the side of the taxi with a glazed look in his eyes and started to slide downwards, only to be grabbed from the back and helped slowly into the back seat of the cab.

Jacobus couldn't believe his luck as he slowly untangled the dishevelled figure onto the seat and watched as he collapsed in a drunken stupor now completely unconscious.

'Holy shit, I've done it. We've got the bastard. Wait till Piet sees this. Oh my god it's my lucky day!'

Just then Creighky threw up all over the back seat.

'I've got him!' a breathless Jacobus squeezed out of his palpitating vocal chords.

'You've got him?' Piet hadn't switched the brain on yet.

Jacobus tried to get another breath in between for the need of oxygen was a high priority after running up all the steps to the apartment. 'I've got him!' he repeated himself in between the wheezing of air intakes.

'You've got who?' Piet still hadn't found the "ON" switch yet.

'The big stupid bastard with the sword!'

'The big stupid…………..Oh, him!'

'Yes, him!'

Piet had a glazed look in his eyes, then all of a sudden the lights came on.

'Oh, him!.............the big stupid
…………..Oh him!' bingo! We were cooking on
gas.'

'Ah……………???'

Well only on a small ring.

'Um, er, ah!'

Jacobus was standing there out of breath
in front of his brother with both his arms on his
hips looking at him waiting for some sort of
acknowledgement and some sort of reasonably
educated reply.

'So?'

'Er, um, ah, yes.'

'Yes?'

'Yes, well, er, holy shit!'

'Christ min!' Jacobus was getting
extremely frustrated as well as out of breath.

'So, you've got him?'

'Christ min, that's just what I said. So
what the fuck do we do with him?'

'Holy shit!'

Jacobus stood in front of his brother
waving his arms at him now in the hope of
getting a bit more out of him than religious
poo.

'Right bru, we've got to think about this
then.'

'That's a good idea, why didn't I think of
that,' a hint of sarcasm there.

Piet's brain was having a spasm. It
hadn't had to think this fast since somebody
had shouted "pass the fucking ball" at him at a
rugby match.

'We'd better do something
quickly……………'

'Yes, and………………' Jacobus was beginning to lose the will to live.

'We'd better tie him up,' what a stonking good idea Piet thought and was quite pleased with himself.

'He's out cold, drunk as a skunk, and not only that he's honked over the back seat as well, the dirty bastard.'

'We'd best get him up here then, bru.'

'Why do you want him up here?' Jacobus wasn't going to carry him up *those* stairs. 'The bloody Gestapo will be searching all over Gaborone for him.'

'Ah, right, then, we'd best get him out of here then.'

'Yes, and where do you suggest?'

'Ah, you've got me there bru,' Piet said nodding his head. 'Let me think about that?'

'Well you'd best think bloody quickly before the kêrels get here with a bit of the old skop, skiet en donner.'

'Christ min, I don't want to get beaten up by the bloody fuzz again.'

'Well, let's get the hell out of here then. Hey, what about cousin Hennie up at Francistown?'

'Bloody brilliant bru. Bloody brilliant.'

They rushed down the steps to the taxi and opened the door to the smell of stale sick and beer with Creighky still unconscious in the back seat.

'Christ bru, it smells a bit in here?'

'Yeah, you know what these bloody English are like. Boy is chommie going to be babbelaased when he wakes up. Come on lets get started, we've got a long drive ahead of us and I've got to be back for the morning or I lose my licence.'

'Yeah, let's go bru. Boy will doos be mad when he sees he's been kidnapped. Hadn't we best tie him up in case he wakes up?'

'Bloody brilliant idea bru, I think there's some rope in the boot. Have a quick look will you?'

Five hours later they arrived at the outskirts of Francistown and turned off into a dirt track up to their cousin's smallholding. At the end of the dusty track they came to a collection of ramshackle buildings just as the sun was rising over the African landscape. The sound of the chickens and cockerels squawking their welcome at their arrival still couldn't deafen the noise of Creighky's snoring.

Jacobus and Piet slowly climbed out of the car and started to stretch after the long drive. The noise of the yard animals together with that of the car arriving eventually hastened the appearance of an apparition that could only be described as something that the make-up department had only half finished in the filming of "The Monster from the Black Lagoon".

Of indeterminate sexuality, although there were some hints: given that it was wearing a dress, the flower print had faded a long time ago; given that it had long hair, well a mixture of barbed wire and straw; given that the voice was a couple of octaves higher than Barry White. (Isn't everybody's), and given the benefit of the doubt there was a high probability that it could be feminine. It's age was difficult to estimate as she was still in the state of semi-consciousness, rubbing her eyes and at the same time yawning.

'Hello Maretha you gorgeous bakvissie!' This is the Afrikaans name for a giggly teenage girl. It was quite apparent that in no stretch of the imagination could she meet any of those criteria.

She replied with the old traditional Afrikaans welcome, 'Who the fuck's that!'

'It's me Jacobus and bru Piet.'

'Who?'

'Your cousins, Maretha, from Gaborone.'

'Oh, you two spuitpoeps.' Another Afrikaans term of endearment which roughly translated meant a gaseous and liquid mix usually found in the form of a brown stain to the rear of the trouser department after a particular traumatic event.

'You're looking lovely too Maretha, is Hendrick here?'

'Hennie? That piece of kak! He's still in town no doubt getting babbelaased as usual. What do you want, money?'

'No, darling, we've brought you a bit of an investment.'

'What you on about, investment. You *bringing* money then?'

'Not your actual money right now, but it will be worth a lot of money soon. More than you can imagine.'

Jacobus went round to the side of the car and opened the back door to show off his investment.

The large waking lady moved closer scratching herself as part of her morning's dry ablutions. She suddenly stopped short of the car and brought her skirt up to her nose.

'Ag man. That doesn't smell like a very good investment to me.'

'He'll scrub up nicely and he's an English bastard. Works at the British High Commission and he's very important and we've kidnapped him and we're holding him ransom for ………………….how much ransom are we asking Piet?'

'Er, we haven't actually asked for any money yet bru.'

'Oh, shit, well, anyway, we're going to, aren't we Piet, and it will be a lot, won't it Piet?'

'Too true, it will be a lot. It will be in the hundreds of pula. Anyway we can't keep him in Gaborone; the kêrels will be crawling all over the place. So we've bought him up here, out of the way. No bugger will come looking for him up here.'

'So, I've been lumbered to look after the bastard. Well I ain't taking him in that state.'

'Pass us that bucket of water. Just throw it over him while he's in the back seat, that'll save me washing the car down as well.'

So Creighky was duly woken up extremely rudely and hauled out of the car and left in the tender loving care of Maretha.

Jacobus and Pieter made a hasty retreat while she was manhandling him into her shack and was unceremoniously dumped into her kitchen cum living room cum bedroom.

Creighky slowly came round and surveying the situation realised he was in big shit. Now having served in the war in Korea he was rewarded for his bravery in the face of the enemy during action but he was pissed out of his brain then. This had a whole new complexion to it and for the first time in his life he had to start seriously thinking about getting out of a fix.

'I'd be much obliged if I could be having a drink of water there me darlin'. The first problem was a raging hangover and a mouth like a baboon's bottom.

'I wouldn't sell you the steam off my piss you English bastard. Not after what Rhodes and Kitchener did to my folk back in the old days!'

'Did you say English me darlin'.'

'You heard me dog breath.'

'Now you have me there, you see I'm not English.'

'Not English?'

'No, you see I'm from Ireland, from the old Emerald Isle don't you see?

Maretha was a tad bit confused here.'
Not English?'

'No darlin', and if you think you had problems with them Roads and Kitchen fellas, that'll be nothing compared to what that English bastard Oliver Cromwell did to us, I can tell you.'

Maretha was still confused but a little bit more compassionate as she poured a glass of water from the tap and lifted it to the mouth of Creighky.

'Here drink that. Now tell me, if you're not English, why did those two stupid buggers kidnap you and bring you all the way up here then. Answer me that smart arse?'

'Well that was going to be my next question.' Creighky drunk the water and continued. 'Wasn't I needing that? Sure you're as kind as me mother from Ireland, and you've those twinkling eyes as well.'

Creighky was formulating a strategic plan here that would help him escape with any luck. And knowing Creighky's luck it most probably would be there in some form or another.

Creighky not only had the luck of the Irish, but the English, Scottish, Welsh, Latvians and Zimbabweans, well probably not the latter. But anyway the plan was only in the embryonic stages at the moment but it concerned the "The Blarney". Creighky had secured a majority shareholding in the Blarney Stone so he might as well utilise his shares in his current situation.

He finished off the water Maretha was holding for him and said, 'now that was like champagne. You must have magical powers; to be sure I bet your name means something like "a beautiful fairy" only I don't speak the old African languages there.'

'Don't you try and bullshit me, whoever you are.' But as she said that a tinge of pink came to her cheeks.

Creighky continued on his campaign. 'I think your friends from Gaborone are getting me mixed up. They never even asked me my name or the time of day. Just took advantage of the sweet wine and popped me in the wrong taxi.'

'So you're not English?' Maretha was still a bit puzzled on that score as she was slowly being induced under Creighky's spell.

'I can see you're an intelligent lady and anybody with brains and beauty like yours would know from my accent I wasn't one of those English bastards. Sure I work for them now and then, but I need the money for me poor old mother back in Ireland.' Creighky had sown a few more seeds of doubt and a bucketful of flattery fertilizer to get those seeds well and truly to fruition.

Maretha said nothing but carried on with tidying up her "house". House being a euphemism for shack.

'Ah, I can see you're a house-proud lady, just like me mother. And I should think so. Sure it's a beautiful wee place you have here and out in the peace and tranquillity of the countryside. And listen to them birds. God it's a beautiful day, just being here surrounded by all this beauty.' Creighky looked around the shack, the flattened earth floor, the corrugated tin roof, the soap box walls.

'It's a charming little home to go with your own beauty, so it is.'

Maretha was now totally confused. She'd never had anybody describe her home as charming and definitely nobody had ever described her as a beauty. She looked hard at Creighky and scratched her head.

'Now then darlin' I have a wee problem so to speak. I need to go to the john.'

'You what?' Maretha questioned.

'I need to point Percy at the old porcelain don't you know. I need a slash,,,,,,,,,,,,,,,,

'Ag, you want a piss'?

'Now, as I said you're an intelligent young lady and you have grasped the nettles by the horns there, so you have. And the problem being as you will so obviously observe is that the old hands are tied behind the back.'

'So?' not quite that intelligent obviously.

'Now as I see it, to empty the old bladder there, if I'm left in the current situation, I either fill the old trouser department and make a mess of your lovely clean house, not to mention the smell. Now we don't want that now do we?' Creighky carried on before she could initiate her brain cells into some form of answer.

'Or of course I could do it outside, but again that's not the best solution as I'd still be stinking the bloody place out. Now you could of course do the honours of taking old John Thomas out for me and pointing him in the right direction, but I know a lady of your breeding would not be doing anything like that. Now would you?'

Creighky jumped in quickly as Maretha was just starting to get some ideas. 'Now the best and the most intelligent answer as you no doubt have already thought of a long time ago, is to untie the hands, let me go outside to your lovely ablutional area, do the business, and when I've finished I'll pop back and let you tie me back up again. How's that's me darlin?'

She wasn't prepared to use up so many brain cells all at once so when Creighky lifted himself upright and turned his back to her the decision had been already made for her, which was much easier than having to think.

She untied the rope eventually and pointed Creighky down the path to the tin shed at the bottom of the yard.

'Now don't you be too long, you hear?' she shouted after him.

'Don't you be fretting yourself me beauty, I'll be right back.'

She gave herself a little smile and turned back into the "house". She sat down and started to comb her hair. This might take some time.

Creighky managed to fight his way through the flies to the "toilet" or hole in the ground, and fight his way out again and then noticed an old bike leaning against one of the outbuildings.

Now did we mention he was lucky?

There was some air left in the tyres and it took his weight as he stated down the track which only went in one direction. "Boy, wait 'till I tell the lads in the "Snort" about this incredible brave and daring escape," Creighky thought as he wobbled down the dusty earth flattened road until it came to a junction with the main road to Francistown.

Now has it been mentioned that Creighky was lucky? Well, here is a prime example. No sooner had he fallen off his bicycle as it hit the main road than who should be passing?

Yes, you guessed it. The Muddlecombe Cricket Club bus on it's way to Francistown. It skidded to a halt as Creighky picked himself off the dusty side of the road, brushed himself down and casually jumped onto the bus.

'I thought there was someone missing,' said Dr Rammy. 'Where the hell have you been?'

Dr Rammy knew Creighky was organising everything but didn't know if he was supposed to be coming with them or not. Not that he would have waited for him anyway. Little did he know that most of the organising was done by the Commissioner's under-secretary who had figured out Creighky's Intelligence Quotient and felt it best to give him a hand. And to try and keep his hands off her.

Creighky told them of his harrowing adventure and his daring escape but by the time he had finished most of his listeners were asleep. They'd had a pretty hard time as well, getting rid of the contingency fund the night before.

They were approaching Francistown by then and the driver had to stop to ask the way to the hotel and the cricket club.

*   *   *

The contingency fund had now literally been sucked dry. Fortunately there was another contingency funding source that Dr Rammy hadn't yet utilised. This had been discussed with Chekov and Mma Xalwo before they had come out to Botswana and would be able to cover *any* contingencies.

After the win at Francistown they celebrated once more and it was now the morning after and Dr Rammy was trying to get his players onto the coach. It was like herding cats.

Francistown was much more friendly than the capital Gaborone and everybody enjoyed a festival atmosphere with a bar set up by De Beers who sponsored the game and brought with them a lot of their workers who had been given a special day off.

Everybody loved Boris who did his usual display of losing balls and breaking bats. The team always wondered why Dr Rammy always kept the old bats, telling them he was going to take them back to the manufacturers for a warranty discount.

So at last they managed to get everybody on the bus and were ready for their safari day with Creighky telling them of his experiences. He was in charge now and off they set. The driver looked a little worse for wear as he had quite obviously taken advantage of a lot of De Beers' hospitality the previous night as well.

They drove north for a few hours until they started getting into the delta area with low swamplands and little lakes with a wide variety of birds and animals to be seen.

This is where things started to go wrong. Or in the case of happenings in Muddlecombe, normal. The coach was veering all over the road, or what constituted a road, and the driver looked a little bit peculiar. So they stopped and Dr Rammy had a look at him as he fainted in his arms.

'Yes, I think it's a case of alcohol poisoning.' Dr Rammy concluded after an initial examination and smelling his breath.

'Who can drive a coach?'

A vacant expression went round the coach until someone slapped Hercules on the back and said.

'That'll be you you old bugger Harry. You drives a tractor. Can't be much different. Got four wheels, a steering wheel and a gear changing thingy?'

'Oh ah, but my old Ferguson only got three wheels.'

'Yeah, but you got an engine and a brake and all that stuff.'

'Well, we'd best have a look then,' said Hercules as he walked to the front of the coach and settled into the driver's seat. After a few minutes and after he had twiddled every knob and pushed every pedal he locked his hands together and bent them backwards with a crack and said, 'well, let's give it a go then.'

He found the ignition key and started it up and then very gingerly pressed a pedal down and tried to move the gear lever into gear. There was a little grinding noise as he pressed the pedal down again and found a smooth movement of the gear lever into place. Slowly letting the clutch out the coach gently moved, backwards.

'Well done Harry boy. We gonna drive all the way home backwards then,' this was followed by much laughter as Hercules braked, disengaged the clutch and tried another gear.

The coach slowly moved forward to a large applause from everyone.

'Ah, got you now me beauty,' Hercules said accelerating to a dazzling five miles an hour. There was another grinding, revving and grinding noise before he found another gear and the coach lurched forward and fairly zoomed onto subsonic speeds.

'Anybody know where we're going?'

'Now don't you bother yourselves about that? Wasn't I up here only last week? I know this place like the back of me hand.'

There was an immediate silence over all on the coach and a little black cloud looked down with a grin on it's face.

*   *   *

'Creighky, we've been driving all over the back of your hand now for four hours and it's starting to get dark.' Dr Rammy asked cautiously. He had an assignation with Mma Xalwo tomorrow and couldn't afford to miss it.

The road had deteriorated to a dusty track by now and this was where things *really* started to go wrong.

Chapter 12. The Angola border incident

Simâo Kitu was all in all a happy chap.
He had just been promoted to Segundo-Cabo,
(Lance Corporal) acting unpaid and life was
very pleasant. He was on border patrol in the
South where most of the fighting had ceased.
His Primeiro-sargento was asleep in the little
hut and it was all very quiet with only the
cicadas as company. He was getting one meal a
day and the fighting had stopped for the time
being while Jonas Savimbi, head of UNITAS
was in negotiations with the MPLA leader Jose
Eduado de Santos over the future of Angola.
He didn't have a Mummy or Daddy, he
lost them in the civil war but he was now the
proud owner of an M16 Carbine. The best the
US Army could supply and he was grown up for
God's sake, he was nearly eleven and a proud
member of the Ovimbundu tribe and could go
home when the fighting was over and get the
full respect due for a war veteran. And all those
chicks he could choose from, whoweee! His

mind was starting to wander when all of a sudden his reverie was broken by the noise of a vehicle coming down the dusty track. It was quite a large vehicle with lights blazing.

"Que diabos é isso descendo a estrada. Trata-se de um tanque ou um transportador pessoal blindado?" He thought to himself in Portuguese. He didn't know "what the bloody hell" was in his native Umbundu, or "tank" or "armoured personnel carrier."

"I'll just try out this M16" he thought and gave it a quick burst…………………. "Shit! It pulls to the left a lot on automatic!"

The Primeiro-sargento Mutope was just about awake and upright with the high probability of smelly underwear when the coach came to a sudden grinding halt in a flurry of dust and squealing brakes about two metres from his beloved hut.

As soon as the bullets whipped across the coach windscreen in a diagonal pattern, Hercules threw himself down out of the drivers seat into the door well causing the coach to stall and slide on another twenty yards towards the firing in a cloud of dust.

Everyone in the coach was down on the floor by now as they waited several minutes for something to happen.

Eventually the door opened and Hercules straightened himself up and stared down at a small boy holding a gun. He was four foot six looking up at a six foot four man standing on the step of the coach.

Sort of David and Goliath, but David had a bit more firepower than a crummy old slingshot. Nobody said anything until the boy said something and gestured with his gun to get out of the coach. Everybody crawled out, shook themselves down and stared back at the boy who was obviously as confused as they were.

The only noise was the tinkling of a field telephone bell as the man in the hut was desperately trying to contact somebody to get reinforcements and a clean pair of underpants.

After some brief conversation on the phone the man in the hut came out very gingerly with a gun and started looking at the assembled startled passengers. No one was quite sure who was the most startled, but eventually the man from the hut said something to the boy and he jumped on board the coach and started searching it.

He jumped down the steps with a shrug of his shoulders and was then directed to the luggage compartment doors. He gingerly opened them up and stepped back and started gibbering something to his sergeant. The sergeant came over and opened up the team basket and jumped back and went rushing back to his hut and started winding the handle of the field telephone looking over his shoulder all the time.

Fortunately Creighky had done some logistics of his own and had loaded the coach with several crates of beer. He pointed them out to the little lad and slowly pulled one crate out and opened a bottle giving it to the little soldier.

'Hallo, field Headquarters here.'

'Who?'

'Primeiro-sargento Mutope.'

'Okavango delta border.'

'You have captured who?'

'You don't know quite who?'

'They're foreign?'

'They have a load of what?'

'Some strange armaments'?

'They look like mortars and little red grenades?'

'Are they putting up any resistance?'

'No?'

'Ok, I'll call operations and ring you back.'

'Hang on, what?'

'The Segundo-Cabo thinks they're English, someone is whistling a Beatles song.'

'I'll come back soonest.'

'Hallo, operations?'

'This is the southern border field headquarters here.'

'Yes, that's right.'

'I've just had a report from one of our border patrols that they seem to have captured a unit of the British Army.'

'Yes, that's right, the British Army.'

'You'll do what?'

'Have to get in touch with the delegation in the conference in Lisbon.'

'Ok, and you'll come back soonest?'

'Ok.'

'Hallo, Jonas Savimbi's office, can I help you?'

'You are calling from where?'

'The southern border field headquarters.'

'And you have received an alarming report…….'

'The border patrol has captured who?'

'The British Army?'

'Can you repeat that for me please?'

'Jonas, sorry to interrupt you sir, but we have just received a very strange report from one of our field units.'

'What's the problem my friend?'

'They say that one of our southern border patrols have just captured the British Army.'

'What!'

'That's what I said, but they repeated it several times.'

'Where?'

'Somewhere in the Okavango delta border area.'

'What the fuck are the British playing at. They're on our side for fucks sake!'

'That's what I said.'

'Where's the British delegation?'

'I think they're in the bar downstairs.'

'Get the bastards up here pretty damn quick!'

'Yes Sir.'

'Sir Gerald, how are you, sorry to interrupt your Gin and Tonic.'

'No trouble Jonas old boy. What appears to be the problem? Your man is in a bit of a flap?'

'Yes, you could call it that. In the middle of extremely tense negotiations I find out that your army have tried to infiltrate our southern border?'

'I beg your pardon?'

'It would appear old boy you have just attacked us?'

'Is this some form of joke?'

'Not according to our border patrols.'

'But for fucks sake old boy, we're on your side!'

'That's just what I said!'

'I,…….I…………I'm lost for words. Holy shit! Leave this to me old boy. I'll get onto the Ministry of Defence straight away. Something's not adding up here at all. Many apologies Sir, looks like we have another cock up somewhere down the line. Be back to you in a jiffy.'

'Yes Jonas?'

'Who's that major in one of our infantry units that was trained by the British?'

'Ah yes, er, ah, that's Faraji de Souza, went to Sandhurst.'

'That's the boy. Get hold of him and get him to look into this will you?'

*   *   *

'Sir Gerald, sorry to disturb you, but I have a little something that may be of interest to you.'

'Look, Sir, I'm terribly sorry about all this but I've been onto the MOD and ………..'

'Just sit down and listen to this. This is a report I have just received hot off the teleprinter from a certain Major Faraji de Souza at our southern border region. Perhaps you may like to read it. How's your Portuguese?'

'I don't suppose you could read it for me old boy?'

'The report is as follows: "Further to your instructions I borrowed the HQ helicopter and made my way down to the Okavango delta border region and located our post at 21.00 hours. Upon landing I reconnoitred the area and found a civilian bus with a few bullet holes in the front windscreen. I eventually made contact with Primeiro-sargento Mutope who was a little, shall we say, tired. He was being held up between an extremely large gentleman who it seems was Russian, and another tall gentleman who I understood to come from Ireland. They were singing "Molly Malone" if my memory at Sandhurst serves me correctly. There were a lot of beer bottles lying around and the majority of the "British Army" were asleep in the coach along with Segundo-Cabo Simâo Kitu who I awoke. He eventually managed to show me to the "Ammunition compartment" of the coach and upon further investigation I found a large wicker basket with the initials MCC painted on the side. Inside were cricket bats and balls amongst other cricket paraphernalia. I took out a bat and showed it to Kitu and reassured him that it was completely harmless along with the red grenades, or cricket balls. The tall Irish gentleman said they were on safari looking for the lions and tigers, but had probably taken a wrong turning and could I point the way back to Gaborone please, sir!" I hope this clears up this little incident. Could I trouble you to ask the British delegation to make contact with Gaborone High Commission and arrange for the safe return of the "British Army".'

'Oh my god. The bloody MCC! I can't thank you enough Jonas. Must apologise most profusely and leave this up to me old boy.'

'There is however a small problem.'

'Oh, oh.'

'Yes, as you said. Unfortunately the press have got wind of this. Someone has leaked this, I'm afraid I don't know who it was but be prepared for some juicy headlines tomorrow.'

'I hope this won't prejudice the conference Jonas?'

'Oh no. Don't worry about that. I've pre-empted that already with a statement for the international press first thing tomorrow morning.'

'Phew.'

Chapter 13. Chaos in the High Commission

'Pass me another Castle bru.' Piet had taken the weekend off and was sitting comfortably in their family apartment in Gaborone. He got up and fetched two beers from the fridge.

'So when do you reckon we will get the money?' Asked his brother.

Piet went quiet for a moment and slowly replied, 'what money bru?'

'The ransom money Pielkop!'

There was another silence and Piet slowly replied, 'oh, the ransom money?'

'Yes, the ransom money bru.'

'Ah, right, the ransom money.'

Slowly his brother sat up and looked at Piet and scowled at him. 'Don't tell me you haven't written the bloody ransom note!'

'Christ bru, I have been working at the bloody mines all week since we dropped the big stupid bastard with the sword off at cousin's place. I haven't had time. I'm really sorry.'

'And?'

'Well, I'm really sorry like...............'

'And?'

'Well......................?'

'You're going to write the bloody note now aren't you brother.'

'Oh, Christ, yeah. I'll get right onto it bru.'

There was a puzzled look on Piets' face as he slowly turned to his brother after picking up a bit of paper and a pencil.

'You forgot that you're the one who can write bru.'

'Give us that bloody paper,' as he snatched the pencil out of Piet's hand. 'So tell me clever clogs, what am I supposed to write?'

'Well, er,,,,,,,,,,,,,,,,,,,,,er, well, that we want the money!'

'Ok, so just that we want the money?'

'Well, sort of, yes.'

'So we just walks into the British Consulate, hands him this piece of paper and says we wants some money like? Shouldn't we give some sort of valid reason? Beggin' your pardon says the British Consulate, and why does you want this money? Oh, sir, to piss it up against a wall sir, if that's all right with you. No problem my man here you are take this bundle of one hundred pula notes.'

'Now you're being silly bru.'

'Oh am I? So tell me what to write then professor?'

'Well, it's ransom money isn't it?'

'Good, that's a start. And who are we holding to ransom?'

'It's that big stupid Irish bliksem with the sword.'

'Oh, good. And does this big stupid Irish bastard with the sword have a name?'

'Well, actually no. Well he probably does have a name, but we don't know it like.'

'How do you spell bastard in English?'

'Christ bru, you're the one with the certificate.'

There was a long silence as Jacobus slowly wrote down all the information he had been given.

'And how much money are we going to ask for?'

'Christ min, I don't know. A couple of thousand pula?'

'Is that all?'

'Well, I don't know, call it ten thousand pula then.'

'Why not a hundred thousand pula?'

'Jesus Christ bru……….'

'Why not ,,,,,,,,,,,,a million pula?'

'Jesus fucking Christ bru. We could be rich with a million pula!'

'Piet, right now we could be rich with a hundred fucking pula!'

'Yeah, you're probably right there.'

'Look, let's just go for broke and then at least we can negotiate down. It's very difficult to negotiate more than you've asked for.'

'Right on there bru. Do it then. Go for a million pula.'

Jacobus started writing again.

'Get me another castle bru. This is hard work.'

After a few minutes Jacobus sat back and admired his work. 'There you go bru, look at that. A fucking work of art.'

'So it is bru. Just like you said.'

'Listen, I just had an idea. What we need is an official sounding name. Like some form of terrorist group.'

'Fucking brilliant bru. Like……………..?

'Afrikaans ……………..'

'Like the Afrikaans Resistance.,,,,,,,?'

'Afrikaans Resistance for…………..?'

'For,,,,,,,,,,,,Social Equality.'

'Fucking brilliant! The Afrikaans Resistance for Social Equality. Shit, that'll put the fear of Christ up 'em, eh bru?'

'Yeah, and then if they don't pay, then what'll happen?'

'He gets' it!'

'That's it. That's fucking brilliant! If you don't pay, he gets' it! That's what they always say.' Piet made a sign of his hand slicing across his throat.

Piet and Jacobus gave each other high fives.

'Let's just get that written down and then off to the British Consulate. This'll put the fear of Christ up their howty towty tietkops, eh, bru?'

'Fucking brilliant!'

'Get us another Castle bru.'

*   *   *

'Pongo old boy. Have you got a minute?'

'Yeah, sure Pinky.'

'Could you just pop into the secretary's office a mo?'

'Thanks Pongo, could you just shut the door please?'

'Sounds a bit official old boy.'

'Yes, well, grab a seat. Now I don't want what we are about to discuss here to go beyond these four walls.'

'I say, all a bit hush-hush old boy.'

'Yes, well, the problem being is that the last thing it is, is hush-hush.'

'Oh.'

'Have you read the papers this morning?'

'No, 'fraid not. Only just finished the soldiers and boiled eggs before I got your call.'

'Sorry about that. Now take a look at these headlines. And I mean headlines. Not the back pages of the sports section, I mean the bloody great fucking big headlines.'

'Oh, I say. Steady on old boy. Don't blow a gasket.'

'Well just have a look for yourself.'

Pongo slowly took in the enormity of the situation after reading through several papers.

'Holy shit!'

'That's what I said.'

'Jesus H Christ.'

'That's what I said.'

'Streuth!'

'That's what I said. Pinky old boy, what the fuck is going on?'

'That's what I said.'

They both looked at each other and started to scratch their heads as Pinky was the first to restart the conversation.

'And I've only had the bloody foreign office on my back demanding a full explanation,'

'Bloody norah.'

'That's what I said.'

'So what did you tell them?'

'I said I would give this my earnest consideration…………..'

'Damn good show.'

'After I'd spoken to you.'

'Holy mackerel. You're the bloody President.'

'Yes, but you're the Chairman of the Board of Selectors.'

'I mean, just look at the Daily Mirror's headlines: " **England's finest sportsmen involved in gun running.** Our reporter at the Angolan Independence talks in Lisbon has unravelled information that the MCC were last night involved in an incident at the southern border when shooting was heard and an army vehicle disguised as a civilian coach was inspected for possible arms equipment. Was this the SAS masquerading as the famous cricket team? Could this lead to the breakdown of the independence talks in which Britain and Russia face each other on either side of the conference table?"

'It's mind blowing.'

'And look at the Daily Sketch: "**MCC bowls a googly at talks in Lisbon.** Our staff reporter at the highly sensitive negotiations understands that the British Army disguised as the MCC was involved in a border incident on the southern border of Angola."'

'You haven't seen the News of the World have you yet. Take a look at this.'

Pinky handed over the paper.

"Old Farts blow up Angolan talks."

'I say, that's a bit below the belt old boy!'

They both sat there looking down at the various papers in total silence not daring to say a word. Eventually Pinky started stroking his chin and came up with a question for Pongo.

'I can't help going back to that conversation we had last week when you muttered something about a Russian and someone called Hercules and us winning.'

'Yes, well, I found that a bit strange as well. You see after I talked with you I overheard some of the chaps who had been listening to old Johnnie Harlot on the old BBC overseas programme and then I gets a call from old Makers. You remember Sir Reginald Makepeace, Makers at school. Jolly decent chap. Used to share his tuck money around.'

'Oh, yes, old Makers. Ended up in the FO.'

'That's the fella, well he gets me on the blower and starts rabbitting on about how our boys had stuffed his local team out of sight and about this Russian chappie who was knocking the ball all over the park, and some Indian chappie who was tying them up in knots and some fella called Hercules who was hurling them down at a horrendous pace…….. .'

'And you say your chums heard this on the radio?'

'Yes, that's what was so puzzling after you said we'd been stuffed out of sight by some whippersnapper.'

'Damn peculiar.'

*　　*　　*

Khuma ran straight into a brick wall. It seemed to appear from nowhere. He was running into the main entrance of the British High Commission when this wall appeared. He looked up to see a large Indian gentleman in a colourful uniform with lots of medals looking down at him.

'And where do you think you're going?' asked the brick wall.

'This big stupid Afrikaans taxi man said I would get paid ten pula if I gave this note to the British High Commission.'

'So, let's see what it says in the note shall we?'

'Not until I get my ten pula.'

'Would you like ten of my size twelve toes in my boot up your arse?'

'Er, no sir,' trembled Khuma humbly realising the effect this large gentleman's boot could have on a small boy. He gave up his pot of gold to the sentry.

The Indian gentleman read it and then looking down at Khuma said, 'come on inside young man and let's talk to these British people shall we?'

He bent down and took Khuma's hand and walked past the big glass doors into reception.

'Mma Gorata, there's a young gentleman here to see you with a note.'

'Thank you Rra Hiresh, and what's in the note?'

Hiresh handed over the note to the receptionist who studied it and then picked up the phone and waited for a few seconds.

'Mma Kagiso, I have something here that I think Sir Reginald needs to be informed about, can you come down please?'

She put the phone down and looked over the desk to Khuma. 'And who gave you this note young man?'

'A big stupid Afrikaans taxi man and said you would give me ten pula.'

'He must have been very stupid to think I would give you ten pula. Let's see what the motlotlegi has to say.'

Eventually the High Commissioner's under-secretary came down and inspected the note and rang up to the High Commissioner's office.

Eventually Sir Reginald came down and looked at Khuma and held his hand out to shake it. Khuma had never met a white boss before and eventually plucked up courage and offered his tiny hand.

'Now then young man,' started Sir Reginald, 'let's see what news you bring us.' He started to read the note out slowly under his breath.

'WE ARE HOLDING THE BIG STUPID ENGLISH BASTARD WITH THE SWORD RANSOM AND IF WE DON'T GET ONE MILLION PULA, HE GETS IT!' He studied the note a bit further and continued.

'It's signed off, ARSE! The Afrikaans Resistance for Social Equality?'

'I presume we are talking about our Military attaché Mr Creighky O'Riley here?'

'It looks very much like it doesn't it' confirmed Mma Kagiso.

'What the blazes is he doing? I thought he was in charge of the MCC touring organisation.'

'Erm, yes,' said Mma Kagiso, slowly looking up to the ceiling. She'd done all the organising for him and for one wasn't going to miss him.

Sir Reginald paused in thought. He looked down at Khuma, 'and who gave you this?'

'Some big stupid Afrikaans taxi man and said I could get ten pula if I gave it to you sir.' He felt a little bit of grovelling wouldn't go amiss here especially as there was ten pula at stake.

'And did this Afrikaans gentleman ask you for a reply?'

'No sir.'

'And did this Afrikaans gentleman give you any idea how we should contact him? A telephone number or anything. An address?'

'No sir.'

'Well young man you seem to have described him down to a "T". Lacking in brain power shall we say.'

Sir Reginald looked at everybody and with a puzzled look on his face said, 'It's not April the first is it?'

'No sir,' said his under-secretary.'

'Or Walpurgis night?'

'No sir.'

'Erm.' He stood in deep thought. 'What's one million pula worth these days?'

'About ten thousand pounds sir.'

'Not asking a lot are they? Mind you I doubt if he's worth even that,' he muttered under his breath.

Mma Kagiso concurred silently.

He continued. 'Now then young man, thank you for bringing this to me. I'll do you a deal. I'll give you five pula now and if you can come back with the registration number of the taxi I'll give you fifty pula. How's that!'

Khuma was gobsmacked. He'd never had so much money in all his life. 'It's a deal Rra, I mean Sir, I mean your majesty.'

'Mma Kagiso, can you lend me five pula please?'

*   *   *

Mma Kagiso walked into Sir Reginald's office. 'I'm sorry to interrupt you again sir but I've just had a message hot off the teleprinter from our head office in London.

'Christ, what the bloody hell do they want?'

She handed over the roll of thin paper and he slowly read it.

"Our delegation at the Angolan talks in Lisbon has just been informed of a border incident in the South involving the MCC. A border patrol ambushed a coach and shots were fired. No casualties have been reported and it appears that the situation is now under control and any misunderstandings have been resolved. It seems they were on safari and got lost but will need a recovery vehicle. The misunderstanding involved mistaking cricket equipment for guns and ammunition.

The press as usual have got hold of this and their stories vary so please prepare a statement as follows: "The MCC touring team on safari in Southern Africa accidentally crossed the Angolan border but have now been redirected and are returning to their team base in Gaborone. The British delegation has passed on their apologies to the other delegations at the Angolan talks in Lisbon."

Sir Reginald sat quite still for a few minutes before looking up to Mma Kagiso. 'Have we got anything in the drinks cabinet? I think I need a large gin and tonic. No, just a gin. A very large gin!'

*   *   *

Sir Reginald, I have a Sir Llewellyn Pinkerton on the line for you from somewhere in Lords?' Mma Kagiso put the phone call through.

'Hallo, Sir Reginald?'

'Yes, that you Pinky?'

'Yes, how the blazes are you Makers old chap?'

'Damn fine, well actually no. A tad stressed out at the mo. My god I was only just talking to Pongo the other day.'

'Yes, so he says.'

'Look, Pinky about the MCC, I've just heard from the FO and we're doing everything possible to sort things out down here.'

'Have you seen the papers old boy?'

'Well, no actually. We don't get them until twenty four hours later.'

'Well, I'll warn you now, get your helmet on old boy. The shits hit the proverbial fan!'

'Yes, the old FO did give me a hint.'

'But perhaps you could help on this matter?'

'How's that old boy?'

'Well first of all where are you exactly?'

''I beg your pardon Pinky?'

'I know it might seem a bit strange but can you tell me just where you are?'

'Pinky old boy, you have just sent a team out here and you don't know where they are?'

'Well sort of. If you can just give me an idea old boy?'

'Well, I'm in Gaborone.'

'And just precisely where is that?'

'Well it's in Botswana of course.'

'Of course it is, how silly of me and just for the record where is Botswana?'

'It's in Southern Africa old boy. Are you sure you are alright?'

'Oh, yes, perfectly ok. So you are not actually in *South* Africa then?'

'No, South Africa is our southern border neighbour. But we are part of Southern Africa, along with Zimbabwe and Mozambique.'

'Ah, I'm glad I've cleared that up. And can you just run through some of the names on the MCC who were playing please old boy?'

'Well I think I can remember some of them. I'm a bit puzzled by all this Pinky old chap?'

'You think *you're* puzzled old boy?'

'Yes, well, anyway, there was this enormous Russian chappie. By god he was the spiting image of old W G Grace, only a bit larger. What was his name now? That's it, Slobovitch, Boris Slobovitch. By god he couldn't half hit the ball.'

'Any more names old boy?'

'Ah yes, the captain was the young Indian chappie. His uncle is the Secretary of the Botswana Cricket Association, Chutnabuttee, that's the fella. Dr Rammittin Chutnabuttee. And then there was a Hercules. Boy he couldn't half throw 'em down, Bloody frightening……………..'

'No Bothams, or Willis' or perhaps the odd Gooch?'

'No,' Sir Reginald stopped and thought for a moment. 'Now you come to mention it, no. I thought that was a bit strange, but I've been out of circulation for a couple of years down here.'

'No Gowers or Boycotts or Truemans?'

'No, none of them. What are you saying old boy?'

'Well, I've just been in touch with our agent in South Africa. We sent the boys down there for a bit of R and R on the old QT before they went off to Australia for the Ashes. He informs me that they are all on a day off and in some safari park somewhere called the Madikwe game reserve.'

'My god that's just down the road across the border from us.' Sir Reginald spluttered.

'Yes, but how far is it from Angola?'

'Oh, I would say a good thousand miles at least.'

'So it would seem they could hardly be involved in any incident anywhere near Angola then?'

'No, so,…………..what are you saying?' Sir Reginald was putting this question very cautiously to Pinky.

'Ah, there you have it old boy. It looks like there are two MCC's.'

The last thing he wanted was to get a reply from someone with a PhD in "the blatant obvious", but unfortunately shit happens.

'And the real one is in,,,,,,,,,,,,,South Africa on safari in the Madikwe game reserve?'

'Looks like it old boy.'

There was a very long pause before Pinky started up again. 'You there old boy, you ok?'

'I'm just looking for something sharp to slash my wrists with.'

'I say, that's a bit over the top, steady on old boy. Remember the school motto………..'

'Fuck the school motto unless it said "find the nearest gin bottle" ,,,,,,,,,,,,,ah here it is.'

'I'm ahead of you there old boy. Given the Pimms a bloody good bashing already.'

'Fucking hell Pinky old chap, I've had the bloody BBC down here. Old Johnny Harlot……………'

'Yes, I know old boy. All the gang were listening to him.'

'So who the fucking hell have I got here then?'

'Ah, you've got me there old boy.'

'Holy shit…'

'That's what I said….'

'Pinky old chap, you wouldn't believe the day I've had so far. I've just been handed a ransom note from some Afrikaans arseholes who have kidnapped the pillock in charge of this whole fucking cock up. That was after the FO were breathing down my neck………….'

'Had the blighters jumping all over me as well …………….'

'Christ Pinky what the hell are we going to do?'

'I'm going to have another drink old boy.'

'That's the most sensible suggestion anyone has come up with today.'

Chapter 14. Dr Rammy has an assignation

"Now where did I put that piece of paper?" Dr Rammy thought as he went through his pockets. The team was now back at Francistown. The recovery vehicle eventually found them. It had to take the normal roads not the "short cut" Creighky had managed to find.

Creighky had taken the cross country route straight from Botswana to Angola, across Namibia through what was called the Caprivi Strip named after a German Chancellor, General Count Georg Leo von Caprivi di Caprara di Montecuccoli who wanted to acquire a strip of land linking the German South-West Africa with the Zambezi River, thus providing easy access to Tanganyika (Tanzania) and ultimately the Indian Ocean.

Unfortunately for the Germans, the British colonization of Rhodesia (Zimbabwe and Zambia) stopped them well upstream of Victoria Falls, which buggered up navigation on the Zambezi.

During World War One the Caprivi Strip again came under British rule but it received little attention and became known as a lawless frontier. No change there then.

Not that any of our intrepid travellers were aware of this incredibly interesting piece of history neither were they aware of the furore they had caused and the reception they would be getting.

Hey ho. Ignorance is bliss!

Dr Rammy managed to get some sleep on the coach as he knew he had a hard night ahead of him. The others were all now blissfully tucked up in their beds in the hotel as he took the piece of paper out and dialled the number on it.

'Hallo? Is that Mma Xalwo?'

'Oh, good. Have you got everything?'

'Ok, you'll come and pick me up? The coach is at the back of the hotel in a big car park. I'll be there waiting for you.'

Mma Xalwo arrived twenty minutes later and Dr Rammy opened up the luggage compartment on the coach and pulled out several broken bats and put them in the bag Xalwo had brought. He closed the luggage compartment; put the bag in the boot of her car, got in and off they went.

They eventually came to an old industrial estate and after opening the garage doors to a workshop, drove the car in and closed the doors after them.

'Where did you find this?'

'Oh, a friend of a friend. An Afrikaans gentleman whose wife has a cousin here who works in the mine in Jwaneng, in the kitchens I think. The big creep has been following me around like a puppy dog. But he has his uses.'

It's a funny old world isn't it?

'Ok, let's get some lights on in here.' Dr Rammy took the bits of bats out of the bag and started to lay them out on the workshop bench. Each bat had a little symbol to be able to match it up with the other half.

'Right, do you have the drill?'

Xalwo took a load of stuff out of the bag where the bats had been and picked out the drill. She then found some drill bits and handed them over to Dr Rammy. He put the largest bit in the drill, plugged it into the wall socket and gave it a quick burst.

'Ok, here we go then. Now if you can just be holding this end of this bat upright so as I can drill a nice hole down the length of it.......that's it. Ok off we go.'

He drilled down through the centre length of the bat to about six inches and then slowly waggled the drill out again slightly enlarging the width of the hole.

'Ok, that's that bit done. Now can you pass over the other part of the bat? That's it over there. Great. Now can I ask you to hold that upright again please...........?' Dr Rammy then drilled down again and out again and gave the hole a perfunctory blow to dislodge any dust and put the two parts of the bats flat on the bench with the broken bits facing each other.

'Ok, I can see what you're doing now,' said Xalwo. 'And I suppose you want something from me now?'

'Yes please Xalwo.' Dr Rammy was starting to sweat a little here as he watched her pull out several small long black velvet bags and lay them out on the bench next to the broken bat.

'Chekov said I should ask you for your list of items, just the number of units only so that they can be verified at the other end.'

'Ok, here's the list and a copy for you to give to Chekov.' She passed over a bit of paper to Dr Rammy.

'What is happening if the numbers are not matching up when they get to Muddlecombe?'

'You are in deep shit.'

'Oh, I am deeply understanding.' Dr Rammy suddenly understood the enormity of his responsibility.

'So I am better to be counting the little items in question then shouldn't I? And Chekov said something about the costings to be worked out on some sort of Rapaport pricing.'

'Yes, that's it. But first of all we have to get the little beauties to England.'

'Right. So now have you got the silicone gun? Good, now let's pour some of these little beauties down the holes into this lovely specimen of the finest Indian willow.' He smiled at Xalwo but the joke was lost to her.

Xalwo took some diamonds out of one of the bags as Dr Rammy started counting them and poured them from the palm of his hand down the hole of the first bat. He then took the silicone gun and filled up the hole stirring the diamonds around so that they didn't rattle.

'Ok, that's that half done, now the other half of the bat.'

They held their breath as some more diamonds disappeared down the drilled hole and were swallowed up by the creamy gel.

'Right,' said Dr Rammy. 'That's the easy bit, now to put the bits together. Have you got the wood glue please?'

Xalwo went to the bag and pulled out the plastic bottle of glue and handed it to Dr Rammy. He squirted a small amount onto the broken ends of each bat and than started to squeeze the two parts together.

They easily matched but for some rough bits sticking out here and there which Dr Rammy sanded down after the glue had dried.

The next four bats were duly drilled, filled, glued and sanded down.

'Right, that looks ok so far. Now for the tricky bit.' He took out of his pocket a large ball of waxed twine and looked for an end. He pulled out about three feet of twine and asked Xalwo to hold one of the bats upright on the bench.

He then made a loop from the bottom of the bat to the top and back down again and then asked Xalwo to hold the bottom of the loop which had a long loose end hanging down. He asked her to hold the top of the loop and to put her finger over the twine as Dr Rammy started winding the twine, first over her finger and then upwards over the loop pulling it tight once Xalwo had released her finger. He then continued winding it very tightly slowly upwards until it covered the join and reached the top of the loop.

He then asked Xalwo to cut off a couple
of inches at the top. She got out the scissors
and cut a bit off and then Dr Rammy passed
the loose end at the top through the loop and
asked Xalwo to pull it tight. He then got hold of
the bottom loose end and pulled it down slowly
with great difficulty through all the binding until
the top of the loop had disappeared into the
binding leaving a bit of twine sticking out at the
top.

'Can you just snip that bit off for me
please Xalwo?'

She cut it off and watched as Dr Rammy
slowly pulled the bottom loose end down
through the binding and a bit further down until
nothing stuck out at the top.

'Phew,' breathed Dr Rammy as he cut
the loose end off at the bottom. 'How about
that then?' he said standing back admiring his
handy work.

'That is a work of art, if I say so myself,'
said Xalwo standing back and admiring it
herself.

'That's a brand new bat.'

'Ah, no. We now have to give it a
weathered look by hitting it with a ball a few
times, gently, just to get some of the red to
come off onto the new twine and then we have
a used bat.'

'How are you going to tell the difference
between these bats and the others at the other
end?'

'A good question. I shall be making a
small symbol on the bottom of the bat with all
the other scratch marks.'

'Isn't some silly bugger likely to start to use one by accident?'

'Well, we are not having anymore games scheduled out here and I shall be canceling all practices at Muddlecombe until our merchandise has been removed.'

Xalwo just stood and looked on in amazement until Dr Rammy brought her down to earth.

'Ok, that's number one. We are still having to finish all the others yet.'

They eventually finished some three hours later and sat down exhausted. Xalwo produced a small bottle of whisky, had a sip and passed it onto Dr Rammy. He gulped it down and ended up in a coughing fit.

He eventually managed to speak. 'Oh cor blimeh, I'm not used to imbibing the Scottish stuff.' He handed the bottle back to her and gave her a long leering look as she had another sip. "Nice legs," he thought.

Xalwo finished the drink and caught the look from Dr Rammy and smiled to herself. "Not bad at all, tall and what a lovely smile. God, these doctors look so young these days don't they?"

'I think we had best get you back to the hotel before anyone starts to ask any questions.' Xalwo helped Dr Rammy pack everything up and put the "new" cricket bats back into the luggage bag.

*   *   *

Dr Rammy staggered back to the hotel at about three o'clock in the morning and was eventually let in by the night porter who asked.' Sorry, but are you Doctor Chucknabuttee?'

'Yes.'

'Ah, there's a message here for you. Reception missed you when you booked in.' He passed the piece of paper over to Dr Rammy who opened it and read: "From the High Commission, Gaborone. Your border trip has caused a political problem. Should you encounter the press, please do not make any, I repeat, any comment to the press whatsoever. Return here ASAP."

'Mmmmm,' muttered Dr Rammy. Then looking to the night porter said, 'thank you. Can you please be giving me an alarm call at seven o'clock?'

'No problem Doctor.'

Dr Rammy staggered off to bed and the night porter settled down in his little office with his unfinished bottle of cheap South African sherry. By the time he was relieved he'd forgotten all about any alarms.

Dr Rammy sat bolt upright, looked at his watch and startled, cried, 'Oh shit. Somebody is being in big trouble.'

He dressed and rushed down to the breakfast room.

Too late!

Creighky was in full flow with half a dozen reporters hanging onto his every word.

'......just as I was telling you, it was just the same in Korea with all them bullets flying around all over the place. We was surrounded but they didn't realise who they were up against, oh no me bucko…………'

'I'm so sorry gentlemen; my patient has missed his medication. Please excuse us.' With that Dr Rammy pushed Creighky out of the room and hissed at him, 'get packed, we're leaving in fifteen seconds or you are being very dead person.'

Creighky got the point and rushed up to his room.

Dr Rammy managed to round up the rest of the team and found the driver and warned everyone not to breathe a word to anyone and get on the bus as quickly as possible.

'Can we stop for breakfast somewhere?' came a plaintive cry from Boris.

*　　*　　*

Mma Xalwo drove back to Gaborone that night had a few hours sleep and went straight into her office the next morning. After sorting out the mail and any outstanding actions, she shut the office door and dialled a UK number.

'Hallo, is that you Brewster?'

'Yes Brewster here, who's that? Ah, is that you Mma Xalwo?'

'Yes, it's me Xalwo. Can you get bold of Chekov for me please?'

'Ok, it'll be about ten minutes?'

'Alright, I'll ring back in ten minutes then.'

'Hallo, Chekov? It's me Xalwo. I have given the items to Dr Rammy, and I must say I am impressed with your "Plan A". Anyway, he has the full listing of the items in question and I have the original.'

'OK, that's good. Let's hope everything will go smoothly. I can't see any problems, anyway, I have sent a bankers draft of ten thousand US dollars to you together with another two thousand for Dr Rammy's expenses. Can you pass that onto him for me please?'

'No problem.'

'Now I will wait here for Dr Rammy to return, check the list of items in question and get them off to Dudley for the Rapaport valuation and bring that with me for you to agree, and I think that should cover everything for Plan A and then Plan B. Have *you* got everything ready?'

'Everything is all ready for the off. I have just got to get hold of Mr O'Riley. So when do we meet up?'

'We'll all meet in ten days time, that's a Wednesday, in the agreed hotel which has all been booked, at about midday, somewhere in the reception or in the bar. OK?'

'Can't wait!'

Chapter 15. Mma Kagiso get's her knickers in a knot

Mma Kagiso knew it was going to be a bad day when she woke up to find she had accumulated several more creases or wrinkles as some unkind people would call them, in her face after a night fighting with her pillow. She then stood in front of her car and remembered she'd left the car keys in the house. Then as she drove away she'd forgotten to pick up the rubbish to drop off at the dustbins. Then she realised she had a twist in her bra strap.

*　　　*　　　*

Xalwo read the headlines in the local press:

"War hero fights off Angolan terrorists" accompanied by a picture of Creighky.

"Oh, shit," she thought amongst other things. Her mind was going over the plan she had discussed with Chekov and Mildred back in Muddlecombe.

She had met up with Dr Rammy at his hotel, given him the money and he had told her about their little incident at the Angolan border and she could see how Creighky had managed to exaggerate it out of all proportions.

Would it matter if Creighky was high profile? Or could she use this to her advantage?

Her mind was going into mach three as she weighed up the pros and cons, and at last came up with a solution.

She was fairly certain that the British High Commission would be embarrassed with Creighky's presence and perhaps she could help there and also this would accelerate Plan B.

She rang up the High Commission from her De Beers office and her reputation got her an appointment with the High Commissioner. She made her excuses at her office and walked down the Mall to the elegant white building.

Mma Kagiso ushered her into Sir Gerald's office. 'Mma Xalwo to see you Sir Reginald.'

'Do come in, Mma Xalwo? Is that correct?'

'Go siame Rra.'

'Ke a leboga Mma, I'm afraid that's about my limit of Setswana. Now how can I help you?'

'Well, it's more about how I can help you.'

'Mmmmm, interesting, and in what way?'

'Mr Creighky O'Riley.'

'You're going to shoot him for me?'

'I'm sorry; I can't do that but...'

'That's a pity, sorry to interrupt you, please carry on Mma Xalwo.'

'Have you read the local papers yet?'

'I've only just finished with the English nationals. Gosh what a bloody mess we're in over a simple game of cricket.'

'Ah, so you haven't read about Mr O'Riley in the local rag then?'

'My God, how did the press get hold of that? We're in a damnable ticklish situation here you know. I'm sorry to have to ask you Mma Xalwo but what do you know about ARSE.....''

'I beg your pardon?'

'Afrikaans something or other to do with racial equality.'

'Have I got a blank expression on my face?'

'I take it that's a no then.'

'Afrikaans wanting racial equality, are we on the same planet here?' Mma Xalwo was just a wee bit puzzled now.

'That's what I thought. The problem being that, as much as I would love to take up your kind offer of doing something to Mr O'Riley, the problem is that I don't know where he is. The last thing I heard about him was in a ransom note from these nutters calling themselves ARSE.'

Sir Reginald held his head in his hands shaking slowly from side to side.

'When was this?' Mma Xalwo was fast accelerating into warp speed confusion.

'Oh, must have been some time last week. God doesn't time fly when you're having fun?' He was nearly in tears.

'Oh, not recently then, say in the last twelve hours or so?'

'Oh, no.' Sir Reginald sat bolt upright.' What *are* you saying?'

'Well according to the local press, he is alive and well and has just taken on the whole Angolan army single handed.'

Sir Reginald just stared blankly at, or through Xalwo for several seconds and then shook his head and said, 'the kidnapping could have been the answer to all our prayers.' He sank back into a deep depression again.

Xalwo lent her hand out and touched Sir Reginald's and speaking very softly, 'perhaps *I* could kidnap him for you Sir Reginald?' She stroked his hand like a nurse would a trauma patient.

Sir Reginald slowly started to get some colour back into his cheeks and started to brighten up considerably. 'Do you know that's the best offer I've had for a long, long time? He was smiling by now. 'I think *I*, sorry I think *we*, need a drink. One to soothe the savage breast, begging your pardon, not being sexist here, and, two, in celebration. What do you say to that?'

'When I get that drink in my hand it will be cheers.'

'Can I offer you some gin, or er,…….some gin?'

'Let's go for the gin shall we?'

*   *   *

'There's a young gentleman in reception for you Sir Reginald, called Khuma, and he says please can he have his fifty pula?'

'I'll be right down Mma Kagiso. Oh and can you bring a large sheet of headed paper and a black felt tipped pen please as well?'

Mma Kagiso was the confused one now. 'Oh, and fifty pula out of the petty cash box please.'

Sir Reginald managed the staircase two steps at a time and slightly out of breath walked up to Khuma and held out his hand.

'Mr Khuma. What have you got for me now?'

'Please sir, I've got that big stupid Afrikaans taxi man's number plate for you sir. And please can I have my fifty pula, please sir?'

'Certainly young man, you've done a good job. Now where's Mma Kagiso? Ah here she comes.' He took the scrap of paper from Khuma, looked at it and held up the fifty pula note. 'Can I ask you to wait another few seconds please my man?'

Khuma had never been called "my man" before. One: because he wasn't quite old enough to be a man. And, two: he didn't understand if it was a term of praise or derision.

'Yes sir, boss.'

Mma Kagiso handed Sir Reginald the sheet of headed paper and he laid it out on the reception desk. 'Now, just let me write this down on this bit of paper.' He made some bold strokes to spell out the following:

"CAN YOU PLEASE STICK THE BIG STUPID BUGGER WITH THE SWORD RIGHT UP YOUR **ARSE**.

THE POLICE WILL BE ROUND TO ENSURE THESE INSTRUCTIONS HAVE BEEN CARRIED OUT."

He rolled the sheet of paper up and asked the receptionist for an elastic band, wrapped the roll in it and gave it to Khuma along with the fifty pula note.

'Now then, what's your name again?'

'Khuma please sir.'

'Now then Khuma, would you like to earn another fifty pula?'

'Would I like to earn another fifty pula?' Khuma said in extreme startled/ecstasy mode.

'I'll take that as a yes then. So when you see that big stupid Afrikaans taxi driver again can you give him this bit of paper?'

'Cor that's easy, I see him nearly every day.'

'Well done but if I find out you haven't given it to him and still want fifty pula, do you know what will happen to you then?'

'Please sir, don't you worry, I won't let you down sir.'

'That's a good boy, because there are a lot of hungry lions out there aren't there?'

'Holy shit, oh beggin' your pardon sir!'

'Now off you go Khuma, there's a good boy.'

*   *   *

'Mma Kagiso can you get hold of Rra Krishna Chutnabuttee's telephone number and make an appointment with him at his emporium ASAP? And after that book me a conference call with Head Office in London. OK?'

How could she refuse?

'OK, I'll just pop out and see Rra Chutnabuttee now then, shouldn't be too long. When is the conference call booked for?'

Mma Kagiso quickly checked her diary, 'Twelve thirty.'

'Great. I should be back in plenty of time.'

'Rra Chutnabuttee, how nice to see you.'

'Oh, Mr Sir Rra Reginald I am wishing it is nice to be seeing you, but I am betting you are coming here to give me good kicking in the bottom.'

'Relax my friend, now where's that charming wife of yours with the old Darjeeling?'

'It will be coming damn sharpish.' With that he shouted 'Dupinda!' which nearly deafened poor Sir Reginald. 'Please to be getting our illustrious guest here some of our best Darjeeling.'

'Now then relax and let's go through this cricket match thing shall we?' Sir Reginald tried out his best calming voice.

'Oh, when I am getting hold of my beloved nephew again I am going to the one giving him the kicking in the bottom.'

'But you must be jolly proud of him surely?'

'Oh, I am so proud to see he is Doctor but he is disgrace to family.'

'Why is that my friend?'

'Because he is getting me much muddled and confused and thinking things are not what they seem and oh, oh, I don't know what to think any more. Who is MCC who is not MCC, who is from Marylebone who is from some bloody stupid little village?...................................'

Poor Sir Reginald put him out of his misery with an interruption, 'so what you are saying is that the cricket team who came out here to play you is not the one you thought it to be?'

'Oh, it is the one I asked to come out here, but because I wanted to see my Dr Rammittin, it is not the team I was expecting.'

'So who did come out here then?'

'My lovely nephew is telling me it is from some bloody village called bloody Muddlecombe. I tell you, my best national team beaten but some bloody stupid little bloody English village cricket team……….'

'Sir Reginald laughed but had to contain himself. 'Poor Rra Chutnabuttee,' he said quickly getting in before poor Chutnabuttee exploded. 'But I think you were beaten by a very good team. I doubt if any first class team could handle such an unusual gang of individuals. Anyway, can you let me have the name of that village again please?'

'Bloody Muddlecombe something, snorting or something, now where did I put Rammittin's business card? Oh, here it is, now let me see, yes Muddelcombe–cum-Snoring.'

*   *   *

'You've booked the conference call Mma Kagiso?'

'Yes Sir Reginald.'

'Now, I want to get hold of that Dr Rammittin Chutnabuttee and make sure Mr bloody O'Riley sees me as soon as he comes OK? Lock him in his office if you have to. OK?'

'Right you are sir. Your conference call is due any moment now.'

'Hallo, that Sir William?' It's Sir Reginald Makepeace here from the Gaborone High Commission in Botswana.'

'Hallo Reggie, so how's it going? I take it you got the wire off the teleprinter re this Angolan cock up?'

'Oh, yes, Sir William but I have some more information that may or may not sort of alleviate the situation.'

'Sounds like you're sitting on the fence a bit there Reggie old boy, but let's hear it anyway.'

'Well, it would seem that the cricket team who are out here in Botswana are not the MCC. Well, they are the MCC but not the MCC as we know it. The real MCC are in South Africa, very adjacent I'll give you that but nowhere near Angola for instance.'

'So who the bloody hell have you got out there in Botswana, the ones causing all the bloody hoo har?'

'Well, that's where all the confusion lies you see. They call themselves the MCC but they're not *the* MCC.'

'Christ Reggie I'm a tad confused here old boy.'

'As is everyone else out here. The team enjoying the hospitality of our lovely country are from a small village called Muddlecombe-cum-Snoring.'

'Who?'

'Muddlecombe-cum-Snoring.'

'Where the bloody hell is that?'

'God knows.'

'That's not all that helpful old boy.'

'Yes I know but I've got the captain of the team coming in and hopefully he will be able to help us out.'

'Listen old boy, I think the best thing we can do is to make them disappear, get them back here a bit smartish and keep them out of the way of the press.'

'Yes I thought of that, but am not quite sure how to go about it. Perhaps you can help me out there Sir William.'

'Listen, get them on a British Airways flight and I'll have a word with the boss at BA and we'll sort something out. A spot of the old diplomatic immunity might come in handy eh?'

'Brilliant idea Sir William. I'll come back to you soonest. Many thanks for your help.'

'No problem old boy. Well that's one in the eye for the old press then. Not the MCC eh? Going to have a field day here old boy. Many thanks for that. Just make sure that team you've got out there are invisible OK?'

*   *   *

Poor Mma Kagiso was about to pull her hair out. She didn't know if she was Mma Martha or Rra Arthur. Trying to get hold of Dr Rammy or Creighky was a nightmare but she had a last traced them. And then Khuma turned up demanding his fifty pula. What a day!

Sir Reginald felt as if he was in a pond full of alligators and somebody had pulled the plug out. Well at least he had got hold of Dr Rammy and Mr bloody O'Riley.

'As soon as they show up send them up to me Mma Kagiso!'

'Yes sir.'

'Oh and by the way as soon as Mr O'Riley turns up get hold of Mma Xalwo. I've got her number here.'

'Yes sir.' She wondered if Sir Reginald was in the mood for sharing his gin.

'Oh and by the way, have a look at British Airways schedules for the next flight back to the UK will you please? And get hold of Dr Chutnabuttee's flight plans and get him onto a British Airways schedule. Ok?'

'Yes sir.' She wondered if he shared his razor blades to slash her wrists.

*   *   *

Poor Jacobus van de Nitwit was confused when the little black boy threw a roll of paper into his cab and ran off. He opened it up but wasn't quite sure if he was translating it correctly.

He rushed back to his apartment and as it was the weekend Piet was back there as well.

He showed the sheet of paper to him. Piet looked at it and shrugged his shoulders.

'Christ min you're the one with the certificate, what does it say?'

'Well I'm not quite sure. It looks awfully important with all sorts of emblems on it like it was from somebody, well, somebody very important.'

'Yeah, and.....?'

'Yeah, well it seems to be saying that we have to get that big stupid bugger with the sword and stick him somewhere.'

'Yeah, and..?'

'Well you know that terrorist group we thought up?'

'yeah, and…..?'

'Well it sort of mentions that.'

'You've got me there bru.'

'And then it says if we don't do that the kêrels will be over to check to see if we have done what it says in the letter.'

'It doesn't say anything about paying us the million pula then?'

'No.'

'Oh. Just run that bit about what we have to do with him?'

'Stick him up our……………………..oh shit!'

'What's up bru?'

'I've just figured it out and I think we're in deep kak!'

'Can I get you a castle bru?'

'I think we need more than a fucking castle right now bru.'

*   *   *

Xalwo had handed in her notice of resignation at de Beers, not that she would be able to work her notice, and had started to pack ready for Plan B. She had finished stocking up the "His" and "Hers" pill dispensers for the journey. She had to make sure she didn't get overtaken from jet lag and ensure she arrived at the destination fresh and ready for the action.

Creighky's itinerary was quite the opposite. She had to ensure that he was "permanently placid and flaccid" throughout the journey to ensure that any wandering hands would at least have their internal Sat Nav and libido turned off. And she wanted him as docile as a damp towel upon arrival.

She had been to the bank, cleared the draft from Chekov and withdrawn the cash. Paid the travel agent the outstanding amount owing for the travel itinerary and then found Dr Rammy and given him his share.

'Thank you Mma Xalwo, well we are off now. I've just had a call from the High Commission to pop in before we leave. I presume we will be seeing you back at Muddlecombe in the near future?'

'Oh, yes. But not *too* soon. I have some other business to attend to before I come back to your lovely little village.'

'Well, you'll always be welcome.'

'Did you say you're going to the High Commission?'

'Yes.'

'You haven't seen Creighky anywhere have you?'

'He's gone to the High Commission as well.'

'Oh, good. Let's be off then. I hope you've got all the bats Dr Rammy?'

'Oh, yes, don't worry they won't be leaving my side; I can assure you of that.'

*   *   *

'Mma Kagiso? It's reception here. I've got Mr O'Riley, Mma Xalwo and Dr Chutnabuttee here to see Sir Reginald.

'I beg your pardon?'

'Mma Kagiso!'

'Oh yes, they're all here. Do what to Mr O'Riley? Mma Kagiso, really! Ok. And send Dr Chutnabuttee up? OK.'

'Mma Xalwo and Mr O'Riley would you mind taking a seat in the office over there for a few minutes please? Can I get you a cup of coffee?'

'You wouldn't be having any of the old Bushmills lying around by any chance there would you now? No what in heavens name are you dong here princess?' He said turning to Xalwo.'

'I've come to see Sir Reggie.'

'Oh, Sir Reggie now is it?'

'And I've come to take you away from all this.'

'Sure you have, you're a tease that's for sure.'

'Come in Dr Chutnabuttee, please sit down.'

'Oh please to be calling me Dr Rammy. I can't remember what I have to be calling you your highness.'

'Sir Reginald will do. Now then Dr Rammy.' He started to look through some papers on his desk.

Dr Rammy had this feeling of déjà vu come over him all of a sudden as if he was back in the Dean's office in the University College Hospital, Jodhpur.

'Dr Rammy, you've no doubt gathered from your uncle that your cricket team has caused quite a stir out here. I must say I've never enjoyed myself so much at a cricket match for a long time. Anyway, I digress. My head office in London has taken a bit of stick from the international press who have mistaken your team for somebody else.'

'Oh, the boys from Marylebone.'

'Quite.'

'I am sorry I am thinking my uncle Krishna is getting his underwear in a knot, ...'

'Yes, quite, as you say, poor old Rra Chutnabuttee is in a bit of a state. Very proud of you though Dr Rammy, but I think he's losing the plot. Anyway, my head office in London wants you and your merry men to disappear.'

"Oh, no, not a hold full of bloody Brahman cows again," thought Dr Rammy. Looks like we're back in pear-shape mode again. Or "tits up" as he preferred to say.

'When are you due to fly?'

''We're off tonight to Johannesburg and then back to the UK.'

'Well, have a word with my PA Mma Kagiso; she has a new itinerary for you now. As soon as you get to Jo'burg, you've to get in touch with the British Airways agent in transit and they have you booked through to Heathrow in first class and you will have full diplomatic immunity to see you straight through all those nasty customs and immigration formalities at the other end..................'

Sir Reginald paused for a moment. 'Where do you come from?'

'Muddlecombe. Muddlecombe-cum-Snoring.' Dr Rammy was biting his tongue with exhilaration.

'Where's that?'

'Well, I'm not that sure myself. It's somewhere in the middle of England.'

'Well, whatever. But whatever you do please do not speak to anyone, especially the press, is that understood?'

'Oh, Mr Sir Reginald, I am most happy man. You are being a scholar and a gentleman.' Dr Rammy could hardly contain himself as he left the office. As soon as he was outside the office he jumped up and punched the air to the amazement of Mma Kagiso and the rest of the office staff outside.

'Xalwo, you are not going to believe this. You are *not* going to bloody believe this.'

'Calm down Dr Rammy. What am I not going to believe?'

'We are having diplomatic impunity all the way home!'

'I beg your pardon?'

'We are getting first class all the way back and not having to go through bloody customs!'

'I don't believe it!'

'That's what I said, and of course the bloody bats are having impunity as well, can you believe that?'

'Come in.'

'Ah, Mr O'Riley and Mma Xalwo, please sit down.' Sir Reginald got up from his chair and shook hands with Creighky and gave Mma Xalwo a kiss on both cheeks.

'Now, Mr O'Riley, I believe you gave a statement to the press while you were staying at Francistown, would I be correct in that presumption?'

Creighky felt the same as Dr Rammy that things were about to go pear-shaped. 'Well, your honour, it was like this, I was just sitting down at the old breakfast there in the hotel and this fellow comes up to me and starts asking questions about the old shindig we was having with them fuzzy wuzzies on the border with all them guns and things and……………..'

'Yes, yes, but still you have talked to the press?'

'Well how was I to know they was from the old papers and that? Sure I thought they was just having a bit of the old craic………'

'Well whatever. The fact of the matter is that you have broken some of the diplomatic rules that you signed when you joined us.'

'Did I now then?'

'Yes, and we cannot let that happen. So we are going to have to put you under "sub judice" for the foreseeable future.'

'Just run that by me again can you there your majesty?'

'Basically it's a judicial requirement that you do not talk to anybody concerning any happenings here during your tour of duty in Gaborone. Normally that would mean putting you under house arrest. However we have a volunteer who has agreed to be your guarantor to that effect and has agreed at great personal expense to ensure that such an event will not happen again. So I am putting you on indefinite leave and handing you over to a chaperone for the foreseeable future.'

'And who would that be?' said Creighky hardly believing his luck that it could be the person sitting next to him. Is he lucky or what? Plan A here we come!

'Mma Kagiso, come in. Have they all gone?'

'Yes Sir Reginald.'

'Thank Christ for that. Now Mma Kagiso would you mind indulging an old man please?'

Mma Kagiso was a bit taken aback but replied, 'why certainly Sir Reginald.'

'Mma Kagiso, would you mind taking your shoes off please?'

Mma Kagiso was struck dumb. "He's lost it," she thought. "It's all this stress. What will he want me to take off next? Is he going to rape me?"

'Would you mind just walking over to that cabinet over there please?'

Mma Kagiso walked very slowly keeping as far away from Sir Reginald as possible and pointed to a cabinet.

'Yes, that's the one. Can you open it for me please?'

"What's his game?" she thought getting into a hysterical state.

'And I want a stiff one!'

She froze. "He *is* going to rape me" she was too scared to do anything else now as she slowly opened the cabinet and stared at several bottles of gin, an ice bucket and some crystal glasses.

'Now pour us both a large one and come and sit down and put your feet up.'

*   *   *

When Mma Kagiso eventually got home she collapsed and started to get ready to go to bed only to find she had her knickers on inside out!

Chapter 16. The MCC fly back and meet some close friends.

'Would you like to come this way please Dr Chutnabuttee and party? Here we go; if you can wait in our first class transit lounge we will call you when your next connection is due. Please help yourself to any food or drinks in the lounge, they are complimentary and there is a telephone and fax machine should you have any business requirements and the latest newspapers and magazines. Enjoy your stay at the British Airways hospitality suite here in Johannesburg.'

'You are being very kind. May I enquire as to the whereabouts of our luggage please?'

'Don't worry about that Dr Chutnabuttee your luggage is automatically transferred straight through to your final destination, which is………….?'

'Oh, ah, yes, Heathrow.'

'Good, so you just sit back and enjoy yourselves. I hear you are quite famous back in Botswana so now you don't have to worry about any interruptions especially from those nasty newspapers people.'

'Oh, you are most gracious. Thanking you for all your help.' Dr Rammy gave the nice lady one of his heart stopping smiles and ushered the rest of the team into the lounge.

'Ok, now, help yourself to food and drink it's all free lads. I'm thinking there is none of Brewster's special bitter for you Boris. You'll have to try something without any alcohol in it. Oh, bloody hell.' Dr Rammy stood transfixed as if seeing a ghost.

'Of all the Goddesses Durga, Kali, Lakshmi, and Saraswati, look who the bleeding hell is standing over there?'

'It's not?'

'It bloody well is.'

Dr Chutnabuttee without further ado walked straight over to this other fellow traveler and said, 'please be to god, you are Mr Botham aren't you?'

'Er, well actually yes, I am, can I help you?'

'Oh, I am being very rude interrupting your privacy but could I humbly request your signature please on this meagre piece of paper?'

'No problem old sport there you are.' he duly signed his autograph and casually asked, 'you on holiday then?'

'Well no, well yes, but we are playing cricket in Botswana but it is seeming like a jolly holiday.'

Botham slowly started to become interested. 'Erm, would you mind if I asked if this was fairly recently?'

'Oh, yes only last week.'

'And could I ask the name of your team?'

'Oh, ah, oh, yes, well we are being called the Muddlecombe Cricket Club.'

'Ah, that is sort of similar to the MCC?'

'Oh, please Mr Botham, I am having much cock-ups with people getting our names mixed up and having much troubles.'

'Hey up lads, guess who we've got here?' Botham shouted to the rest of the travelers sitting around the lounge.

'It's only the bloody MCC!'

'Not the MCC?' replied the other people as if in one voice. They all got up and started to come over to where Dr Rammy and his new friend were standing.

'Oh, please,' Dr Rammy started to blush. 'I am being most upset about the spelling of our poor little village cricket club.'

'And did this poor little village cricket club just happen to stuff the home team?'

'Well, we are making lots of luck and just managed to scrape a win, but it is the first game of cricket we are playing.'

'That was the first time you have played a game of cricket?' Botham said very slowly, completely stunned.

'Oh, yes please but we are having many practices and we have special training methods you understand.'

There were now about thirty people standing round poor Dr Rammy who was being joined by his own team.

'I don't believe this,' said Botham incredulously. 'And what's so special about your training then?'

'It is Brewster's special best bitter. Our beloved landlord from the "Snort and Truffle" is quenching our thirsts after we are practicing and we are giving pints to good players and bad players are having to pay for pints.'

Botham put his arm around Dr Rammy and looked around the lounge. 'I think we need to try your training techniques, but, my friend we listened to your game with much interest while we were getting stuffed by the South Africans here.'

'You are the bloody MCC?' Dr Rammy couldn't believe his luck.

'That's us, the MCC, but we didn't win *our* matches and we've been practicing for bloody years.'

Dr Rammy was still in a state of shock. 'You are the boys from Marylebone?'

Botham nodded along with Geoffrey Boycott and a few others.

'And we were on bloody radio?'

'Oh, yes, and what a fantastic game.'

'Bloody British BBC radio?'

'Oh, yes my friend, bloody British BBC radio all over the world.'

Dr Rammy promptly fainted and Boris came over and picked him up like a rag doll and placed him on one of the plush leather sofas.

'And you must be Mr Slobovitch, Boris the basher?'

'Oh, da, da, yes, yes, I am cricketeer for village and you are?'

Botham gave him a large smile and tried to put his arm around the now upright Boris. 'Boris my friend can I have your autograph please?'

Dr Rammy eventually regained consciousness in the arms of one of the attractive British Airways stewardesses, soothing his brow with a cold flannel.

'Oh, goodness gracious, I have reached Nirvana, in the arms of the goddess Gaja Lakshmi and in the company of the high gods from Marylebone.'

"Smooth talking bastard," somebody muttered as the stewardess slowly unwound Dr Rammy's encircling arms and managed to escape from any further engropement.

He was just in time to say goodbye to his new friends from Marylebone on their way to Australia. Not before they had exchanged contact details and been invited to come and play at Muddlecombe.

'Please to be ringing this number. This is the very fine Mr Brewster who has only telephone in village and we are looking forward to seeing you and showing you how to play cricket.'

This brought titters all round as they said their fond farewells.

Chapter 17. Plan B

'Come along Creighky darling we are going off on a dirty weekend.'

'Just run that by me again would you please?' What he really meant was that it looks like he was going to get his Plan A up and running at last.

'Come along, let's get you all packed up. We've a flight in three hours.'

'Aren't you going to handcuff me like Sir Reggie said then?'

'Don't worry big boy, we'll be having plenty of fun later.'

Creighky had that strange feeling in the groinal area again.

Xalwo recognised his look and realised she had some hard work ahead of her.

*   *   *

Xalwo had planned to take the pretty route as they had ten days before they were due to reach their destination and she had a lot of work to do to ensure that Creighky arrived at their destination in the correct state of mind.

Comatose.

So after their initial connection to Johannesburg, it was onto Dubai, then Bangkok and Hong Kong before a twenty three hour

Cathay Pacific flight to their final planned port of call.

Their body clocks were a bit out of phase to say the least, but Xalwo had managed to maintain some form of natural rhythm with judicial usage of her full range of pharmaceutical packages and had managed to ensure Creighky's natural rhythm was completely all to cock. Well, that's probably not the best way to put it, but shall we say that Creighky's Plan A was no nearer completion.

She managed to get his sleeping patterns completely out of phase and they were now on the last lap of the journey as she raised a glass of champagne to Creighky (after administering the necessary "upper" or "downer") and they drank to their holiday in paradise.

So far they were on schedule, not that Creighky was aware of any schedule. Not that Creighky was aware of anything.

*   *   *

Mrs Dimmock had taken advantage of the absence of Boris during a cricket practice and Dudley who was immersed into compiling the Rapaport report for the Borisky Diamond Company to call an extraordinary meeting of the Inter Planetary Standards and Ethics Committee in Primrose Cottage.

After everyone had settled and laid into Mrs Dimmock's home made cakes, Gerantinium O'Deighty brushed the crumbs from his beard and started the proceedings.

'Mrs Dimmock, I presume there is a reason for the meeting?'

'When was the last time we had a festival in the village?' Mrs Dimmock came straight to the point.'

'Ah, a good piss-up,' replied Gerantinium.

'Chair!' Mrs Dimmock's look could have halted a division of panzer tanks during the Blitzkrieg of Poland.

Gerantinium only gave her a snigger like a dirty old man in an old people's home lustfully leering at the bouncing cheeks of matron's bottom.

'Decorum wouldn't go amiss here Gerantinium. What I was about to say was, that we haven't had a good party for a long time.'

"You mean a good piss-up," what was Gerantinium wanted to say but felt it probably was not the best time to reiterate his feelings again. It came out as, 'and you feel there is some sort of occasion to warrant this Mrs Dimmock?'

'Well, yes. Our cricket team seem to have done very well and they may be having a proper match soon and inviting some important people here. And then there may be other occasions for some sort rejoicing.'

'Such as?'

'Well, I don't have anything in particular in mind.' Which meant she bloody well knew exactly what she had in mind.

'Oh, and a church service might be included in the festivities, don't you think?'

'The old cassock and surplice job then Mrs D?'

'Oh, yes Gerantinium, you'll need to get scrubbed up.'

'Well, I can't see any reason why we shouldn't let our hair down a bit? What do the rest of the committee think?'

'Well, why don't we tie it in with the cricket match? Let's ask old D'Arcy Landacre if we could use Muddlecombe Hall, just like the old summer fête? Not quite sure where the church fits in but why not. Get everyone dressed up to start with and then sort of, well, relax a bit, eh?'

'And get Brewster to sort out a buffet?'

'What a good idea, shall we minute that then?' Mrs Dimmock's idea was going exactly to plan.

*　　*　　*

Brewster picked up the phone. 'Hallo, Snort and Truffle, can I help you?'

'You want to speak to who?'

'Oh, you mean Dr Rammy?'

'Ok, and who shall I say is calling?'

'Both who?'

'Oh, Ian Botham?'

'Hold the line. He's out on the pitch at the moment, can you hold?'

Dr Rammy eventually got his breath back and got hold of the phone. 'Hallo, is that Mr Botham?'

'Oh, goodness gracious me. I am so excited. And how did it go in Australia?'

290

'Oh, fantastic. You have burnt something?'

'Oh, you have the Ashes, I am very pleased for you, and you what?'

'You want to come and play here?'

'Oh, bloody hell. Oh I am so sorry, I am so excited.'

'You have a spare weekend when?'

'Oh, we will be having a special day; Mr Brewster will be having to get some extra special brew in for you.'

'Oh, and you will be stuffing us?'

'Oh, Mr Botham you are being a very funny man.'

*   *   *

Xalwo and Creighky landed safely at Las Vegas and cleared customs and immigration by three 'clock. Xalwo's first assignation was at five 'clock. Her second assignation was at seven o'clock and her third at nine. She was dead on schedule.

They booked in at the Sands Hotel and she managed to get Creighky up to their palatial room where he collapsed on the enormous bed.

'Come on big boy, let's get freshened up and go down to the bar for a drink. I could murder a decent glass of champagne.'

'Sweet jeysus darlin', I'm fair banjaxed, could we not get some sleep?'

'Come on, there's plenty of time for that later big boy. Last one in the shower is a sissy.'

The sight of Xalwo slowly peeling off her clothes very nearly got the old groinal area twitching, so he managed to follow her into the bathroom after she had finished and got himself spruced up ready for the old Plan A.

'Look at that darling; they only have your favourite Bushmills here. And I'll have a nice cooling glass of bubbly.'

How could he refuse? Xalwo stood back from the bar and watched as Creighky slowly managed to get up enough strength to ask for some drinks. She felt sure the Irish Whisky mixed with all the pharmaceuticals he had taken would do the trick. He got the drinks and slowly sipped his nectar while Xalwo relished her iced cold glass of champagne.

Then all of a sudden Creighky turned a paler shade of ghastly white. He dropped his drink and ran for cover behind one of the reception area's large sofas. He was now kneeling as Xalwo went over and looking down at him said, 'what's the matter darling?'

'Holy mother Mary, sweet fecking Jeysus. Have you seen what I've just seen?'

'No, what's that darling?'

'It's only the fecking Missus. Holy shit, it's only fucking Mildred! Sweet Mother Mary are we in the shit. What the fecking hell do we do now?'

Xalwo left Creighky kneeling behind the sofa muttering to himself and walked over to greet Mildred as Creighky peaked over the top of the sofa in total amazement. He saw her embrace Mildred and then a tall swarthy looking man standing next to Mildred gave her a kiss on the cheek.

He was sweating by now as they turned and slowly walked back towards him.

The three of them stopped and looked down at this gibbering idiot on his knees.

'Hallo Creighky,' said Mildred matter of factly. 'I don't think you've met Chekov have you?'

Creighky was in no condition to do anything other than stare blankly up at the threesome looking down on him.

'Chekov, this is our Korean war hero Lt Col Creighky O'Riley MC OBE. Creighky this is Chekov. Lt Col Chekov Yeboleksi, late of the Russian Army, say hallo.'

Chekov leant down to grasp Creighky's hand which vaguely resembled a bit of wet fish as he shook it and let it go swiftly. Creighky's arm swung limply back to his side as his glazed look tried to make head or tail of what in heaven and hell was going on.

'Come on Creighky, let's hit the town,' Xalwo said bending down and trying to lift him to his feet. Between them they managed to get him upright and get his legs in some semblance of walking mode.

Not only was he jet lagged and drugged, he was now completely traumatised as they dragged him off down the "Strip".

*   *   *

Creighky slept for thirty six hours once they got him back to his bed at four o'clock in the morning after having painted the town red amongst other things.

Xalwo, Mildred and Chekov had done the Grand Canyon by helicopter, the Grand Hoover damn and various shopping malls whilst Creighky slept and they now came back to see how their fourth member was doing.

It was now six o'clock in the evening as Xalwo went up to their bedroom and slowly managed to wake him and offered him some light refreshments.

'Hey, big boy. You're awake then?'

'Holy mother of Mary, where the feck am I?'

'You're in Las Vegas darling?'

'What the feck am I doing here?'

'You're on holiday darling, remember?'

'Sweet jeysus, I had this terrible nightmare.'

'Tell me about it my dear.'

'Well, who should turn up but the bloody missus? Mildred with some fella and we all gets taken outside to this bloody great limousine. Jeysus, I tell you it must have been the size of Croke Park in Dublin, and there's drinks and televisions and then we gets driven off to some office or other and we all gets inside and there's this chap with a black smock sitting behind this bloody great desk with a load of certificates on the wall and blow me down doesn't Mildred come and sit beside me and he takes out a load of papers and gets me and the missus to sign a load of bumf and then you and this other fella have to sign something or other to do with witnesses or something.'

'And then I get's dragged back outside to this bloody great limousine again and there's champagne all over the bloody shop and then we arrives at some sort of church. Only the vicar must have been hard pushed for a decent congregation, you couldn't get more than a dozen people in there if you all breathed in.'

'And the bloody flowers, Jeysus I've never seen so many flowers crammed into such a small place, you could hardly breath and then there was this strange fella in a pink suit playing the bloody organ if you please and them darkie mamas all dressed in pink swaying about and jumping up and down wailing and giving the halleluiahs a good old bashing and clapping. Jeysus what a mad house.'

'And then this geyser in a white smock comes out with a book in front of him and under this arch of bloody flowers he gets you and me up with Mildred and this other fella holding me up on the other side. Well this boyo in the white smock starts blethering on and this fella what's holding me up gives me something to give to you and the ponse on the organ is going berserk along with the big fat darkie mamas and they're getting right on my tits I can tell you. And then this geyser in the white smock says I can kiss you.'

'Well, that's jolly decent of you I thought to myself. I can do that at anytime, so what's the big deal about this place? Do I have to get permission every time I want a snog? I'm just about to land him one when this fella on me right guides me over to this table where you and me sits down and this fella in the white smock turns up with a load of more bumf to sign and Mildred and this fella has to do some more witnessing.'

'Well, I can tell you I'm about out of me mind what with all the noise and flowers and that fella on the organ is going to get it I'll swear, and then I'm up again and this fella is holding me up on me left side with Mildred on the other side with you and then the fella in the smock starts all over again.'

'Then this fella gives me something that I have to give to him back again, what the feck is all that about? And blow me down doesn't the old boy in the smock start preachifying all over again reading from this book in front of him. And then I gets asked for that thing back again and can I remember where I put it?'

'Well, that caused a right old commotion and Mildred's fella nearly lets go of me but I find it eventually and then bugger me doesn't the geyser in the smock tell this fella *he* can kiss *Mildred* now. What the hell is going on?'

'So they have a small peck. Sweet mother Mary, that's not much of a snog even if it was with me missus and he drags me over to this table again where him and Mildred sign something and you and me has to do the witnessing bit.'

'This bloody fella on the organ has lost it by now and the bloody mamas was with him and I couldn't get a word in edgeways and if I don't get a drink pretty soon I'm going to lose it too. And then out it comes, the champagne in a bloody great bottle, thank Christ for that says I, I've a thirst on me like the Sahara desert. And we gets taken into a little side room and bugger me there's a cake on a table with four toy people on top and you and me have to cut a piece and then Mildred and this fella has to cut a piece and I have to sit down and eat it before I faint.'

'No sooner had we finished off the champagne and the cake and this fella lifts me up and off we go again outside and there's this bloody great limousine waiting for us again. And then it's off to some posh place and into a bloody great big restaurant only there was a stage there and all the tables was on different levels and me bucko has difficulty in getting me up all them steps to our table and at last I can sit down. And then we starts off on the drinking again and everybody is drinking to everybody else's health and then a waiter comes round and asks us what we want to eat. And there's this list of food but I'm buggered if I can tell what it says, just the half a cow I says to the waiter and we all has a good laugh.'

'Well, we gets stuck into the food and then they put the bloody lights out! How the hell can I see what the feck I'm eating and then the curtains on the stage open and bugger me there's a whole bleeding orchestra sitting up there?'

'And they start playing and then this geyser comes out in a white tracksuit with a load of sequins all over the place and boy, how much Brylcream did he have on? Well he starts the old singing bit and he must have had a problem in the old underwear department 'cause he couldn't keep his arse still but the ladies seemed to like it so much they all went up to the front of the stage and was holding out their arms and some of them was holding up bits of clothing. Holy sweet jeysus, what a carry on.'

'Well, I lost it after that and that's about all I can remember of the dream but it all seems so real.'

'Doesn't it just,' said Xalwo holding up her left hand and blowing onto a large diamond ring with a gold ring next to it.

'Do you know, I never noticed that before?' said Creighky incredulously. 'You never told me you was married, who's the lucky fella?'

'You are Creighky. You are. Say hallo to the new Mrs O'Riley.'

The last thing he was thinking about then was his Plan A which went straight down the pan as Creighky tried to figure out what the merry hell was going on. Much too difficult for a man in his condition. So he fainted.

Comatose.

Plan B however, was right on schedule.

Chapter 18. The proper wedding

Creighky managed to survive the rest of the week. He trailed round after Xalwo like a puppy dog on an invisible lead, whereas Mildred and Chekov were inseparable. Twined around each other like ivy round a tree.

They saw all the lights of Las Vegas and all the floor shows, the casinos and various excursions out into the desert.

At last they boarded a direct flight back to Heathrow and were collected at the Heathrow airport by Brewster.

'Welcome back Mrs O'Riley,' said Brewster as Mildred involuntarily took a step forward but managed to stop herself.

'Thank you Brewster,' said Xalwo leaning forward for a kiss on the cheek.

'And how are you Mrs Yeboleksi?' Mildred smiled and allowed Brewster to continue his welcoming routine.

Poor Creighky was still in a state of confusion, watching somebody kiss his wife; well not his actual wife but one he had been married to for some time. And then there was this other wife of his. That was a puzzle for sure.

He couldn't even remember asking her to marry him, not that he could remember much that had happened in the past couple of weeks anyway. But not so much as a by-your-leave, or even "do you fancy getting married?" did she say.

"Let's tie the knot," never came up in any conversations that he could ever remember.

"It must be the old African tradition?" Creighky thought to himself. "She must have realised I was a good shag and that's probably all she needed to think to get married in African."

"Or was it something I said when we was on the old safari there, under the old moonlit stars and all that malarkey. It'll be that bloody bottle of Bushmills no doubt. I must have got carried away, that'll be it."

But he still wasn't convinced, all very confusing and nowhere nearer to any Plan A either. He sat in the back of Brewster's Range Rover on the way back to Muddlecombe trying to puzzle all this out and all he managed to get was thirsty.

'I'm getting sick of driving down here. That's twice in a week,' Brewster muttered as they found their way out of Heathrow and onto the motorway.

'Of course you had to come down and pickup the cricket team?' Chekov made an initial enquiry with plenty more questions to follow.

'Jesus Christ, that was some to do, I can tell you. Bloody police all over the shop. I had to go and make myself known to them, as they must have known I was coming down for the boys. And then we get taken around all the back streets of the airport and straight out onto the tarmac and there's their plane. All the passengers are getting off as we are kept waiting and then a bit later off comes young Dr Rammy and the lads and he has to go round to the hold and identify the team bags and all their luggage.'

'What happened then?' Chekov was about to burst in frustration.

'Well, he pointed out their baggage and then some official looking bloke gave the bags all a big tick with a piece of chalk.........'

'Christ man, and then what happened?' Chekov was nearly out of his seat pulling his hair out.

'Well, I thought, oh bloody hell, as they picked out all our baggage and put it in some large grey van with no windows, only slits, like the prison vans.'

'Oh shit!' Chekov couldn't stand much more of this.

'Then this copper comes over to me and gets in the minibus I'd hired, and "Oh shit" I thought to myself, we're for the bloody chop now as he pointed to where he wanted me to drive and looks behind and we have to wait 'till the boys are all off the plane and they all have to get in this grey van.'

Chekov couldn't contain himself any longer. 'Bloody hell, what happened man?'

'Well, bugger me but this other cop car pulls out in front of us and we starts driving off and they starts the blue light flashing and all that. Well, my underwear was slowly changing colour,,,,,'

'Just like mine,' said Chekov.

'So we start driving round all this perimeter road and ends up at some side gate at the other side of the airport. This copper flashes something to the security guard and he opens the gate and bugger me we're on the slip road to the motorway.

"Where to sir?" says this copper to me casual like? "Erm, well, we have to get onto the M1 north please, if that's alright with you officer?" I said casually as if I do this every day of the week.'

'Who we got in there then?' He says to me. 'A load of asylum seekers?'

'Well, no actually, I said. 'It's only our cricket team just come back from Africa.'

'You're not the MCC are you?'

'Well, yes and no.'

''Ere, you're not that lot out in that African country like John Harlot was on about?'

'Well, yes, actually, now you come to mention it.'

'With old Basher Boris?'

'Oh, yes, our Boris. We're proud of young Boris.'

'And didn't you get involved with some sort of arms smuggling in Angola or somewhere in Africa?'

'Not quite. The press made a right balls up there. The team lost it's way and went across the border and I understand there was only a young soldier and his sergeant who'd never heard of cricket and mistook our bats for mortars and the balls for grenades.'

'Well, the press made it sound like you'd made a right pigs ear of the talks that was going on, somewhere in Portugal was it?'

'Yes, I read the papers too. I couldn't believe my eyes and then the lads rang back and we had a right good old laugh, I can tell you.'

'So you are the MCC then? Thought you were off to Australia?'

'Well, not exactly. We're only a village team.'

'What village is that then?' he says as we get onto the M1 and heads north.

'Muddlecombe,' I told him.

'So you're not the real MCC then?'

'You know, that's what a lot of people keep telling us. But we don't understand why we got asked to go out to Africa to play and why the BBC came out to see us play and what all this bother is about now?'

'I think there must have been a few cock-ups along the line somewhere? I don't think the old Foreign Office are that chuffed with your exploits in Angola, well that's what we heard in the briefing anyway. But you still stuffed that African country eh?'

'Oh, yes, and that was only our first game of cricket.'

'You're joking. Holy shit. Now listen, we have to drop you off at a service station once we're on the M1. Can you get Boris' autograph for me? I'm in the Metropolitan Police Cricket Club and the boys had a right laugh listening to that game.'

'No problem there officer,' I said trembling.

'I tell you what; we must have a game with your lot sometime. I'll have a word with our secretary.'

'Well, that'll be nice,' I said to him with my sincerest smile and my tongue stuck right in my cheek.

'So what happened next?' Poor old Chekov was nearly drooling.

'Well, we stopped off at a service station, and all the boys get transferred from the prison bus to the minibus together with all the luggage and after lots of autograph signing we said our tearful goodbyes and drove off waving goodbye to all the nice policemen.'

Chekov leant back in the seat, 'phew!'

'That's what Dr Rammy said, and he had a right old sweat I can tell you.'

'I bet he did,' echoed Chekov sitting back and relaxing for the rest of the journey.

They were nearly at the turn off to Muddlecombe when Brewster started talking again as the bodies in the back of the car struggled to wake up.

'We've got the decorators in at the moment and we've had to move you out of your room Xalwo into the spare room. I hope you don't mind. It shouldn't be too long.'

Plan B was going nicely on schedule.

'Oh, what a shame,' said Xalwo trying not to smile. 'And where's my brand new husband going to sleep?'

'He's in with Boris in Primrose Cottage,' Mildred piped in very quickly, having already moved all his stuff out a long time ago.

'There you are darling, it won't be long and then we'll be together.' Xalwo patted Creighky's knee playfully, but not for too long.

Creighky was still in a state of shock. Call it jet lag, call it trauma, call it post marital bliss, (no, that would be too much) anyway he still wasn't firing on all brain cells just at this moment of time. His Plan A was slowly going down the pan but Xalwo's (and Chekov's) Plan B was running smoothly and had to continue in this condition for some time yet.

They were just coming up to the turning off to Muddlecombe as Brewster broke the silence.

'Oh, by the way, Mrs D has organised a festival in which you will be partaking.'

'Oh, and how will we be partaking?' Mildred said in amazement.

'Ah, yes, well you will all have to go to church?'

'To church?' it was a long time since any of them had done anything religious.

'Yes, I think you will have to go and re enact your wedding vows. Sort of dressed in white.'

'Oh, my god. You mean the full wedding thing?'

'Yes, the whole village is involved. The wedding breakfast will be at Muddlecombe Hall. Fiona and I are doing the catering and running the bar and you should see the village. It's all decked out in flowers, everyone has gone bananas. You are celebrities now.'

'Good old Mrs D,' sighed Mildred in resignation. Not a lot one could do once Mrs Dimmock had ordained it.

*   *   *

As Creighky was down at the "Snort" and poor Dudley hard at work on the shop floor in the diamond factory, sorry, the Community College, Primrose Cottage was free for another committee meeting.

'Thank you for coming to this extraordinary directors meeting at such short notice but quite obviously we need to move and change some items of administration. Can we proceed please chair?' Chekov looked to Boris as if he could say no.

'Da, da, yes, yes.'

'Thank you chair. Now moving swiftly on I would like to propose the following amendments, and we do need them putting in the minutes. Is that alright Mildred?'

'Oh, he's so forceful, isn't he?' A little titter ran round the room in Primrose Cottage.

'And the first item is that Mrs Mildred O'Riley be struck from the records as Company Secretary.' Chekov demanded in one of his loud commanding voices.

'You beast!' Mildred smiled

Another titter. Mildred started taking notes in between purring.

'And replaced by Mrs Mildred Yeboleksi.'

A round of applause went round the table as Mildred's purring visibly increased in volume.

'All those in favour?'

A rhetorical question if ever there was.

'Passed unanimously, ok chair?'

'Chair?'

Poor Boris was still in Botswana hitting sixes.

'Oh, da, da, yes, yes.' It will soon be practice time he thought.

'Now,' Chekov looked over to Mildred who was just finishing the notes, 'now we come to the part where we must reinstate Mrs O'Riley.'

He looked round the room to a beaming Xalwo and a snigger started to gather pace in Crikey's absence. Plan B so to speak.

'I would like to propose that we invite Mrs O'Riley that is Mrs Xalwo O'Riley to become an executive director. Can I have a show of hands please?' Mildred immediately took her hands off Chekov's thighs and blushing, she raised her hand in a voting gesture.

'Thank you.' Chekov gave Mildred one of his sultry looks and passing round the rest of the gathered attendees at the table continued. 'That's another unanimous vote then is it? Chair?'

Somebody kicked Boris who quickly jumped in with a 'da, da, yes, yes,' although he wasn't quite sure what he'd just agreed to.

'Ok Mildred?' asked Chekov as he watched her write down all the details in the minutes. He got the nod from her and continued once more.

'Now, I hope you all have the Rapaport report that young Dudley has prepared. By the way, I feel he has a big bonus coming because of all the work he has put into this report. All in favour?'

'Da, da, yes, yes,' jumped in Boris quickly to impress everyone.

'Good. Now where was I? The report. Does anyone have any questions about it?' As if anybody had the faintest idea what Dudley was on about?

'Briefly, as I understand it, the report looks at each size range of diamonds which has it's own price grid matrix. For smaller sizes under 0.30 carat, the price grids refer to parcels of diamonds with colour and clarity ranges. For stones larger than 0.30, each colour/clarity combination has a price. All prices are in hundreds of U.S. dollars per carat.'

What wasn't mentioned was that this was the trade price and that there was a Muddlecombe factor wherein a fifty percent cut had been taken in order that the shareholders get a decent dividend.

Chekov surveyed some very glazed looks. 'Good, I'll take that as no questions then. Now, in his report he concludes that the latest shipment received from the Muddlecombe Cricket Club,' a large applause was heard around the room, 'the value of this shipment is one million five hundred thousand, nine hundred and forty US dollars.'

A large intake of breath was very nearly heard the other side of the cricket pitch. Xalwo sat beaming.

'I would now like to propose a share issue of the equivalent in sterling to our new executive director Mrs Xalwo O'Riley,' Chekov said and then as an afterthought which had been given considerable thought earlier, 'and of course there will have to be the nominal expenses of the operation to be deducted from this……….'

'Naturally,' confirmed Fiona quickly.

'Naturally,' reconfirmed Xalwo giving her blessing as a similar afterthought upstaging Fiona.

Everyone stood up and applauded Xalwo who was very nearly in tears. In actual fact after a few seconds she was blubbing profusely and was comforted by Mildred until all dampness was removed from her face and she waved everybody to sit down.

'You don't know how much this means to me. How much heartache I have been through ………'

'Christ, she even had to marry Creighky!' Mildred put her penny's worth in and eased the tension as everyone laughed.

'I don't know how to start to thank you all. The Muddlecombe Cricket Club Plan is the most professional operation I have ever come across.' She forgot to mention that the Plan B was going pretty smoothly as well.

'Da, da, yes, yes. I break many bats and then I come back and have to break bats all over again,' chuckled Boris.

Xalwo kissed Boris on the head. Fortunately he was sitting down and she was a very tall lady.

'I have never felt more at home in the world as I have here in Muddlecombe and have my dearest friends here.'

She nearly started everyone else off into tears.

'But please be assured I shall be spending a lot of my time and money here.'

'You'll have to wait a few months for your first dividend Xalwo,' chirped in Fiona. 'But I'm sure we can arrange a short term loan at a very reasonable rate.' Being Scottish and an accountant hadn't stopped Fiona from bringing things back down to earth.

'I don't see why the bloody husband shouldn't look after her,' Mildred muttered under her breath, knowing full well where most of *his* income would be going.

'Now I know Boris has to go to cricket practice and break some more bats before the MCC come up here next week and I know we all have to go to our practice in the church before our big day as well. So I'll propose that this meeting now be closed,' Chekov finalised.

'Da, da, yes, yes. I got a bloody big thirst like doggies bottom in Australia.'

'Thank you for that Boris.'

*   *   *

Life in Muddlecombe-cum-Snoring had never been more hectic. All the villagers had been invited to the wedding and all of them had a specific task allocated by Mrs Dimmock. All the table and chairs from the school had to be moved to Muddlecombe Hall together with those outside the "Snort".

All the grass had to be cut and all the fresh flowers cut and arranged for the church. Most of them were already in use brightening the village up but Mrs D had a word with the gardening club and a few words with the "boss" and lo and behold a whole new crop of brightly coloured flowers appeared as if by magic. You didn't mess with Mrs D!

The bridal party all had to go down to London to get their dresses and uniforms which by some miracle had been pre-ordered and measurements already given minimising the alterations necessary. Fiona and Lucinda D'Arcy Landacre (the wife of the owner of Muddlecombe Hall) were bridesmaids, with Mrs Dimmock as the Matron of Honour.

Brewster was to give Mildred away and Dr Rammy to give Xalwo away.

Poor Betty Boring had to make do with the choir and the church organ and looking after Gerantinium in his starched cassock and surplice.

The wedding practice went very nearly to plan. Somebody with a sense of humour had Boris down as a page boy (only because she wanted to see him in a nice clean outfit for a change) but he complained bitterly that he couldn't see any wedding trains to play with.

Mrs Dimmock had to fit out Boris in his crushed velvet leggings with the buttons down the side of the calf and the patent leather shoes with silver buckles. The main problem being the blouse which really needed the assistance of a sail maker but Mrs D did the frills on the front.

Brewster had to set up a marquee to keep all the beer cold in the shade and to have a bar for the comely Blossom Deecup to stand behind and serve and keep the local lads and Creighky at a safe distance.

And also to the keep the till safe, not that any cash would be used, just to keep a tab on the bill to give to Chekov at the end of the day.

Poor Chekov had been grudgingly persuaded to pay for the whole affair by

Mildred and so he had to dip into his Mafia slush fund and the remaining contingency funds left by Dr Rammy. That probably amounted to enough to buy some of the tent pegs for the marquee.

*   *   *

And so the great day arrived. It was another beautiful day in Muddlecombe (yawn, as usual) as the normal sounds of the village heralded the beginning of a new day. The cockerels cock-a-doodle-dooing, the pigs honking, the dogs barking and everybody screaming at each other trying to find the clothes they last used many years ago for such special occasions.

The previous night was a sort of bachelor do in the "Snort and Truffle", no different from any night really, but everybody had a bloody good excuse for drinking. Creighky and Boris held the floor for most of the evening until Creighky realised it was a waste of time trying to keep up with Boris and subsequently got carried back to Primrose Cottage. His Plan A was getting nowhere. The decorating in the pub seemed to be going on forever and so he was cordoned off from Xalwo into Primrose Cottage. But tomorrow night everything would change after the proper wedding ceremony and then, whey hey!

All the men regathered in the morning in the pub for sherry and waited for their beloved ones to join them eventually.

Harry Hercules had cleaned up is tractor and decorated his trailer with ribbons and flowers with four chairs for the brides and grooms and room for the rest of the party to stand and wave as he drove them all of four hundred yards to the church from the pub picking up the brides and their entourage at their respective homes or residences.

The grooms went straight into the church while tradition demanded that the brides kept them waiting. Lots of oohs and aahhs came from the church congregation packed like sardines into the narrow pews with most of the village outside clapping and shouting at every new arrival.

Gerantinium was standing at the altar fully scrubbed up with his beard hoovered, in his official robes as stately as a king awaiting the start of the proceedings with full pomp and circumstance.

Betty looked up from the organ playing some innocuous melodies and nodded her head to the entrance of the church to see if the brides were coming in.

Gerantinium craned his head to try and see the ushers and get some early warning until eventually he heard the dulcet tones of Harry's tractor and waited for the screech of brakes and sound of chairs falling off the trailer and the curses flying about.

The brides managed to re-establish some sort of composition and started in towards the church dusting themselves down and rearranging their hair and then an usher ran in and gave the thumbs up signal everybody had been waiting for.

Betty started up the Trumpet Voluntary as the bridal group came into the church. Lots more ooohs and aaahhhs as Brewster and Mildred led the way with Dr Rammy and Xalwo close behind and then the bridesmaids and the "Page boy" and the Matron of Honour bringing up the rear.

They eventually managed to form a line in front of Gerantinium who started talking and then looking to Brewster and Mildred asked, 'and who gives this woman away?'

Brewster gently ushered Mildred forward as Chekov resplendent in his uniform of the Russian Army stepped in to fill the void.

Gerantinium then looked at Dr Rammy with the same question.

Hardly anybody noticed Dr Rammy's right hand gently stroking the contours of Xalwo's pert left buttock and then launching it away together with the rest of the body to the altar as his gesture of "giving the bride away".

Xalwo never batted an eyelid.

But nearly everybody noticed Mrs Dimmock's right hand grabbing a considerably larger buttock belonging to Boris who was too busy concentrating on carrying the wedding train.

Gerantinium collected his thoughts and looking down on his notes continued until he came to the part where he asked Mildred and Chekov their names and asked them to reply:

'Do you, Chekov Yeboleksi take you Mildred O'Riley to be my wife to have and to hold from this day forward, for better or for worse, for richer, for poorer, in sickness and in health, to love and to cherish; from this day forward until death do us part'.

'I do,' came the brief reply with Mildred fairly drooling up at Chekov

Mildred then replied and as they had already rehearsed that there was no need to do the rings bit in lieu of a best man, Gerantinium continued with, 'I now pronounce you man and wife,' and then they were asked to kiss each other.

You could hear the hankies coming out and the sniffling starting.

Mildred and Chekov moved back to allow Xalwo and Creighky to take their place. It was all going far too smoothly.

Gerantinium then went back to his original notes and started to ask Creighky his name.

'Do you, Creighky Aloy………….?'

Gerantinium started giggling, well spluttering which was bound to end in giggles.

'Do you, Creighky Aloy………….?'

'Aloysius,' hissed Creighky.

'Do you, Creighky, Aloysius, Bun………….?' He lost it totally. The giggles completely took over.

'Bunion,' hissed Creighky vehemently.

Gerantinium managed with supreme effort to regain his pomp and circumstance and took a deep breath.

You could feel earth moving in the church from people trying to hold their bellies from lurching up and down and stop themselves going into convulsions.

'Do you Creighky, Aloysius, Bunion O'Riley….?'

Before he could finish Creighky jumped in with a resounding, 'Yes, I do!'

'Thank God for that muttered,' Gerantinium between splutters. Then drying his eyes he continued trying to gain some composure.

'Now, do you, Princess Xalwo,………' Gerantinium lost it again but this time asked for help.

'Just read that bit for me my dear will you?' Gerantinium said wiping away the tears.

'I, Princess Xalwo Edjigayehu Asfa-Woofson Sellassie,…..'

'Thank you my dear. Now do you, whatever you just said, take whats'isname here, to be your lawfully wedded husband………?'

'Yes, I do!' Xalwo jumped in quickly to save a lot more embarrassment.

Phew! There was an almighty outtake of breath around the church as Gerantinium quickly concluded asking them to kiss each other.

Betty hit the loud button on the organ and gave it some welly while Creighky started his kissing. In his state of mind he was going to get whatever he could towards his Plan A whether it be in front of a full congregation or not. Xalwo managed to disengage him resting her knee gently in his groin and increasing the pressure until he got the message. Creighky joined everybody else in tears. He started with an ache in the groinal area and now had a pain in the groinal area.

The church business completed they marched stately down the aisle nodding and waving until they reached the sweet fresh air outside the church and waited until the congregation joined those already outside to marvel at the proceedings and all the finery on display. The villagers had never seen such a multitude of satin, silk, voile, epaulets and plumed helmets.

Creighky had shown his diplomatic pass to the ceremonial dress hire company and demanded his "chicken" feathered helmet together with his ceremonial sword.

Chekov looked resplendent in his Russian uniform, jodhpurs and shiny boots together with all his campaign medals. He was awarded one for each ten confessions he obtained from his interrogatees.

It was amazing how the dress hire company had been given all these details a few months ago.

How *does* Mrs Dimmock do it?

Mrs Dimmock had strategically placed herself six yards down the path away from the church door and was glaring at anybody within a two yards radius as the brides got ready to throw their bouquets.

Up went the bouquets into the air behind the brides and just guess who caught both of them.

Mrs Dimmock glowed demurely and sidled up to Boris regaining her stroking of the buttock process much to the applause of everyone else and to the total embarrassment of poor Boris.

Harry started up his tractor and trailer but everybody felt it best to walk the five hundred yards across the cricket pitch to Muddlecombe Hall.

And so the procession walked through the wrought iron gates and down the avenue of trees to the lawn where all the tables were laid out bedecked with flowers.

The beer marquee was immediately swamped and the majority of the bridal party were seconded to help the tidal wave of thirst.

Eventually everybody's thirst was sated and most people found themselves a seat. Some of the villagers had to be moved from the top table not fully understanding the etiquette of weddings having never been to a proper one before.

The hog roast had been on the go since early morning and the smell now overtook the guest's thirst requirements.

Everybody eventually sat somewhere and the wedding breakfast proceeded. Poor Brewster had taken over the best men's role, and toastmaster as nobody else (apart from Creighky) wanted to get up and speak so he recalled one of the old marriage jokes about a man and a woman who had never met before finding themselves in the same sleeping carriage of a train. After the initial embarrassment had passed, they both managed to fall asleep - the woman on the top bunk, and the man on the lower.

In the middle of the night the woman leaned over the edge of the bunk and said, "I'm sorry to bother you, Sir, but I am terribly cold and was wondering if you could possibly pass me another blanket?"

The man looked up with a glint in his eye and said, "I've got a better idea... why don't we pretend we're married?" "Why not?!" giggled the woman. "Good," he replied. "Get your own damn blanket!"

This bought on the usual marriage anecdotes, some funny, some extremely rude and poor Brewster had a job to control the hecklers with lots of catcalls for speeches from "Aloysius Bunion", but fortunately Creighky didn't take up the offer, as Xalwo had pinned his legs to the chair.

Brewster then shouted "food", which shut them up and started them off banging the tables as the young girls from the village Brewster had hired (the minimum basic wages bill hadn't arrived at Muddlecombe yet) ran round with the carvings from the hog roast and all the other trimmings. Silence eventually fell over Muddlecombe as everybody stuffed themselves, raising their glasses now and then to a toast.

Fortunately for Brewster the local victuallers of the "Snort and Truffle" had come up with a fantastic offer on South African Champagne so he could be extremely generous with his toasting.

Fortunately for Brewster most of the villagers had never tried champagne before. Even *he* was a little taken aback with the first mouthful but carried on manfully until he didn't really care as was the case with everybody else.

Gerantinium managed to reinfest   his beard from the detritus of his food together with the spilt wine as everyone polished off the various courses and relaxed with the children frolicking in the pleasant sunshine and everybody thoroughly enjoying the festival atmosphere.

The local band or group had eventually, after considerable quantities of champagne, managed to get into tune. The village in-breeding shone through here as most of the musicians were squinty-eyed banjo players but they got everybody up dancing anyway.

On the dance floor, Mildred was up to warp speed in purring looking up into the eyes of Chekov who was by now completely besotted.

It would be hard to imagine that only a short time ago he was a ruthless and cold blooded interrogator for the KGB and then converting to drug running, prostitution and money laundering and now under the "Muddlecombe spell" was a director of a very-nearly-legitimate diamond company as was his old trusty retainer and hired assassin Boris.

The only thing Xalwo could see in Creighky's eyes was lust. He was having great difficulty with his sword and the pain in the groinal area but was kept alive with the thought of his forthcoming conjugal rights or Plan A.

Xalwo was thinking of an early bed for Creighky tonight as well after administering considerable doses of her witch doctor's medicine in his drinks. Plan B was nearly coming to fruition.

Mrs Dimmock had managed to get Boris onto the dance floor but had given up and was now sitting back relaxing and thinking what a wonderful little world it was here in Muddlecombe and admiring everybody enjoying themselves on a beautiful sultry Muddlecombe summer evening amidst all the flowers and massaging the toes Boris had stepped on.

*   *   *

The next day was the big day of the cricket match with the real MCC. The front lawn of Muddlecombe Hall resembled a battlefield in the First World War. But people were starting to wake up and generally giving a reasonable impression of human beings and the mess was starting to be cleared away.

The priority was to get the tables back to the village green cum cricket pitch ready for the big occasion.

By midday the green was ready, but where were the players?

One by one they appeared ready for practice with Dr Rammy and Boris leading the field.

The procession of morticians' dummies eventually gathered into some semblance of a cricket team.

Brewster, who was completely exhausted from last night's festivities but not one to pass over a good profit, opened up the pub if only for the black coffees. Boris was not to be overwhelmed at such setbacks and immediately demanded his usual best bitter.

As the practice continued Fiona got her motivational blackboard out and started on the credits and debits.

There was however one small problem of course. The MCC couldn't find Muddlecombe could they?

Epilogue

After the wedding, Lieutenant Colonel (Acting) Creighky O'Riley, OBE., MC, and all round pain in the arse and groinal area, was immediately recalled by the foreign office to Botswana to help police with their enquiries concerning his kidnapping and had to stay on for several months for witness duties in the court case.

As you can imagine his poor wife was bereft in his absence and had to seek medical assistance. Dr Rammy managed to console her, if console is the right word, but she was a very satisfied and content lady during her husband's absence, so much so that upon his return she served him notice of divorce on the grounds of non-consummation of the marriage.

The medical evidence of this was supported in a report from a leading member of the gynaecology team of the University College Hospital, Jodhpur (failed).

So the moral of this story is if Plan A has a cock-up go to Plan B.

Lightning Source UK Ltd.
Milton Keynes UK
UKOW02f0633291015

261643UK00001B/4/P